Sweet Georgia Brown

Also by Cheryl Robinson

It's Like That
If It Ain't One Thing

Sweet Georgia Brown

cheryl robinson

 NEW AMERICAN LIBRARY

New American Library
Published by New American Library, a division of
Penguin Group (USA) Inc., 375 Hudson Street,
New York, New York 10014, USA
Penguin Group (Canada), 90 Eglinton Avenue East, Suite 700, Toronto,
Ontario M4P 2Y3, Canada (a division of Pearson Penguin Canada Inc.)
Penguin Books Ltd., 80 Strand, London WC2R 0RL, England
Penguin Ireland, 25 St. Stephen's Green, Dublin 2,
Ireland (a division of Penguin Books Ltd.)
Penguin Group (Australia), 250 Camberwell Road, Camberwell, Victoria 3124,
Australia (a division of Pearson Australia Group Pty. Ltd.)
Penguin Books India Pvt. Ltd., 11 Community Centre, Panchsheel Park,
New Delhi – 110 017, India
Penguin Group (NZ), 67 Apollo Drive, Rosedale, North Shore 0632,
New Zealand (a division of Pearson New Zealand Ltd.)
Penguin Books (South Africa) (Pty.) Ltd., 24 Sturdee Avenue,
Rosebank, Johannesburg 2196, South Africa

Penguin Books Ltd., Registered Offices:
80 Strand, London WC2R 0RL, England

First published by New American Library,
a division of Penguin Group (USA) Inc.

First Printing, January 2008
10 9 8 7 6 5 4 3 2 1

Copyright © Cheryl Robinson, 2008
Readers Guide copyright © Penguin Group (USA) Inc., 2008
All rights reserved

 REGISTERED TRADEMARK—MARCA REGISTRADA

LIBRARY OF CONGRESS CATALOGING-IN-PUBLICATION DATA
Robinson, Cheryl.
Sweet Georgia Brown / Cheryl Robinson.
p. cm.
ISBN: 978-0-451-22228-2
1. African Americans—Fiction. 2. Marital conflict—Fiction. 3. Radio talk shows—Fiction. I. Title.
PS3618.O323S84 2007
813'.6—dc22   2007025784

Set in Granjon
Designed by Alissa Amell

Printed in the United States of America

PUBLISHER'S NOTE
This is a work of fiction. Names, characters, places, and incidents either are the product of the author's imagination or are used fictitiously, and any resemblance to actual persons, living or dead,
business establishments, events, or locales is entirely coincidental.
    The publisher does not have any control over and does not assume any responsibility for author or
third-party Web sites or their content.

*To all of the dreamers who believe in what a
difference one day can make.*

Keep on!

Sweet Georgia Brown

PART ONE

Struggle No More

Shit happens.

Georgia Brown stood in the teeny upstairs bathroom.

Her mind raced as she peered at her reflection in the cracked mirror and raked her fingers through her thick mane.

She was deep in thought—first, about that morning's sermon at Greater Everlasting Faith Church. Bishop L. T. Anderson had given her much to think about.

And then she thought about her husband, Marvin, and his obsession with striking it rich.

Georgia glanced down at her bare feet pressed against the cold linoleum. The bishop had stamped his foot hard on the pulpit when he said, "Your faith has to be planted so deeply that you know all things are possible, because you know God. You know you are able to do all things through Christ. He strengthens you. Don't you know He's preparing you? While you're crying and asking, 'Why hasn't this or that happened?' I can tell you why: It's because you're not ready yet. You need to have faith and let it be unwavering."

And then a man with a voice as powerful as Fred Hammond's walked onstage, holding a cordless microphone and singing "No Weapon."

Georgia had risen to her feet and said, "Amen." With her eyes shut, she lifted one hand toward God and said, "Thank you, Father."

Georgia's two small sons, Edrik and Haden, were in the church nursery, while Marvin stayed home. As usual, he had skipped the Sunday service to work on his comedy routine. The night before, he had rehearsed his new act, entitled *Shit Happens*, in front of her, and he would be performing it onstage at Bea's Comedy Kitchen that evening if she didn't say something.

And she wanted to tell him the truth.

She didn't like it. Not at all.

There was just too much profanity.

And she didn't want to come off as being "all Christian-like," as Marvin often accused her. But the truth was, she didn't understand why he was changing his own style, which had been free of the four-letter words. He had always shied away from the N-word and the B-word. He didn't discuss politics, religion, race, or a person's sexual preference. His routine consisted mainly of impersonations. And he knew how to handle hecklers well, because at nearly every show there was at least one drunken patron who yelled out, "That shit ain't funny." Marvin's comebacks would make the audience laugh more than his planned jokes did. But Marvin was no Richard Pryor, no Eddie Murphy. Marvin was Marvin. And the Marvin she knew cursed only occasionally, and rarely onstage.

But now he wanted to change his image totally.

"Clean comedy is safe but doesn't go over well," he'd told her one night. "Not in clubs." He rattled off half a dozen names of comedians who had started with him—whose routines had never been clean—who were now in Hollywood making movies while Marvin was still in Detroit living with his parents.

Georgia reminded him that he had opened for the Gospel Explosion in Hart Plaza, a gig he had gotten only because his comedy was so clean. And he reiterated that, despite that booking, they were still living with his parents.

Shit happens.

The title of his routine was appropriate for their life—that much Georgia couldn't argue. Because the shit that had happened to them a few years earlier was the same shit that caused them to now live with his parents.

She heard the television blaring outside the bathroom—heard her voice and their laughter, hers and Marvin's, on tape. She knew he was watching that home video again—the one that brought back so many memories.

"Turn that shit down!" Marvin's father shouted.

Her father-in-law's shouting nearly made Georgia

plug her ears. She opened the bathroom door and peeked around it.

"Marvin, please turn that down," Georgia said. "Don't get him started. Not today. I can't take it. My spirit is so filled up right now, but once he gets on a roll, I'll end up deflated. You know how he can be."

"It's not even that loud. I feel like a ten-year-old kid in this house."

"I know, baby, but it is their house, so we have to do what they say."

He sighed and shook his head, biting his bottom lip as he tried to control his frustration.

"I said, turn that shit down now! If you want to hear some surround sound, go to the damn movies! But right now, I want to hear myself think!"

Marvin was sitting on the edge of the bed, watching the video of their earlier life, their wedding, and the move into their first home.

"Marvin, please," Georgia pleaded. "I just want one day of peace." He picked up the remote control and lowered the volume. She sighed in relief. "Thank you."

"Are you getting ready to go somewhere?"

"Just to Farmer Jack's. I need to grocery shop for our Christmas dinner. Two days 'til Christmas, baby," Georgia said as she sat in a small chair in the corner of their bedroom and put on her socks and gym shoes.

"Yeah, two days before I'm reminded of how big a failure I am."

"How do you figure that?"

"Because I don't have shit."

"There you go with that word. Shit, shit, shit. Between your father and now you, that's all I hear in this house. Do you want to go shopping with me?"

"I need to get my new routine down if I'm going to perform it tonight. Baby, I swear. I'm going to get us out of here and into our own place real soon." He turned his attention back to the television.

"Can I say something?" she asked, ready to share her honest opinion with him about the routine.

"Yeah." He turned to face her, and when his sincere eyes met hers, she was lost for words.

"I can't believe you're watching that again. That's the past. We're trying to move forward."

"It's our life, baby . . . when we had it good."

"We still have it good."

"Well, when we had it better."

She sat beside him to view a little of the video, taking a few moments to reflect. She smiled when the exterior of their West Side Detroit brick colonial flashed. Georgia remembered all too well how much pleading she had to do just so Marvin would put a bid on the house. He felt it was much too small, and he always set his sights big. But since it was the house Georgia wanted so badly, he wanted her to have it. It was a simple home, but she had fallen in love with the kitchen with its built-in nook and a window over the sink. *Such a shame we lost it after Marvin was laid off from his factory job,* she thought.

Even though they had filed Chapter 7 bankruptcy to try

to keep their home, they had already fallen so far behind on payments that the mortgage lender asked the bankruptcy court to lift the automatic stay to begin foreclosure proceedings. Now, Georgia and Marvin had been living with his parents for over two years. It was tough for them to save when Georgia, earning twelve dollars an hour at a call center taking phone orders for a major mail order company, was the breadwinner. She had a good man in Marvin, one she loved and respected very much. Of course they argued, like any couple did, but for the most part, they were happy and would be so content if they could just stop struggling so much.

She rubbed his knee. "Do you want anything from Farmer Jack's?" He shook his head. "Are you sure you're okay?"

"I'm sorry."

"Sorry for what?"

"You deserve so much more than this."

"You're scaring me. You're starting to sound like your father."

"He's right. I need to start looking for a real job. This comedy thing . . . I don't know . . . nothing has become of it so far. There are so many guys who started with me who are doing way better. They're in Hollywood filming movies while I'm still performing in the same club I started in."

"Don't ever doubt yourself, Marvin. You're a dreamer and that's who I fell in love with. Don't ever stop dreaming. We're doing okay."

He leaned his face forward and kissed her. "I love you. I love you so much. You are so patient and so loving and kind. You are a good mother and a great wife . . . a wonderful lover. How did I luck out?"

She shrugged. "You caught me at a weak moment."

"I probably did. I'm probably a rebound."

"No, you're not, silly. You're my one and only man. The first man I truly loved. This too shall pass, honey. Always remember that. Cheer up, we're only two days away from Christmas. And I'm only three days away from turning thirty-five." She leaped from the bed. "Let me hurry up so I can get back . . . and maybe we can play tonight." She winked.

"Maybe we can? Oh, we will."

Georgia was pushing a race car shopping cart with three-year-old Edrik and one-year-old Haden down the beauty aisle at Farmer Jack's when it dawned on her.

She and Marvin really were poor.

She tried not to think about it, but Marvin's sulking and that video of their former life made the reality of their situation sink in. For the first three and half years of their marriage they were living okay. When Georgia got pregnant with their first son, they decided to move from their apartment off East Outer Drive to a home in the same area. Then the baby came, and they were a happy little family enjoying a decent life. They had a home, a healthy baby, and a great marriage. But out of the blue came some massive layoffs with the automakers that also extended to their suppliers and Marvin worked for one of the suppliers. One thing led to another and now they were homeless, but still fortunate enough not to be living on the street like Georgia's brother, Peter.

She and Marvin were too poor to afford their own place or a new car or even the full coverage insurance that went along with having one, especially for Detroit residents. The insurance alone could set a person back as much as, if not more than, the car payment. But they needed reliable transportation because their Dodge Shadow, which was the only car they had, was on its last leg. Marvin had been saving up for a down payment on a new car because he was tired of his wife making the daily hour drive back and forth to Troy, Michigan, with a car that had a bad muffler and transmission problems and had already conked out on her twice. Mechanics were amazed that the ten-year-old car with over a hundred and fifty thousand miles was still running at all.

She dug her chipped nails underneath her knitted winter cap and scratched her itchy scalp through the two inches of new growth while perusing the box perms. She needed a touch-up badly, but paying sixty dollars at the salon was out of the question. She reached for a no-lye perm kit and studied it for a few seconds before setting it back down, taking heed to her hairdresser Millie's warning not to use a box perm unless she wanted all of her hair to fall out.

She edged her cart up to the checkout line.

Nervous about what was to come.

She wanted to remain positive and believe that their

dreams of one day having money and digging themselves out of their hole would come true, but she'd been hanging on to that fantasy for what felt like forever.

She studied the subtotal as the young woman scanned the ham first followed by a bottle of champagne that Georgia wanted to crack open on New Year's, because if she couldn't be rich at the start of a new year, she might as well be buzzed. Nearly a dozen more items were added to the total, and as the amount on the cash register steadily climbed, Georgia put back the champagne that would have to wait until payday, and a football Edrik had grabbed from the toy aisle. At least she didn't have to worry about a turkey. Her job passed one out to each employee on Friday right before the memo went out stating they were discontinuing the holiday bonus. The big bird was a nice gesture, but it couldn't possibly substitute for five hundred dollars.

"No!" Edrik screamed. "That's mine!"

"Santa is coming soon," Georgia said through gritted teeth, "and I'm sure he'll bring you one for Christmas." After having kids, Georgia understood why parents instilled a belief in Santa Claus—a built-in excuse for why they weren't going to buy something around the holidays— because Santa surely would.

"No!" he shouted even louder, flinging his legs uncontrollably. "You *are* Santa. Granddaddy said."

"Calm down," she said, smacking his little leg while she continued to watch the subtotal. "I am not Santa. Santa lives in the North Pole. And you will get this for Christmas. I promise."

Haden glanced over at Edrik and began crying as well. Now Georgia had two screaming kids *and* an escalating grocery bill to contend with.

When she heard the cashier announce the total—one hundred and eighty-three dollars and thirty-nine cents—Georgia felt faint, her hand trembling slightly as she wrote out the amount.

She attempted to get away with dating the check for Friday, hoping the woman would be more concerned with the growing line to notice, but instead the cashier proclaimed loudly, "We can't accept postdated checks."

"Oh, I'm sorry, I know that. It was a mistake, really," Georgia said as she corrected the date and initialed the change.

"Mmm-hmm, you be sure to have a blessed day." She tore off the receipt and handed it to Georgia, who shoved it in her knockoff Coach bag as she pushed the cart toward the exit. She stopped at the automatic doors, bundled up the boys, and braced herself for the cold air awaiting them. As she rolled the cart out of the store, the freezing air smacked her in the face causing tears to roll. Living paycheck to paycheck was no way to live, and even though she knew the majority of Americans did, she didn't want to be like the majority.

"Excuse me, ma'am, but can you spare some change?" asked a man with a dirty wool cap covering his head, tattered clothes, and busted shoes.

"Peter? Is your name Peter?" Georgia hadn't seen her brother in several months, which wasn't unusual, because he was prone to disappearing out of the blue.

"No. I'm not Peter."

Georgia studied the man closer. His hollow eyes were blue, the brown tone to his skin was dirt—he was a white man.

Georgia took out all she had, a five-dollar bill, and handed it to the man.

"God bless you."

"I wish I had more."

Once back home, Marvin rushed out to help Georgia with the kids and the groceries. He took the boys in the house first and returned to the driveway to help retrieve bags from the trunk of their car.

"We're getting a new car," he told her as they pulled out plastic shopping bags.

"Marvin, we've gone over this already. We just can't afford a new car. I wish we could."

"If *we* can't afford one, tell me how the Johnsons just got a new car." He pointed across the street to the Pathfinder parked in the driveway. "He doesn't work at all and she's on disability. If *we* can't afford it, how is it that Candice Martin and her ex-con boyfriend, who doesn't work either, can get a brand-new Camry?" he asked, referring to their neighbors in the corner house.

"I'm not concerned about them, Marvin. I just know what we can't afford. Maybe we should just buy another used car from Steve's lot."

"I'm not dealing with a buy-here-pay-here lot again." He pulled out four grocery bags. "I have a friend who sells new cars. He can hook us up. I'm tired of you driving that raggedy car to work. That makes me look bad. I'm the one who's supposed to be the provider. So let me provide."

"I'd rather have our own place."

"That's coming . . . trust me. We're going to have a house in Grosse Pointe Farms."

"Oh, honey." She shook her head with laughter. "You're such a dreamer." She stroked the side of his smooth face. "It's so cute. And so are you."

"I'm being serious. I'm not trying to be cute. You know the house I want. Or have you forgotten already? Do you need to take another run back down there?"

"Your father will have a heart attack if you pull up in his driveway with a car. You know we can't do that . . . and still live in their house."

"All right."

"Marvin, please don't come here with a new car."

He closed the trunk of the car. "I said all right."

She eyed him skeptically. She knew her husband. Knew that whenever he made up his mind to do something, he usually did it, but this time she prayed he would listen to her for a change.

"I thought I saw my brother."

"You thought?"

"It wasn't him, but I need to get in touch with him again. Not a day goes by that I don't think about him. My mother is probably turning in her grave, knowing that a child of hers is living on the street." Tears started to fall from Georgia's eyes.

He put the grocery bags on the trunk of the car and held Georgia in his arms, kissing her forehead. "We'll find him, baby. He'll probably call you soon. He always does eventually."

"Have you ever been so fed up with your life that you had to ask yourself, 'When is this misery going to end?' " the televangelist asked. Her energetic voice blared through the four stereo speakers strategically placed around the small living room—two on opposite sides of the leather Art Van sectional, another lying sideways on one of the bookshelves, and a fourth resting on top of the glass wet bar. "You want your life to change. You need a change," she shouted. "You're tired of living paycheck to paycheck and being unappreciated . . . tired of crying over spilled milk. You want the world at your disposal. Tell yourself that your misery ends today. Take control of your life right now. Turn to two people and say, 'My misery ends today.' "

"My misery ends today," Georgia said to the spaces on either side of her.

She was in the living room standing on a stool with her back to the television as she prepared to place the angel ornament on top of the live Christmas tree—the finishing touch.

After leaving work early, she had driven nearly two hours to Frankenmuth, Michigan, to browse through Bronner's Christmas Wonderland, the world's largest Christmas store. The entire two hundred dollars Marvin had given her from his last comedy set was supposed to go into their bank account, but instead she used some of it to buy gas to get her to Frankenmuth and back to purchase the angel. And while things were tight, and all the money was supposed to go into their account, for once Georgia wanted to do something that would make her happy.

She had made it home a couple hours earlier. And she was happy because the trip was well worth missing a full day's pay. Even though her car had overheated and she was afraid it might conk out on the highway, it pulled on through. And the best part was that she didn't have to write a rubber check, because her angel—the exact one she wanted—was on sale for twenty-one dollars from the original sixty-five, and she was able to pay cash. Of course, she told no one—including Marvin—where she'd gone. They wouldn't understand why she would drive that far for an ornament. And they would definitely think she was crazy for leaving work without getting paid for the day as badly as she and Marvin needed money.

She hummed from the satisfaction of it all, amazed that something as small as a Christmas decoration could make her feel so good. In that way she was like her mother whose favorite holiday was Christmas, and who always believed in doing three things for the big day: displaying beautiful decorations that she'd find on sale, putting up a live tree, and blasting Johnny Mathis holiday music throughout their modestly furnished home. In 1966, Georgia almost became her mother's Christmas gift. Born at 12:04 AM, Georgia was just five minutes late of having the December twenty-fifth birthday her mom had hoped for.

"*Your* misery ends today?" her father-in-law asked, chuckling. Georgia's thoughts were immediately inter- rupted once he trudged into the living room. "Does it re- ally? What, did y'all hit the lotto?" He grabbed a fistful of microwaved pork rinds from the bag he was carrying, stuffed his mouth, and plopped down on the plastic cov- ered sofa. "Because only money can end your misery, and Marvin doesn't have any. When you gonna make that man get a job?"

"He . . . has one."

"My son doesn't work. *You* work. *I* work. His momma works. His sister works. Most of his damn cousins work, even Pookey, who was in jail for damn near ten years, has a job, a house, and a new car. What is wrong with my son that he thinks he doesn't have to work? Why does he think he can go down to some club on the weekends and do stand-up comedy? There's no future in that. Make him get a real job, Georgia, or else tell him you're going to quit

yours and start shaking your ass at the Black Orchid Caba-
ret for a living and see how he likes it. That way y'all can
both be working in clubs at night and sleeping during the
day."

"Don't talk to that child like that!" Marvin's mother
yelled from the kitchen where she was busy finishing a
full meal even though the next day she would prepare an
even larger one with Georgia's assistance. Marvin's mother
couldn't sit idle for long. She worked two part-time jobs
cleaning hotel rooms and then left work for home where
she cleaned some more. Georgia wondered how Marvin's
mother garnered the energy.

"First of all, she ain't no child. And I'm trying to talk
some sense into her. I'm doing this because her folks aren't
around to do it."

"Well, not like that," Marvin's mother said. By nature,
Marvin's mother minded her own business and was quiet
most of the time—that is, unless Marvin's father said something inappropriate and she was forced to speak up. Lately,
she had been speaking up a lot.

"Marvin needs to give up on his fantasy of making a
living as a comedian. Eddie Murphy, Martin Lawrence,
Chris Rock, and all the rest of those fools trying to imi-
tate the great Richard Pryor are just lucky. That's all. They
don't have any real talent."

"Well, then, why do you buy their DVDs?" Georgia
asked sarcastically.

"Because they're funny, and when I come home from a
long stressful week of *work,* I want to drink my beer and

laugh, but that doesn't mean they have talent. They just got money. Money that Marvin ain't never gonna have—not like that." Marvin's father was cynical, the type who hated seeing others do well, with Oprah being his least favorite person.

Georgia shrugged and shook her head. "Marvin makes you laugh. I've seen you fall out at some of his jokes."

"I'm not saying the boy doesn't have a few good jokes in him, but he ain't gonna make no living from it. For one thing, his act is too damn clean, trying to act like he was raised in the church. . . . Not in this house he wasn't."

"And whose fault was that?" Marvin's mother yelled from the kitchen. "Not mine."

"All I'm saying is that he needs to start putting in applications at some of these places that are hiring."

"Will you please stay out of their business, Charles?" her mother-in-law yelled. "They are grown with children of their own. Stop treating her like a child."

"As long as they are living up in my house, their business is my business. And Marvin needs to give up on all that foolishness. He needs to think about his wife and his children and stop acting like a child."

"There's only one problem, Pops," Georgia said, bending down to pick up a string of lights. She turned to face her father-in-law and give him the same pep talk she gave herself daily. "I don't want him to give up on his dreams, because if he gives up on those, what else will he have to look forward to?"

"He can look forward to raising his children and being

a good husband, which means a steady provider. That's what I had to look forward to. So what's wrong with that?"

"Yeah," Georgia said as she sighed and turned toward the tree, stepping back on the foot stool to continue decorating, "but we want a different kind of life."

"What kind of life is that?"

"A life where anything is possible."

"Well, when do you think it will be possible for the two of you to get your own place?"

"Soon, Pops. Very soon."

"I don't understand how you can act so la-dee-damn-da like everything's fine. Most women would have snapped by now, been all up in his face. Stop acting like a white woman."

"Like a white woman?" Georgia said with laughter. "Something is wrong with you."

"I mean I know you're trying to hold on to your man like most women do, but living with his folks, struggling to pay the bills, driving a raggedy ass car. Is it worth all that? No man is worth that. And you can lie to me, but you can't lie to yourself. You know you're frustrated. Can't help but be. Have you ever heard that saying, 'I can do bad by myself'?"

He switched the channel from the uplifting Christian Network to the depressing six o'clock news that began with tales of yet another murder on the "dangerous" streets of Detroit, dubbed "The Murder Capital."

"Hey, I was watching that," she said as she turned toward him on the stool too quickly and almost fell off. She breathed a sigh of relief and then focused on the news reporter and breaking news.

"This just in. According to authorities, two missing Macomb County brothers have been abducted from a Simmons department store on Gratiot near Twenty-Six Mile. The victims have been identified as seven-year-old James Bright and five-year-old Kyle Bright. Police are now on the lookout for a silver 1992 Dodge Shadow being driven by a white male believed to be in his early to mid-thirties and who authorities believe also dresses in women's clothing. The brothers were last seen playing in the toy department." A photo of the brothers flashed. "If anyone has information about this crime, please contact your local police department. We'll have more on this urgent story at ten. Bob, back to you."

Georgia shook her head. She couldn't even imagine how the parents were holding up. She went back to her tree, but her thoughts stayed with the story and the pictures of the two small boys. *A silver Dodge Shadow, the same year as ours just a different color,* she thought, *wouldn't be hard to remember.* Nor would the innocent youthful faces of the brothers or the fact that their abductor was a cross-dresser.

She stepped back on the stool, but lost balance again after seeing Marvin pull into the driveway in a brand new Nissan Maxima. The shock caused her to tumble into the tree, knocking her masterpiece into the curtains. The angel and several ornaments flew in various directions. A few branches broke off. Georgia, too distraught and frustrated to cry, felt that moment ruined what she had hoped to classify as a fairly decent day.

"Every day for a week you been messin' on that tree," her father-in-law teased, "and now look what happened. The shit done fell down. It's too much trouble anyway. We've had the same Christmas tree for years and nothing was wrong with it. Fake ones last forever. Why you had to go out and buy that shit is beyond me, especially when you could have saved that money on the down payment you're going to need for your own place."

She pried herself from between the branches and brushed off the needles from her face and sweater.

"Marvin's outside with a new car," Georgia said, stunned.

"No, Marvin is not outside with no new damn car. He better not be, because if y'all can pay a car note, you sure in hell can pay me some rent. Your eyes better be playing tricks on you," Marvin's father said as he tossed the almost empty bag of pork rinds onto the coffee table and stomped to the front window to peer out. "Well, I be damned. He better just be on a test drive."

Georgia grabbed her coat from the closet and walked out in her fluffy pink house shoes. "What's that?" she asked, pointing at the car, as she approached Marvin.

He had a cell phone glued to his ear. "And this?" she said, tugging at the phone. "What's going on, Marvin? I told you not to get a car."

He motioned his hand in front of her face to quiet her down, and then mouthed, "Let me finish up this call."

Georgia stood with her arms folded, freezing and sneezing, waving to neighbors as they drove past in their new cars. She followed Marvin into the house, listening to his conversation about opening for an established comedian who was flying in from the East Coast, but she couldn't catch the name. After he entered the house and his father began mouthing off about the car and getting a job, he abruptly ended his conversation.

"Listen, I bought a new car because Georgia needs some reliable transportation. I'm tired of worrying about her every day and wondering if she's going to make it to work without breaking down."

"They let you buy a car even though you don't work?" Marvin's father asked.

"Pops, I do work, and besides, I had all of Georgia's information with me."

"All of Georgia's information. See, what I tell you?" he said to Georgia. "So how much is the note?"

"How much is the note?"

"That's what I said."

"One of my boys works at the dealership and he hooked me up. We qualified for zero percent interest. And we didn't have to put any money down—"

"Did I ask about the interest or the down payment? I asked about the damn note. And you didn't qualify for shit. Georgia did. How much is Georgia going to be paying?"

"*We're* going to be paying four hundred and ninety-eight dollars," Marvin said quickly and as soon as he did, his father went off.

Georgia sat at the dining room table, fanning herself with Haden's tiny Christmas stocking.

She was almost in tears.

"We can't afford that," Georgia said as she began talking to herself while Marvin and his father argued. "If we could afford a new car, we should be able to afford our own place. Last year at this time, we were supposed to be in our own place. I'd rather have my own place than a new car."

Marvin's father shook his head in disgust. "You're a sorry excuse. I tell you what . . . y'all got to get out of here by the New Year. I hate to do it to you, baby," he said to Georgia, "but your man over here needs to step up and be one."

"That's fine," Marvin said, brushing his father's comments off as if they didn't bother him, but they did and always had. Marvin blamed his parents—his father mostly—as the reason he hadn't yet succeeded in life. All he needed was someone to believe in him and his dreams. Georgia was that someone.

"It's *fine*, Marvin?" Georgia asked. "How is it fine? Where are we going to go?"

"Did you think we were going to live here forever? I'm working on some things. It's fine. Trust me. We have forty-five days before our first car payment is due, and you won't have to pay it, because I will."

She wanted to trust him, but she'd trusted him for six years, holding on to his hopes that some would call pipe dreams. Now, for the first time, Georgia was having her own doubts.

"You do trust me, don't you?"

"Yes, Marvin. I trust you."

Georgia sat in her boss's office, her worst-case scenario finally realized as the day ended the same way it had started—not good. Not good at all.

The day before, on Christmas, her father-in-law had continued insulting Marvin about his recent car purchase and his lack of a stable job—the usual. Georgia received the shock of her life after Marvin handed her a large box with a red bow tied around it. Inside was a long wool dress coat with a five-hundred-and-seventy-nine-dollar Saks Fifth Avenue price tag dangling from the sleeve.

"You didn't need to buy me anything."

"That's your Christmas and your birthday present rolled into one," Marvin said.

"He left the tag on to let you know how much the coat

cost. Not that he paid that much for it," Marvin's father said. "Did you buy it off one of those boosters at your barber shop?"

"No, Pops, *I* bought it."

"Stop being so negative, Charles," Marvin's mother said.

"Marvin, we can't afford this," Georgia said as she hugged the coat.

"It's cashmere. Did you see the regular price? Twelve hundred dollars. I really wanted to buy you a mink, but that's coming one day."

"I don't need a mink. I don't even like fur coats. And you paid way too much for this wool one. Saks, Marvin? You know we can't afford anything in there."

"Well, that's where your coat came from, so I guess we can." What Marvin hadn't told Georgia was that he had taken the last twenty dollars he had to his name to the Motor City one night after his routine and won close to a thousand dollars off the poker slot machine. It was his first time gambling, and he actually won. He was happy with himself that he knew when to stop.

The next morning, Georgia woke up with her husband on top of her. Her eyes strained to open just as he made the sound—the one letting her know when it was all over. And in this case, it was over at the same time her alarm sounded at six.

She didn't feel well—whether her illness was mental or physical, she really couldn't say. But one thing was certain: She didn't want to go to work, especially the day after Christmas, even with a new wool coat.

Her head hung off the side of the full-sized bed and she stared at her flower-print head scarf on the floor. Half of her black sponge rollers had fallen out of her hair, and she now knew that the generic sleeping pills from the dollar store worked because she had slept through most of Marvin's lovemaking.

He thrust his dick inside of her one last time, a move that caused Georgia to fall off the bed entirely and land on the cold, hard wood. By the time she had gathered her hair essentials from the floor and made her way into the bathroom to hurry for work, Marvin was fast asleep and snoring.

It was freezing outside.

The snow had just started to fall as Georgia backed her Shadow out of the driveway, gas needle teetering between a quarter of a tank and empty, when it dawned on her that she could drive the new car. She pulled the Shadow back into the driveway and took the Maxima to work instead, but a new car and a new coat still didn't equate to a new life.

She looked down at her fingers, the red polish chipped on all but two of her nails. She twirled her loose-fitting, tarnished wedding band and wondered if all of the struggling had truly been worth it. But Georgia was just doing what she'd always done—be a good woman by supporting her man emotionally, financially, and sexually. She had to keep the faith that Marvin's dreams would come true. But still, the question remained . . . what had being good ever gotten her?

At work, she mainly kept to herself. She worked through her lunch, eating a snack or two at her desk to avoid the office gossip that occurred in the lunchroom. The further away she was from controversy of any kind, the more secure she felt with her job, because the last thing she needed was the one thing she feared most—unemployment.

For the past several weeks, at least two or three people had been escorted to their desks to gather their belongings and then ushered out of the building by security. For this reason, Georgia started taking most of her personal effects home so that if her D-day were to ever come, she wouldn't have to face any unnecessary embarrassment. She could just leave.

The rumor circulated that this last wave of firings was due to time card issues—claiming overtime not worked. Georgia, though, knowing most of those accused, found it hard to believe. JoAnna, especially, was a die-hard corporate type who lived, slept, and breathed the core values. It all just proved to Georgia that no matter how well liked you were, no job was secure.

Five o'clock came quickly, but a last-minute call kept Georgia a few minutes over. When she hung up the phone, she noticed that her team leader, Ernie Dixon, stood by her desk.

"May I see you in Mr. Marshall's office?" he asked.

Georgia nodded quickly, signed off of her computer, and followed Ernie to Mr. Marshall's office in silence.

The office was down a long hallway at the very end of a row of managers' offices. The door was closed, but when

Ernie opened it, Georgia saw three people waiting in the room: Mr. Marshall, the company's human resources manager, Mrs. Fallen, a group leader, and a male security officer.

Georgia knew before anyone said a word that her worst case scenario was finally realized—she was getting fired.

But for what? she wondered.

Mr. Marshall began speaking after Georgia took a seat.

"We had cause to tap into your computer because our corporate security team identified your ID address as visiting several unauthorized Web sites, particularly thelastlaugh.com. We have proof that you submitted an application online through our Web server for your husband, Marvin Brown. We also traced several calls you made from your work phone to Burbank, California. You also utilized our overnight packaging service to send mail directly to a Los Angeles studio and billed it to our company. For this reason, Georgia, we must terminate you on the grounds of disorderly conduct."

"Okay," Georgia said. What more could she say? It was all true, and she knew it was against company policy. Since they didn't have a computer at home, she had taken a chance, and that chance had cost Georgia her job.

They had papers for her to sign, but Georgia, feeling like she might faint at any moment, had only enough strength to turn in her badge before hurrying out of the building for some much-needed fresh air.

She heard them mention withholding her last check until she signed the termination papers, but her goal at that moment was to not pass out.

She made it out of the building and into the parking lot, her head spinning and her stomach queasy. Once inside her car, she sped away, her wheels skidding on the newly formed ice as she made her way onto Big Beaver Road.

At the first light, she leaned over and removed her pre-paid cell phone from her purse, but with just one minute of talk time remaining, she couldn't even place a call. Now she was outraged about the car and the so-called free cell phone the dealership offered as an incentive—the phone was free but not the monthly service. She was an hour away from home. An entire hour she had to wait before telling Marvin that she had lost their primary means of survival because she had tried to help further his career. So either his dreams needed to come true, or he needed to find a job and let Georgia sleep in for a change. She was officially tired of having all of the burden fall on her shoulders.

Once she made it home, she didn't have a chance to drill into him, because Marvin greeted her at the door with a glass of champagne and cause to celebrate. Aside from the fact that it was Georgia's birthday, after two months and three mailings to the producers of *The Last Laugh*, including a videotape of Marvin's performance, he had been selected as one of a hundred to audition live on-air during their season premiere.

"We're on our way, baby," Marvin promised. "Wasn't this the best birthday present I could give you?"

Now it was Georgia's turn, but her news was far from joyous.

"Today is my birthday and I was fired, Marvin. Called

into the human resources office the day after Christmas and terminated. I can't explain how humiliating that was or how scared I am right now. I don't want to live like this. I don't want our kids to live like this. I was looking forward to the new year, but now what do we have to look forward to . . . a year of unemployment and more bills?"

"You're not going to have a year of unemployment," he said, trying to encourage her.

"You're right, because you only get six months. All I know is there's a whole world out there much bigger than this, and that's the one I want to live in. We've struggled enough."

"And that's the one we will live in," he promised. "When I hit LA, I'm coming back to Detroit as the winner of *The Last Laugh*. And we're going to get our own place. It's going to be that mansion in Grosse Pointe Farms with luxury cars in the garage, the best schools for our kids, anything and everything that money can buy."

"Happiness?"

"Of course, happiness," Marvin said, embracing Georgia. "You stuck by my side, and I'm not going to let you or the boys down. We're always going to be together and we're always going to be happy. We're never going to be poor again. That much I promise."

They headed east from Detroit toward Grosse Pointe Farms, riding in silence along scenic Lake Shore Drive in their Dodge Shadow with its bad muffler. The rattling had become such commonplace that they no longer heard the noise. With the loss of her job, Georgia made Marvin take the Maxima back to the dealership. They tried to give him a hard time, but with Georgia never signing the contract, nothing was binding.

Georgia faced Lake St. Clair while Marvin's eyes bounced from one multimillion-dollar estate to the next. He had always wondered what people did to afford to live like this; he wanted to be one of them. There was only one thing he knew how to do well—make people laugh. But sometimes he thought he didn't even know how to do that well enough. He had started performing stand-up in comedy clubs around the same time as Chris Tucker, Jamie Foxx, and Martin Lawrence. He vividly remembered gracing the same stages on the same nights. Now to think all three had hit the big time while he was still an unknown. The very idea dominated Marvin's existence.

"Damn, it's so amazing to see how the other half lives. Sometimes I just want to go door-to-door and ask them what in the hell they do. If we can't live like this, what's the use in living at all? Baby, one day we're going to live here. One day soon. I'm winning that contest. I'm bringing that million dollars home, and I'm getting ready to show you the house we're going to buy with that money."

She snickered. She'd seen his dream home several times before. Driving to Grosse Pointe had become as much a ritual as dreaming about living there.

"What, you don't believe me? You don't think we can live here? My father must be convincing you I'll never amount to shit."

"Of course not, Marvin. You know better than that."

He made a left turn at a median. The street was relatively clear with the exception of a few cars that he allowed to pass before he proceeded. "Look at me." He placed his hand on her chin and turned her head toward him. "You do believe me, don't you? We're on our way now, baby. Next week I'm in LA. Can you believe it?"

"I believe it. But living like this?" She shrugged while her eyes perused the well-manicured, expansive lawns. "Sherwood Forest would be fine."

"Sherwood Forest? If you're going to dream, dream big. Shit, I already know people who live in Sherwood. But I don't know anyone who lives here, baby."

"Anita Baker."

"I don't know Anita Baker," he snapped. "Do you?"

"Why are you pulling up in this driveway, Marvin? You know how the police are around here. You better hurry up and back out of here."

"This is our house." He shifted the gear into park, pulled the keys from the ignition, reached for his disposable camera underneath the seat, and snapped a picture of the house. "Let's get out and see how it looks on the inside."

"Go inside? Are you crazy?"

He would have to pry her out, with the way she looked. She'd thrown on an old pair of sweats, some worn-out sneakers, and a down-filled jacket. She wasn't even wearing her new cashmere coat and hadn't applied the least bit of makeup or put a comb through her hair. This was supposed to be a leisurely drive with no stops. Marvin had promised.

"Come on, baby. They have an open house. It's for sale. My dream house is for sale."

She shook her head and folded her arms. She was prepared to fight. Three expensive cars were parked in front of their raggedy one, cars with symbols and numbers on the back and no names. She sighed, knowing that the owners of those vehicles could afford more than just mere dreams.

"I'm not going to go in there looking the way I do. If you knew you were taking me to an open house, why didn't you tell me?"

"I didn't think we were going to go in, but now that we're here, I want to. Baby, you look fine. It's an open house. Aren't you a little bit curious?"

"No. You go ahead without me. At least you're halfway dressed." He was wearing a pair of black slacks, a pullover sweater, and the leather jacket Georgia had given him on Christmas.

"I'm not going in if you're not. This is going to be our house, not just mine." He flipped her vanity mirror down. "Just throw your hair in a ponytail, put on a little makeup, and let's go. It's not like you're trying to catch a man. You got one. The only people we need to worry about impressing are each other."

She smiled. It was nice to have someone who loved her regardless, which was the way she loved him—regardless. Regardless of whether he had any money and whether they had to live with his parents. He had big dreams, and she was willing to ride them out because she knew he wouldn't leave her like her father did.

"I don't know, Marvin. I don't want to be embarrassed. I do the yard work in these gym shoes."

"Look, I don't care what anybody thinks about us. Those same people who laugh at us today will be envious tomorrow. Come on."

"You're right." She rambled through her purse for some

powder, lipstick, and liner. It took her several minutes to fix her hair and spiff up her face.

An anxious Marvin and a nervous Georgia stood at the door and waited for someone to answer their ring. A well-manicured woman with a navy suit and a realtor pin greeted them, her smile collapsing quickly as the two came into view.

"Did you need something?" she asked, blocking the entrance.

"Yeah," Marvin said. "Isn't this an open house?"

"Yes, it is."

"Well, can we come in?"

"Are you in the market for a home of this magnitude?"

"Of this magnitude? Well, we won't know until we're allowed to see its magnitude." Marvin grabbed hold of Georgia's hand and brushed past the stuffy agent. "Do you want to start upstairs or down?"

"Up. Far away from her."

They waltzed up the spiral staircase. The accents and detailing to the home were awe inspiring. "It's too big. We don't need anything like this," she whispered, her voice carrying throughout the open spaces.

Marvin stopped midway on the staircase, taking in an aerial view.

"I don't like it as much as I thought I would." He shook his head. "Not nearly as much as I thought I would. We'll have to build."

"Okay. But for now, can we just leave?" Georgia rushed

back out into the cold and back to the comforts of their Dodge Shadow.

When Marvin took his place behind the wheel, he turned to Georgia and said, "Do this with me."

"What?"

"I read about this somewhere. About the power of visualization. Close your eyes." He turned toward Georgia and waited for her eyes to close before he continued. "What's your favorite car?"

She shrugged while her eyes were closed. "I'm not sure. I guess a Saturn."

"A what?" Marvin shouted.

"What's wrong with a Saturn? I like Saturns."

"Think big, baby. Bigger than a Saturn."

"Okay." She squeezed her eyelids together. "How about a Ford Explorer?"

"Are you kidding me?"

"I love SUVs. You know that."

"Well, then, why didn't you say a Lincoln Navigator?"

"Because right now any new car will do."

"Just imagine you can have any car you want. Sky is the limit."

She thought for a moment and then smiled. "Oh, I know, I know." She began slapping Marvin's thigh out of excitement. "What's the name of that new SUV that Porsche just introduced this year? The Cane?"

"Cayenne."

"Is that it?" she asked, her eyes remaining shut.

"Yeah, baby, imagine you are sitting behind the wheel

of a Porsche Cayenne and you pull out of the driveway at your posh Grosse Pointe Farms home and head for the spa. Do you have that picture locked in your head?" She nodded. "Open your eyes, Georgia." She opened her eyes and Georgia smiled. There wasn't anything wrong with dreaming. And she sure wished his dreams were about to come true.

Georgia could not sit still.

She thought about all those nights she had prayed to God to bless her family, and now her husband was on national television with the chance of a lifetime—fame and fortune.

She was in and out of the kitchen, occupying the thirty minutes before the results show of *The Last Laugh* with refilling drinks and arranging trays of finger sandwiches. She was pleased with how many people came over to lend their support for her husband, but there were almost too many for Marvin's parents' small bungalow.

Considering she didn't even have a house of her own, Georgia felt guilty as she noticed all the repairs it needed. Who was she to criticize? But it did need a new roof that wouldn't leak every time there was heavy rainfall. And the stained carpet, which should have been pulled up years ago, smelled of mildew. Georgia had to use nearly half the package of Country Garden Glade carpet and room deodorizer while she vacuumed to disguise the odor.

She wanted everything to be just right. She was superstitious in that way, thinking bad luck would result if something was wrong, missing, or out of place. It bothered her there were not enough seats for her guests. Well, *his* guests, Marvin would say, all of them hoping he'd win, because they'd be ready to ask for a handout. She prayed he would move on to the next round so she could visit him in L.A. As much as she hated the thought of flying, especially after what had happened on September 11th the previous year, she tried to put away her fears so she could support her man and his plans.

Georgia sat on the living room floor holding Haden in her arms while she tried to quiet Edrik as he ran around the house carrying his football and yelling, "Touchdown!"

"That's Daddy," Edrik said, finally stopping when he noticed Marvin on TV. "How did he get in there?"

"Daddy's in LA," Georgia said as she pulled Edrik away from the television and told him to sit quietly and watch Daddy perform. But no one was quiet while the three remaining comedians performed the same material they had done the night before. Their neighbors, friends, and relatives were all talking, sipping on wine, guzzling down beers, grabbing two and three finger sandwiches at a time. Crumbs fell on the freshly vacuumed floor, and Georgia's skin crawled. Finally, after nearly forty minutes of noise so loud she could barely hear herself think, let alone make out what the host of the show said as he stood with an envelope in his hand, she shushed everyone. "They're getting ready to announce the finalists."

"Moving on to the final round of *The Last Laugh* is Idaeus Hilarus . . . and . . ." The pause was too long for Georgia, who now stood with Haden on her hip.

"Marvelous Marvin," she said at the same time the announcer did. The bungalow erupted with cheers. Georgia sighed with relief. They weren't there yet, but they were so close.

Marvin had started writing new material before he left for Los Angeles. Most of his jokes centered on married life. Essentially, he made jokes about Georgia, but nothing she couldn't handle—nothing that didn't make her laugh. The routine was all a part of a character Marvin created called Marvelous Marvin—an obnoxious, egotistical, chauvinistic know-it-all whom he had fine-tuned each week on the show, beating elimination.

The kids stayed with Georgia's sister Kendra while Georgia, her father-in-law, mother-in-law, and sister-in-law, Kayla, all survived the plane and bumper-to-bumper taxicab ride to the Los Angeles Marriott. It was just several miles from the famed Shrine Auditorium where the live finale for *The Last Laugh* would be held at the end of the week.

Three rooms had been reserved at the hotel through the studio. But what Georgia didn't know, and was surprised to learn, was that her room was the only one on a completely different floor from the others. She asked to be moved, but the hotel was full, and so Georgia, too tired to argue, took her card key from the front desk attendant and headed for the elevator.

Georgia, worn and exhausted from the long flight, threw down her bags, kicked off her heels, and headed for the bathroom as soon as she entered the room. It was more like an apartment, with a small sitting area and kitchenette. She stopped with her hand on the bathroom doorknob after hearing Marvin's voice.

She walked around the wall past the sitting area and toward the bed where she found him.

He stood to greet her. "Surprised? I really missed you."

"Oh, Marvin," she said, rushing into his arms. It had been weeks since they'd seen each other.

"You're ready, aren't you?"

"Yes, I'm ready."

"Well, I guess I'm ready, too." His pants had ballooned as a result of his erection.

"I missed you so much. I'm so proud of you. You are so incredible."

"We haven't even done anything yet, and I'm getting ready to come. Keep talking."

"You are, Marvin. You really are marvelous." Her lips danced across his face, down his neck, and over his chest as they collapsed on the bed.

* * *

By the end of the week, Georgia and her in-laws were sitting in the first row of the Shrine Auditorium.

Kayla sat on the edge of her seat on the other side of Georgia. She couldn't keep her head still. "Isn't that the guy from *The Wayne Brady Show*?"

"Who, Wayne Brady?" Georgia responded sarcastically.

"Yeah."

Georgia squinted to bring him into focus. "Do you need glasses? I think that's Damon Wayans."

"That's what I meant to say—the guy from *My Wife and Kids*."

"Sure you did," Georgia said. The lights dimmed and her stomach leaped—it was in knots from the anticipation. The red light glowed atop the main camera. Tonight was a two-hour show, meaning the first hour would be packed with guest spots from past winners and runners-up. Georgia didn't know if she could make it a full two hours.

"Hello, America, my name is Ian Conley and I'm the host of *The Last Laugh*. We are live from the Shrine Auditorium in Los Angeles, California, where our final two contestants, Marvelous Marvin Brown from Detroit, Michigan, and Idaeus Hilarus from Seattle, Washington, are battling it out to see who will have the last laugh. Tonight, America, your vote will make one of these contestants a millionaire and help launch an acting career. And we're going to get started . . . right after this commercial break."

The show started off with the host attempting a few jokes before Marvin and the other comedian came onstage to flip a coin determining the order of their performances. Marvin called heads, and heads it was. He chose to perform last, and the show began with his competitor's fifteen-minute routine. Then a commercial break, after which last year's winner performed. There was a clip of all he had done over the past year, which included guest spots on television shows, a pilot set to go into production, and a movie scheduled for release in the coming year. He had obviously arrived. Kayla, though, seriously doubted if they would let another black win.

"It's the audience vote," Georgia pointed out.

"Do you really believe that?" she asked Georgia. "The producers decide who's going to win."

Georgia quickly dismissed the negative comments, because winning this competition was their only way out. After last year's winner finished his routine, the show went to another commercial break.

Marvin stood backstage near the curtains. Usually, he wasn't the type to get nervous, but tonight he was. He had butterflies in his stomach. In two and a half minutes he would be on television telling the jokes he had worked on all night. He felt like he was dreaming, the world riding on his shoulders. And for Marvin, the world was his wife and kids. He knew he wouldn't have made it this far if not for Georgia. He owed her so much, which was why he wanted to win the competition so badly. The money and the acting opportunity would change their lives forever.

"Welcome back to the final round of *The Last Laugh*.

I'm your host, Ian Conley, and right now I'm bringing to the stage Marvelous Marvin Brown."

With his hands behind his back, he dropped his head for a second and said a quick prayer. He knew Georgia would have been proud if she had seen him, because she was one to always count her blessings.

Marvin walked onstage as Ian walked off in the opposite direction.

"I've struggled all my life," he said as he stood in the center of the stage behind the microphone stand. He couldn't see faces, only lights and cameras. He grabbed the microphone from the stand and started pacing. "All my life. Do you hear me? And I'm tired of struggling. It's one thing to be poor when you're by *yourself*. It's a whole other thing to be broke and married with children. That would be the name of my sitcom—*Broke and Married with Children*."

The previous night, he had talked about Georgia's weight and their sexual encounter from the day before. How holding up her legs was like lifting a pair of three-hundred-pound weights over his head, how after a few seconds he had to throw them down because it was too dangerous without a spotter.

And back at the hotel, Georgia had let him have it.

"You had to talk about my weight. Did you have to go there? And our sex life? Are my legs really that heavy?"

"Those were just jokes. Did you see how the people responded? All the laughs I got?"

"At my expense."

"But, baby, when we win, will you really care?"

"You better hope you win." Georgia walked into the bathroom and slammed the door behind her.

Marvin stood in front of the bathroom door. "I'm sorry, baby. You know I didn't mean it."

"How do I know you didn't mean it?" she asked from the other side of the door. "Just promise me you won't do that crap anymore."

"I promise."

Georgia opened the door and stood in front of Marvin with a skeptical look on her face.

"Really, I promise."

After Marvin finished, the show cut to a commercial break. Georgia released the breath she had been holding, and wiped her sweaty palms on her pants. She had surveyed the expressions on the judges' faces, watching how they smiled and clapped. He had tamed down his routine and didn't once slander his wife . . . or her cooking . . . or even their sex life. Georgia knew his routine because she had made him rehearse it in front of her that morning.

"He might have won," she told Kayla. "But what if you're right? What if it's rigged?"

"It is. I know what I'm talking about. But still, something good will come from this, with all the exposure Marvin has gotten."

If that something good wasn't instant cash, it wouldn't

help their current situation any, and so Georgia, feeling slightly defeated, sunk into her seat.

When the show returned, there was a film clip of the auditions and how they had arrived at the final two. Then Marvin took the stage. Georgia watched the judges. Their smiles appeared even larger and their applause louder. They nodded and whispered in one another's ears.

"I don't know. I think Marvin may have won," Georgia said as she turned to face Kayla.

"Why do you say that?"

"I just get that feeling."

Before the results were announced, there was another commercial break. Georgia was in agony.

"And now, the moment America has been waiting for," Ian said as he stood between Marvin and Idaeus Hilarus holding a white envelope. "After the largest nationwide vote in *Last Laugh* history—more than fifty million callers—you have decided the fate of our contestants." Ian opened the envelope and read. "With seventy-nine percent of the vote, congratulations . . . Marvelous Marvin! You have the last laugh!"

Marvin looked stunned. "Are you serious?"

"Absolutely."

"Yes!" He jumped from excitement and hugged the host before shaking the other contestant's hand. He rushed offstage into the crowd as thousands of balloons rained from the ceiling. "I told you, baby. Did I not tell you?" He swept Georgia off her feet and twirled her around. "We won a million dollars, baby. We're on our way. We can get our own house. No more raggedy cars." He set Georgia down. The realization of winning was too much for him to handle at that moment. "You believed in me. And now we're here. Thank you."

There were tears in all their eyes—Marvin's, Georgia's, his mother's and sister's. Even his father held a handkerchief.

"You better go back onstage and get your check," his father told him, then turned toward his mother. "Dummy almost forgot his check."

Marvin gave his father a high five and ran back onstage. He stood between the host of the show and the president of the network with a check in his hand and a smile on his face.

All Marvin could think about was the home on Lake Shore Drive in Grosse Pointe Farms, Michigan, that he was going to buy for his family, and how he no longer had to ask the people who lived there how they earned a living. It no longer mattered.

PART TWO

Mo' Money Mo' Problems

Five years later

Come December, which was a little less than two months away, Georgia would turn forty-one. She and Marvin now lived in Grosse Pointe Farms—not in his dream house, but in another, three houses down, that was more to their liking on the inside, and both she and Marvin drove their dream cars.

They moved to the wealthy suburb immediately after Marvin won the one million dollars on *The Last Laugh*, but his development deal quickly fell through. A disappointed Marvin put his plans on hold for Hollywood stardom and moved back to Detroit for what he hoped would be a temporary period. His plans to become the next Bernie Mac halted when Georgia suggested that Marvin look into doing radio. Within a year, he had taken over as a morning show host for a small local station with its sights on syndication. Within two years of going live on-air, 102 Hitz was the number-one rated morning show thanks to Marvin's wild antics—the fan-favorite Monday prank calls; Talkback Tuesday, when listeners called in to speak their minds; his generous giveaways; and his outlandish comments about Georgia.

But Georgia couldn't helping feeling she and Marvin had lost something—a little piece of what kept them grounded.

Their life was full of bling. Yet Georgia's was just a blur.

Fancy cars and expensive clothes just didn't cut it for Georgia. Materialism wasn't something she strived for. She was looking for acceptance. Marvin had been accepted— by his fans and of course by her. He was Marvelous Marvin in the Morning on 102 Hitz; he was both popular and controversial on the air and on MySpace. He made outlandish comments about everything—from celebrities, to current events, to his wife—that he never apologized for.

Georgia accepted what he said, because he claimed he was just joking about most of it. Georgia's unwavering love for Marvin went deep. She needed to be loved. Part of it stemmed from her childhood, having never known her father—not her real one. So Marvin was more than a husband: He was her everything.

Entertainers knew her husband well and seemed to have more access to him than she did. She stayed home to cook and clean even though they could afford a maid and personal chef. She might have had the ability to rival Martha Stewart, but she was no Beyoncé.

Now the years had packed on pounds that Beach Body exercise tapes, Curves, and Weight Watchers couldn't help her control in the same way an extra-firm support girdle could.

If Georgia ever had dreams, she had forgotten them. She lost herself in *Oprah* and reality TV. Her life consisted of making up cheers for her family. Hooray for Marvin. Hooray for Edrik and Haden. *But who will hooray for me?* she often wondered.

She was living Marvin's life, not hers. They had struggled for years, and it had been bad, but not as bad as she had thought, now that she was on the other side and had something to compare to. Before, looking at a price tag made her strive for something, and striving made her feel alive—she had a goal to achieve. Now price was never a concern, because money was not an issue. And if it ever became one, Georgia wouldn't even know, because Marvin handled all the finances.

And what of the rumors about Marvin's infidelity?

How had they affected her?

Not much . . . not much at all.

She liked to tell herself.

He had been coined a "serial" cheater by his listeners when he admitted on air that he frequented strip clubs. Georgia heard Marvin describe his favorite dancer, who performed for him in the champagne room. His cohosts, Big Fella Mike and Milt Merlin, couldn't stop laughing, while Cammy, the only female member of the team, tried to get a word in edgewise to chastise him.

Georgia was stuck in a life she had not designed.

She was a wife.

She was a mother.

And she was in search of herself and a life she had some say in.

It was 5:50 A.M.

In ten minutes, Marvin would be live on air with his number-one rated, nationally syndicated radio show—*The Marvelous Marvin Morning Show*, on 102 Hitz. He stood in the studio wearing a turquoise suit with gray pinstripes and a pair of turquoise gaiters. His matching fedora hung from the hat rack.

He was living on top of the world . . . or was he?

He had money now, but as the late Notorious B.I.G. said, "Mo money, mo problems." Marvin was a gambler, and the stakes were high on all the bets he placed. He won often, but lost even more. And somehow, through it all, he had managed to keep his addiction a secret from Georgia. One wrong move, though, could break the bank, and if that happened, he would just as soon blow his brains out than live like a pauper again.

More money, more problems.

The woman he was messing around with was trying to monopolize his free time. But she wasn't his real concern, because she could be appeased with money and gifts. His real problem was his growing gambling debt. He had to get it under control. He had just paid the last installment of a high-stakes loan—nearly two hundred thousand dollars—when, within a matter of weeks, he nearly doubled his old debt.

Had this been six months earlier, he wouldn't worry so much, but the FCC was cracking down on a few things—mainly "pay-for-play," which was Marvin's biggest side hustle. In a given day, he could earn ten thousand dollars under the table just for mentioning certain artists or playing certain songs. Sometimes it was products being launched or dealerships announcing special sales. Marvin felt like he was hustling, but instead of drugs, his commodity was airtime. This was common in radio, but now he had to be careful.

Marvin had weaknesses: women and poker, mainly, but occasionally alcohol. For the most part, his drinking was under control, but women and gambling—those habits were hard to break. One time, he left the casino with seventy-five thousand dollars in profit. Other times, he left double that amount in the hole.

He stood in front of the controls with his headphones wrapped around his neck and a microphone extended in front of him. After taking his seat on what he affection-ately called "his throne," he slid the headphones over his ears and adjusted the microphone so that it nearly touched his slender lips before he sipped his Starbucks venti-sized white chocolate mocha.

One song.

That's all it ever took to blow up some unknown artist. It was the power of radio.

Marvin looked at the CD jewel case of Miss Ella J. She really wasn't all that. But he had to hype her up. Her label had wanted a Beyoncé type, and Marvin felt they should have kept looking. The only thing Ella J and Beyoncé had in common was their complexions. And possibly their weaves. Aside from that, Ella J's sound didn't come close.

Marvin had agreed with the A&R rep to play the same song every hour he was on air, starting the day the single dropped until it climbed to number one on the Billboard chart. Marvin received a bonus when the single reached number one, which was more motivation for him not just to play it but to pump it up. Marvin knew if idealistic Georgia knew what he was up to, her world would crumble.

You mean stars are made? Airtime is bought? Listeners are manipulated?

Georgia still believed that good old-fashioned luck coupled with raw talent won out. Didn't happen. Not these days. Marvin believed it wasn't about having talent but, rather, having connections.

And he was a connection.

Marvin's BlackBerry vibrated during his first segment

and it never let up. Since he knew Georgia didn't call him while he was on air unless it was an emergency, he didn't bother to see who was trying to reach him.

"Marvin, you have a call on the red phone," his intern said.

"I have a call on the red phone?" he asked. "Tell whoever it is I'm busy. I'm about to go back on the air."

The intern went to the phone and repeated Marvin's message.

"They said they'd hold."

After the segment ended and they went to another commercial break, Marvin picked up the red phone, hoping to hear a dial tone.

"Marvin, how are you, man? You haven't forgotten about the nice little sum you owe us, have you? Because it's way past time to pay up."

Marvin's blood ran cold as he cleared his throat. "No, of course I haven't forgotten. I know."

"I mean, we love doing business with you, man, but waiting four or five months isn't working for us at all. This time, we want our money. All of it. And the sooner, the better . . . for you."

Marvin hung up the phone, too distracted about what he owed to go back on the air.

"But it's Monday. Who'll do the prank?" Cammy asked.

"Just replay the one from last week."

He had Cammy fill in for him while he headed to his bank to inquire about a home equity loan. Georgia wasn't on the original deed, so she'd never find out. In seventy-two hours, over five hundred thousand dollars would be deposited into Marvin's private account, one Georgia didn't even know existed. He would use the majority to pay off the debt he owed to the loan sharks. He had that much equity after having put more than half of his winnings into buying the house.

Now, not only did he have to pay his primary mortgage, but he would also be responsible for a second mortgage that was nearly as high. But at least he would have the mob off of his back for now . . . until the next time he got his urge.

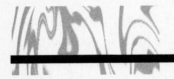

Georgia fumbled with her ringing cell phone as she pulled her Porsche Cayenne into their three-car garage between Marvin's Corvette and the space that usually occupied his Mercedes S600.

"If your husband slanders my name or mentions my ex-husbands one more time on the radio, I'll slap a lawsuit on his ass so fierce that you and yours will be forced to move back in with his parents," Kendra barked.

Kendra, Georgia's oldest sibling, was on her third divorce. Her first marriage had lasted only six months. The second time around, she was twenty-five when she married a fifty-year-old man, staying with him long enough to collect part of his pension. After their mother passed, Kendra turned to plastic surgery for her therapy, wanting to escape her own existence. With a new face, she could perhaps invent a different life.

Georgia's worn voice dragged. "You're getting ready to get married *again,* so what problem could you possibly have now?" The last time Georgia's sister called sounding that upset, it was after a botched breast job.

"You know damn well what I'm talking about. You listen to your husband's lame ass morning show. Trying to be the Tom Joyner he's not. So you should know what he's been talking about all morning on 102 *SHitz* . . . besides you."

"I didn't tune in to his show this morning. I haven't listened to it in quite a while. What did he say?"

"He's still on the air talking about *my* family, laughing like something's funny. My life is getting ready to explode and your husband has jokes? Talking about my plastic surgery, which by the way, he shouldn't even know about unless you told him."

"Why is your life getting ready to explode?"

"Because Robert is putting up a fight for my house." Robert was her third husband, and the house was actually his. She had been married to him for four years and they had just recently separated. "And your husband isn't helping my legal matters any by putting my business out in the street. Robert doesn't know I'm engaged, and the last thing I want that man to have is some ammunition."

Georgia quickly tuned in to the morning show and heard nauseating laughter—mainly Marvin's—ringing so loudly through her fourteen Bose surround-sound speakers that she hurried to turn down the volume.

"My sister-in-law looks like a cross between La Toya Jackson and Lil' Kim. Maybe they all went to the same plastic surgeon," Marvin said. "She's getting ready to get married for the fourth time. The first time, her marriage lasted six months. Her second marriage lasted ten years—long enough for her to collect his pension. And her third marriage is still legally binding."

"I don't see how you do it," Kendra said to Georgia. "I'm mad as hell at Marvin for disrespecting me just one day, but he does it to you every day. You don't have to put up with that. Everybody knows Marvin's fuckin' around on you. Everybody but you. I get calls all the time saying, 'I saw your brother-in-law here or there.' "

"He's in radio, so he knows a lot of the artists and goes to a lot of events and gets photo ops."

"She may look thirty," Marvin said, "but she's a long way from it. Like twenty-three years from it."

"Oh, that's it! I'm calling his ass right now," Kendra screamed, "and they better put me on the air."

"Hello," Georgia said, but Kendra had already hung up.

Georgia removed an endless array of shopping bags from the back of her SUV, all from high-end retailers located in Somerset Mall. Kendra didn't know what she was talking about; Georgia was fairly confident Marvin was not having an affair. All the mess he said on-air was just for ratings. At least, Georgia prayed it was. Sometimes she wasn't so sure.

To keep her mind off of what her husband might be doing those nights he crept in so late, Georgia shopped . . .

and ate. And then shopped and ate some more on the weekends with her best friend, Claudette, or with Beverly, the wife of one of the station owners. And sometimes with her next-door neighbor, Art, a corporate attorney turned stay-at-home dad who had time during the day to catch sales at the mall with Georgia.

Life was going well. Or was it?

Georgia wanted more from her life. More than the luxury cars they changed out every six months, the sprawling estate they owned, the fancy functions she stopped attending two years earlier after Marvin stopped asking her to join him. She thought about the past five years that had brought her husband fame and fortune, how so much had changed. Marvin and Georgia's new life, eleven years in the making, had finally arrived, and she expected to be happy. Until she could accomplish some of her own goals, though, she wouldn't be. And what made matters worse, she had no idea what those goals were—aside from getting her brother off the streets. That would be a lifelong goal.

She knew her family and friends all talked behind Georgia's back about how Marvin was doing her wrong and how she never confronted him. And even though Marvin would always apologize, Georgia knew he wasn't sorry. But for now, she decided, Georgia was going to keep on being Georgia—sweet. She had faith that one day it would all pay off.

That night, when Georgia finally decided to retreat to their bedroom, Marvin lay in bed butt naked underneath the sheets, stroking his penis and anxiously awaiting her arrival. But how could she get excited about sex, knowing that what went on in their bedroom was often recounted the next morning on-air?

"Remember to put on that thong and bra set that I bought for you."

She stood in the bathroom, staring at the full-length mirror. She saw every angle and every dimple on her thighs, and tried to reassure herself that she was sexy. Fifty-plus pounds had been added to her body since she said, "I do." At one time, she could easily fit into the sexy Victoria's Secret outfits like the one he had wanted her to put on. But not this time. The thong and bra were both too small, but she somehow managed to squeeze into them.

Sex between the two of them had always been good, something neither one could get enough of in the first five years of their marriage. But lately, they rarely enjoyed intimacy and she wondered who was taking care of his insatiable appetite since she was never in the mood and he rarely pressed the issue.

"Hurry up, baby, *we're* waiting for you."

"I'm fat, Marvin," she yelled.

"Well, bring your fat ass out here, then."

"Please don't make fun of me." She inched her way out of the bathroom with a terry cloth robe covering her.

"Take it off, baby."

"Turn off the light."

"Why? I want to see you. I'm tired of doing it in complete darkness."

"Marvin, please, just turn off the lamp."

"No."

She climbed in bed with her robe on. "I'm going to sleep."

"You can sleep. But while you're sleeping, I have other plans," he said, tugging at the sheets.

"No, Marvin," she said as she snatched the sheet back from him, and they began an intense form of tug-of-war. "I'm not in the mood."

"For once, I am in the mood, so you better get some while you can."

"Sometimes, I can't stand your ass," she blurted.

"Oh, really, you can't stand my ass sometimes?" he asked, tickling her stomach. "How come you're not laughing? Is all that fat hiding your tickle bones?" He began squeezing her love handles.

"Marvin, stop. I'm really not in the mood. I want uninterrupted sleep for a change. Please."

A few hours later, she awakened to find Marvin's head buried between her legs. His tongue swirling around her clitoris reminded her temporarily just why she could take so much of his mess. Marvin climbed on top of her, bending her legs back so far they were nearly touching the headboard. His quick movements made the bed squeak. With each thrust, the springs sang loudly.

"I'm getting ready to come," Marvin said.

Georgia turned her head to the side with her eyelids tightly clinched, trying to bear the burning sensation. He was going faster, and she knew that any minute, he would be ready to explode inside her. He grunted several times, moaned, and then loosened his grip to allow Georgia's legs to relax. "Maybe you need to start exercising and work on your flexibility."

"I'm flexible enough." Georgia sat up, tossing the sheet over her like a cape.

"I'm just saying you have gained a lot of weight. Some of it looks good, but some of it," he said, jiggling her stomach, "you can definitely stand to lose."

She shoved his hand away from her belly, and said, "I know what I need to do, Marvin, so please stop constantly reminding me. I have feelings, too, you know."

"I mean look at me." He slid his hand across his six-pack abs.

"And in case you've forgotten, I gave birth to your two kids."

"Working out is a good way to relieve stress. And fat." Marvin turned on his side and within seconds was snoring. But Georgia, who had always been self-conscious about so many things—her hair, her complexion, even the fullness of her lips—retreated back to the bathroom to stand in front of the full-length mirror, worried that her weight may be something else to add to her growing list of personal dislikes.

"Have you ever seen a cow in a thong?" Marvelous Marvin asked. "I did last night when my wife walked into our bedroom and dropped her robe." The booing sound effects played in the background. "I know I'm going to get in trouble with some of my full-figured female listeners. I'm just telling the truth. Hell, I had to fantasize I was with another woman just to stay hard. I pretended I was in the bed with Beyoncé—I had to do with my mind what my wife needs to do with her body—some serious stretching."

"Now, wait a minute," Cammy said. "That was so rude. How are you going to say something like that about your own wife?"

"Would it be better if I said something like that about

somebody else's wife? When don't I say things about Georgia?"

"My point exactly. I've met Georgia, and she is not at all the way you describe her, so stop lying to the people."

"You're always trying to take up for her. But the truth is the truth, and I'm just giving my listeners the truth . . . and a chance at one thousand dollars if you're my tenth caller this morning."

"Marvin, I feel pregnant every day I work with you."

"Why is that?"

"You give me morning sickness. The things you say really make me want to throw up. Have you ever heard that old saying, 'If you don't have anything good to say, don't say anything at all'?"

"I've heard it, but that can't apply to married men, because we rarely have anything good to say about our wives."

"Oh, whatever. You know that's not true. Don't try to group all men in a doggish category with you. I'm a single woman, and I want to believe there are still some good men out there."

"There are. And certain women don't have to worry about getting dogged. Like Beyoncé and Ciara—even Janet Jackson."

"What do you mean 'even Janet Jackson'?"

"Her age is starting to show a little bit. That face is starting to crack."

"You must be crazy!" Cammy shouted. "Janet looks

good. Maybe I'm getting older, or maybe I'm getting wiser, or maybe I just don't want to hear your mess anymore."

"Can we talk about the new hairstyle?"

"Oh, you don't like my braids?"

"Braids are a lazy woman's hairstyle. No, I don't like them at all."

"Whatever, Marvin. You don't like braids. And what about a weave?"

"A weave done correctly can be a turn-on. Like Janet Jackson's."

"Just a few minutes ago, you said she was cracking."

"I said she was starting to crack. That doesn't have anything to do with her hair. She has the best weave in the business. I think whoever does her weave is on her personal payroll with a signed agreement that they can't do anyone else's hair, because I have never seen a weave look that good."

"I don't even think Janet Jackson has a weave. And if she does, I want to know who does it so I can make an appointment."

"Anyone who remembers Janet Jackson from *Good Times* knows she has a weave."

"Not true. A person's hair does grow over the years."

"She has a weave. And I don't mind a weave that looks good. Ladies, listen to Marvelous Marvin. If you're going to get a weave, make sure you do it over your entire head. Please do not have half of your head silky straight while the other half is nappy."

"Tenth caller. I'm so sorry to keep you waiting. All I need you to do is tell us what station gives away more cash, keeping it locked in the number one spot."

"102 Hitz," the woman said.

"That's it, baby."

Corliss Riggs was on her cell phone talking to her best friend, Tiffany, while peeking through her vertical blinds to observe the black Escalade parked in front of her apartment building. A female sat behind the wheel—the same woman who had been calling Corliss's home all evening to speak with Dante. According to Dante, the woman was his cousin.

Dante had just strolled out of the apartment building, approached the SUV with a smile, and hopped in the passenger side as the two whisked off.

"See, this is the very thing Marvelous Marvin was talking about on his show all last week—unfaithful men. And Dante is one of them. I can't believe this broke-ass Negro has just disrespected me like this," Corliss said to Tiffany. "The next man I date will be a white man."

"You should have said the next man you date will be Jermaine," Tiffany said. "Stop wasting your time with those other fools, and try to work on fixing what you broke with him."

"I don't think he'd ever forgive me for cheating. I messed up."

"A man once told me that if he actually saw his woman with another man, he would never be able to forgive her, but if he just knew about it, then he may be able to."

"I guess it's coming back around to me, because Dante is definitely cheating, and I am so sick of this shit." She walked away from the window, kicking the side of her leather sofa. "Damn. He had the nerve to have his other woman pick him up at our apartment—a so-called cousin. If she's his cousin, why does she have to wait in the car? Why doesn't she just come up and wait in the apartment and introduce herself? Why do I even deal with that fool?"

"What are you really mad about? Because I know you don't care this much about Dante."

"I miss my man. I want Jermaine back."

"There's one question I never asked you—why did you cheat on him?"

"I honestly didn't have a good reason. He worked long hours at the dealership, and I was lonely. But that was no excuse. He brought the money home and took care of me and Jelani. No, the sex didn't blow my mind, but he was a good man. . . . He is a good man. Girl, I was such a fool."

Jermaine was the only man who had stayed a decent

length of time in Corliss's life—three years off and on—but now he was gone, too. "Let me talk to you later. I need to get my mind together."

"Okay, girl, but if you need me, I'm here for you—always."

Corliss sat on the arm of her sofa. At thirty-one, she was a single mother struggling to take care of her four-year-old son. She sold Avon for a little extra money. And even though she had been through a string of relationships, it was Jermaine, her baby's father, whom she loved. He wasn't romantic—not the type to send her flowers for no special reason at all. But she had never had any man do that, which was why she sent herself roses. He never forgot the special occasions—birthdays, Christmas, Valentine's, and the Great Lakes region's observance of Sweetest Day.

Jermaine was a good man—hardworking. He started his career as a car salesman for a Chrysler dealership when they first began dating, and even though things were tight while working on straight commission, he built up his clientele and became one of the top salespeople, eventually getting promoted to a new-car sales manager at one of the largest dealerships in Michigan. Now his income was much more stable, and he owned his own house in Novi, a suburb of Detroit.

Corliss thought about all the men currently in her life. Her son was with Jermaine and would be home shortly. Dante was with his other woman, and who knew when—or if—he was ever coming home? She was by herself, which had always made her feel uncomfortable.

Her eyes felt strained from all the stress. She wanted to take off her false corner lashes and her hazel contacts because she knew it would relieve some of the tension, but she didn't like herself with stubby lashes and dark brown eyes. She slid onto the sofa and lay across it with her feet dangling off the ends as her eyes slowly closed. She had been sleeping for close to an hour when banging at the door caused her to spring up.

"I'm coming," she shouted. She looked through the peephole and saw Jermaine and Jelani. She made a quick detour for the bathroom. What should have been seconds turned into a twenty minute mini-makeover, and before long, both Jermaine and Jelani were banging. "Sorry," she said as she rushed to let them in.

"Getting made up," Jermaine said as he pulled his son into the apartment. He shook his head. "Some things never change."

"You're right," Corliss said. "Some things never do."

Jermaine stared Corliss down. "We need to talk."

"About what?" Corliss asked with attitude.

"I don't want to talk around my son, but we definitely need to have a conversation about that dude."

"I'm not in the mood for all that. My business is my business, and your business is your business. That's how it goes down when two people are no longer together," Corliss said, pretending their breakup didn't bother her. They had been apart for nearly a year.

"Yeah, and whose fault is that? It sure in the hell ain't mine." He looked down at his son. "Little man, go on to your room and close the door."

Jelani ran to his bedroom with his hands covering his ears.

"You got that dude living here, don't you?"

"That's none of your business."

"The hell it is some of my business. Why did you lie and tell me he wasn't? Why did I have to find the truth out from our son?"

"Are you going to believe a four-year-old over me?"

"Don't do that. Don't act like our son is lying."

"Okay, I won't do that, because you already knew he was living here."

"The hell I did. Why would I think you would let that dude live with you? Isn't it bad enough you cheated on me with him? I don't want Jelani exposed to all that. I know we're no longer together. You've moved on and I've moved on—"

"Oh, you've moved on. So you have a girlfriend now?"

"Please don't question me. I've moved on. And I understand you have needs and all that. I mean, I know you're a young woman, but to have a man living up here with my son? That's not cool. Not at all."

"I don't know what you think this is, but you can't be calling the shots up here. If you can have someone, I can have someone."

"Who says I have someone?"

"You just said you moved on."

"I date, but I work too many hours, and I'm trying to do too many things to have a serious relationship. I'm just trying to look out for you and our son."

"Me?" Corliss questioned.

"Yes, you, because a lot of these dudes today are just out for what they can get. And they're playing some serious mind games. Some of these dudes out here are just looking for a place to lay their head. They're not thinking about you or your feelings. And the way it is now in Detroit, with all these folks without jobs, houses in foreclosure, you just have to be careful. Don't let a man take food from our son's mouth."

"Now, you know when it comes to Jelani, I don't play that. No one's taking anything from his mouth."

"I know you're a good mother, but anybody can get played."

"Mmm, well, not this anybody, so don't you worry. Is that all?"

"Yeah, that's it." He started walking toward the door.

"Oh, I need you to pick up Jelani from latchkey tomorrow. I'm working late," Corliss said.

"You sure have been working late a lot."

"You're right, I sure have. Why, is that going to be a problem?" She opened the door for Jermaine and the two stood in the hallway talking.

"Shouldn't be," he said.

"No later than five or they charge, and if they charge, I won't be the one paying for it—you will." Corliss didn't have to work late. She had just told Jermaine that for two reasons. One, she wanted to see him again, and two, if Dante made it back home tomorrow, she was going to collect his half of the rent for last month and then kick him out.

"I'll be there by five. I'll just take my lunch late."

"Four o'clock lunch?"

"Most nights I'm at the dealership past nine. You know that, or have you forgotten already?"

"I knew it was like that when you were in sales, but as a sales manager—"

"It's the same. But don't worry. I'll be there."

Corliss closed her door and watched him through the peephole, then ran over to her window and waited for him to walk out of the building and over to his brand-new Chrysler Aspen with a dealer license plate.

"Mmm. Things are looking up for him, and I'm still struggling."

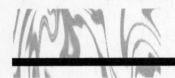

Georgia was curled on the sofa, nibbling on cheese and talking on the phone with her next-door neighbor, Art, when the doorbell rang. She picked up the remote control to lower the volume on the television.

"Art, are you still outside?"

"I'm at my mailbox. Nothing's in it except a mailer for two missing boys. They've been missing for years now— the ones who used to be on that billboard off I-75."

"The two brothers. I remember that story. The man who abducted them drove a Dodge Shadow, just like the car we used to have."

"You used to have a Dodge Shadow? My, you've come a long way. Do you want me to check your box?"

"No, but can you check my door and tell me who's there?"

"Two women."

"Two women?" Georgia walked toward the front of the house. "What do they want?"

"Well, they don't look like Girl Scouts, so I'd say they're not trying to sell cookies. And there's a cab parked in your driveway."

"A cab?" Georgia opened her front door.

"Is this the Brown residence?" the tall, large woman asked. She wore a glittery jacket with fake fur around the collar.

"Possibly," Georgia said. "Why?"

"Either this is the Brown residence or it's not." The woman rocked on the sides of her high-heeled snakeskin boots. Her fancy multicolored nails had cubic zirconias on them and were long and curved, reminding Georgia of the crazy straws her sons loved to drink from.

"Yes, this is the Brown residence. And who are you?"

"Are you Marvin's wife?"

"Yes," Georgia said reluctantly.

"Mmm. You're nothing like I pictured." The woman motioned to the cab driver to wait for a minute and then pushed the young girl standing beside her into Georgia's home. "Not the way Marvin talks about you on the air. I expected to see Aunt Esther on the other side of this door."

"Wait a minute. You can't just barge into our house like this. Who are you?"

"I'm Bernadette," the woman said as her head swirled, looking at the grand entrance of the home. "And this is my daughter Chloe. Mine and Marvin's."

"Yours and Marvin's? How old is she?"

"Thirteen. Don't worry, I had her before you and Marvin got together."

Chloe faked a smile and revealed a gold and diamond grill that spelled out her name.

"Please tell me that's removable," Georgia asked.

"Yeah, it comes out," Bernadette said, "but good luck trying to get her to take it out." Bernadette walked through the large marble foyer with her head tilted toward the vaulted ceilings and the massive chandelier hanging from it. "That shit had to cost a fortune. I saw one just like that on *MTV Cribs*. I think it was in Lil Jon's house, wasn't it, Chloe?"

"Lil Jon ain't got no shit like that in his house. That ain't even his style."

Georgia's eyes bugged after Chloe spoke.

"You're right. It was a white person's house, wasn't it?"

"Probably. Look like that's where that shit needs to be—in a white person's house."

Bernadette and Chloe began laughing.

"You don't mind her using profanity?"

"I use it," Bernadette said. "Anything I can do, she can do."

"Really?"

"Yes, really."

Chloe stood in the foyer next to her mother and studied Georgia, her eyes freezing at Georgia's curly hair. Georgia noticed and began playing with her spiral curls to loosen them a bit.

"And Chloe is how old again?"

"Thirteen."

Georgia quickly did the math. Georgia and Marvin recently celebrated their eleven year anniversary, and prior to marriage, they dated for a year. So Bernadette was right: Chloe happened just one year before they met. Georgia took a sigh of relief, but still wondered why Marvin didn't tell her. Having Marvin get a paternity test was the next thought to pop into her head.

Bernadette was quick to explain to Georgia why they were there. The two of them needed a place to stay. A house fire destroyed everything they had, and now they were homeless. Georgia, who panicked over small things like misplacing a shopping receipt, was really freaking out. She told them to wait while she tried to get Marvin on the phone. Her heart raced as she hurried into the kitchen with the cordless in hand. Art, still on the line, had overheard every word. Unmoved, Bernadette and Chloe continued to survey the grand entrance.

"Are they rich?" Chloe asked.

"Oh, yeah, their ass has plenty money. And, hey, it's your daddy, so that means since they are rich, so are you. And me, too, because he owes me a whole lot of back child support."

"Art, let me call you back." Georgia hung up on him and quickly dialed Marvin's cell phone. It was one o'clock in the afternoon, and he'd already left the radio station to work out at Gold's Gym. "This is not the time to have your cell phone off, Marvin," Georgia said to his voice mail.

"Did you know you had a baby? Well, she's not a baby now—she's a teenager. Thirteen, but she looks like she's twenty. You need to come home right now."

Georgia walked back to the large foyer, keeping a fair distance between the woman and her child. The Browns had money now, and Marvin always said they had to be careful of people coming out of the woodwork—people they didn't even know claiming to be long-lost relatives. But as Georgia studied Chloe's features—her deep dimples and mocha brown skin with thick jet black wavy hair— she knew Chloe was Marvin's child. She was a strikingly beautiful girl and tall for her age. *Not quite tall enough to be a runway model and not polished enough to be one either*, Georgia thought.

Bernadette was a real piece of work, clutching her knockoff Prada bag as she paced the entrance with her nose turned up and her eyes darting. Georgia and Bernadette had a brief stare-down before Bernadette broke the silence. "I don't expect you to put *me* up, but Chloe needs to stay here with y'all for good or at least until she turns eighteen. More and more men today are raising their kids, and it's time for Marvin to be one of them."

"Marvin has two kids he's raising right now," Georgia explained.

"Well, Chloe will make three," Bernadette said as she looked over at Chloe, who popped her gum in front of Georgia.

"But this is November. It's well into the new school year. You can't just come to someone's house like this. Just come back. Come back after I've had a chance to talk to Marvin about this. Maybe we can provide child support."

"Maybe?" Bernadette challenged. "There's not no maybe to it. You will. Living like this? Oh, you definitely will."

"I mean we can. And we will."

"Shit, he should've been doing that for thirteen years. It's not as if he didn't already know he had a daughter."

Georgia was now even more confused. She had already excused her husband, assuming Bernadette, who carried herself very loosely, had been a one-night stand. That was until Bernadette explained she and Marvin had been together for four years before she had finally dumped him.

"By the time I finish adding up all that back child support, we might be living in this house instead of y'all."

"That I doubt very seriously."

"To a woman like me, men like Marvin come a dime a dozen. And what you don't understand, sweetie, is you ain't even his type. You're a little too homely looking. Marvin likes things that glitter like gold."

"Isn't your cab waiting?" Georgia glanced down at her cell phone to make sure the ringer was turned up loudly.

"I'll leave, but I'm not taking Chloe with me." Bernadette exited, leaving her daughter behind, but not before complaining that the fare had steadily climbed while she had been inside waiting for Marvin to call. Georgia, feeling obligated, handed her a hundred-dollar bill to pay for the taxi, which she was sure would be more than enough. Bernadette snatched the money from Georgia. "Just let Marvin know that my attorney will be in touch to draft up the custody papers and reach a settlement for all that back child support. It must be really nice living so large." She turned to face her daughter. "Well, Chloe, baby, you can tell your momma how nice it is, because you about to find out for yourself. Aren't you?" The two grinned, carved from the same mold. And just as fast as she appeared, Bernadette left.

Marvin's cell phone skirted across the nightstand.

"Mmm. Is it time to go home already?" Destiny asked as she rolled over and rested her chin on Marvin's chest, plucking at his hairs.

Destiny was twenty-two—exactly half Marvin's age. She had lived a fast life, becoming a stripper at seventeen. She never turned tricks, but had considered giving massages with happy endings ever since learning she could make a lot of money that way. She was a Southern girl who took the Greyhound from Arkansas to Detroit, bound for the big city, after graduating from high school. New York and California had seemed too big, and she had relatives in the Motor City who worked for the factory, people she'd spent summers with and cousins she could stay with. She did at first, but before long she was living in a rental house on the West Side, paying her own bills and stripping for a living.

She had met plenty of men who claimed to have money. Some were athletes who frequented the club, but she knew better than to fool with them. All they wanted to buy was a good time—nothing serious—and Destiny was ready to settle down after taking off her clothes for money for five years.

Marvin was the man she wanted—even if he was married. He was fine, with jet black wavy hair, a bronze complexion, and dark eyes. To Destiny, he looked like a Native American or someone from the islands. She liked how he dressed in flashy bright-colored suits and matching gators. And she just loved him.

She stared at Marvin while he lay in his favorite sleeping position on his back with his hands crossed over his chest. His eyes were closed, and he seemed unaware that his phone had been vibrating for several hours.

They'd had sex all morning, done a few lines of coke, and had some drinks. He didn't do coke often, but when he wanted to heighten his sexual experience, he would indulge. Since Destiny was an admitted casual user, he had someone else to get high with.

"Let's see who this is. Again. As if I don't already know." She reached for his BlackBerry. " '911. Come home. It's urgent.' Oh well." She pressed down the track wheel and deleted the message the same way she had done to all the others. A devilish grin spread across her face. "All's fair in love and war."

"What?" Marvin asked as he struggled to pry open his eyes. She tossed his phone underneath her bed.

"Nothing. Just ready to go again, that's all." She pressed her full lips against his thin ones and rolled her long pierced tongue inside of his mouth.

"Oh, really? I thought I gave you the best fifteen minutes I had."

"And you did, but what's wrong with a woman wanting fifteen more?"

"Nothing. Nothing at all," he said, preparing to go for another round.

Destiny started kissing his chest and working her way down. He closed his eyes and imagined where her lips would land. While Marvin enjoyed the oral sex, his phone began vibrating.

"Let it ring, baby," Destiny said, taking a break to exercise her jaw.

"I better answer. It's probably my wife." He searched the nightstand with his eyes. "Where's my BlackBerry? Have you seen it?"

"Maybe it fell."

Marvin leaned over the side of her bed and ran his hand along the edge, pulling out his phone and a sandal, an aqua blue thong, a hair comb, clip-on human hair, and an empty condom package. He didn't trip about the condoms because he knew the deal and actually was happy to see that she used protection. But the call, along with all her junk under the bed, killed the mood and he stood up, deciding to head home for the evening.

"Why do you have to go home?" Destiny took Marvin's hand and pulled him back on the bed.

"Don't start. Please. Not today. You know the deal."

"I may know the deal, but I don't like the deal. And in fact, it's time to renegotiate that deal."

Marvin had balls. He sported his latest fling through the streets of downtown Detroit and openly dined with Destiny at restaurants he had never taken Georgia—places she had asked to go, like Lola's in Harmonie Park. The Catalina seafood stew, the very dish Georgia had wanted to try since reading a rave review about it in *The Detroit News,* was the same one Destiny had eaten on several occasions.

"You know what I was wondering?"

"What's that?" Marvin asked.

"Why can't I go on the air with you? I'm your woman— or so you say—but yet, I'm still stripping. I'd rather be on the air. That way, I can spend even more time with my man and stop sliding down poles for a living." She was rambling, and Marvin hated to hear a woman go on and on, especially when what she said was nonsense. Besides, Marvin would never put Destiny on his radio program. "I could be way better than that chick you got on there now. She's not even cute. I checked her out on your Web site. Put my pictures on there and see how many hits you get. I want us to be together, and you promised we would."

He cleared his throat. *Why can't life be simple?* Marvin wondered. *Even the strippers want quality time now.*

"Cammy is under a contract that doesn't expire for two more years."

"Buy her out of it. Do what you have to do so I won't be forced to do what I have to do."

"What would you be forced to do?"

"Go to your wife."

"My wife? You would go to my wife? Now you're talking crazy. Don't mess with my family. If you ever go to my wife, it will be a mistake. A big one."

"What? You act like you still love her or something."

Marvin was having a good time with Destiny, but they had been seeing each other for only a few weeks. And she earned a living shaking her ass. There was no way he would leave his wife for a woman like that, even if she was everything Georgia wasn't sexually. He had to be careful how he told Destiny the truth, which was that he would never leave Georgia. He wanted to explain it so she'd understand somewhat, but not fully, so he could continue sleeping with her.

For Marvin, it usually boiled down to the other woman's ultimatum—the moment she gave one, he moved on. But Destiny was a bit more unique. To put it bluntly, she was good in bed. Maybe good wasn't the best word. Exceptional was more like it.

"Don't I turn you on? Don't I make you feel real good, Daddy?"

"Yes, baby, you do. But you have to understand . . . actually, I thought you did understand. I can't just leave my wife and kids."

"Why not?"

"Because I just can't. I have two sons and a history with my wife. Be for real."

"Be for real? I am being for real. You're the only one fakin' it. Why do you even fuck with me then if you're not planning to leave her?"

And this was where Marvin's extramarital affairs became complicated, even for him. Georgia was a good woman who had changed his life—even with her addiction to reality TV. Their intimacy had vanished shortly after their financial situation had improved. It was rare when the two made love; nights like the one several days ago came few and far between, and neither Georgia nor Marvin kept track any longer. They had simply become partners instead of lovers—two people dedicated more to their children than to each other. Marvin supplied the money and Georgia supplied the love. Somewhere, there needed to be a balance.

He loved his wife. He really did. He loved her as much as a man with issues could love a woman. But it wasn't enough to stop being unfaithful, not enough to live up to all of his promises aside from the one Georgia considered most important—never leaving her.

"So when you go on the air dogging her out, what's that? Just for laughs? You need to make up your mind who you want: me or your wife. But in the meantime, Marvin, I'm sick of stripping. You need to put me on your show before I go on someone else's with some confessions."

Destiny was serious about joining his morning team. Either that, or she would start talking. Marvin decided that he would let her join and before he left, he told Destiny that he would work it out. He just needed a little time. He had to somehow get rid of Cammy and take the heat for replacing her with Destiny. He thought it might actually be a good move—controversial no doubt, especially since Cammy, who was the only female member of his morning team, had been with the station longer than he had. Listeners loved her and loved hearing her now famous line, "I'm not mad at you, but I am mad with you." But oh well. It was Marvin's show, and he could do whatever he pleased.

It was three o'clock in the morning when Marvin made it home.

"Why haven't you been answering your phone?" Georgia said as she stood in the garage beside Marvin's convertible Corvette. He pulled his workout bag from the trunk. "I know you got my messages."

"You left me messages?" He fumbled with his Black-Berry. "Messages? You sent me one text."

"Marvin, check again, I called about a dozen times and sent over two dozen text messages, six e-mails, and four or five voice mails."

"Okay, well, what's so urgent?"

Georgia inspected her husband, who wore his workout gear, his duffle bag swung over his shoulder. She wanted to ask him where he had been, but she already knew he would claim the twenty-four-hour gym.

"Your daughter is here."

"My daughter? I have two sons. I don't have a daughter."

"Oh, yes, you do have a daughter. The daughter you and Bernadette had together."

"Me and who? I haven't seen that tramp in years. I know that woman isn't over here claiming I got a kid by her."

"No, she left, and left your daughter here for us to raise. You had a four-year relationship with that *tramp*, Marvin. And *her* kid looks just like *you*. You can't deny her. Besides, Bernadette said you knew she had your baby."

"Now the two of you are best friends or something? Yes, I knew she was pregnant, and she claimed I was the father, but that didn't mean much the way that woman got around." He walked into the house through the kitchen. "I don't even know the girl's name."

"Your daughter's name is Chloe, and she's upstairs in one of the guest rooms, sleeping." Georgia trailed Marvin. Raising a teenager, especially when they were avoiding their other problems—like Marvin's affair—was not convenient at all. She reached for his arm. "What are we going to do?"

"I don't know. You're the one who let them in. And you're the one who let her mother leave without her. So I guess, since you're the stay-at-home mom, you're going to stay home and raise her."

"But, Marvin, she's your child."

"And what's mine is yours." He tossed his gym bag in the laundry room. Seeing his long-lost daughter was the furthest thing from his mind. Instead, he fixed a cup of coffee and sat at the breakfast table, flipping through *The Detroit News*, which lay on top.

Georgia was speechless. She stood by the sink with her arms crossed, studying his duffle bag. "You think I'm your maid and not your wife, don't you? Oh, and by the way, I found a diamond earring in your car today." Marvin took a sip of his coffee while turning a page of the newspaper. "One diamond earring that's not mine, but it's nice. At least a karat. So whose is it?"

"It's mine."

"Your ear isn't pierced, Marvin."

"Damn, did I let my hole close," he said, touching his earlobe.

"This isn't a damn joke. I'm being serious. Who are you fucking? Because it isn't me."

"You need to keep your voice down. Have you lost your damn mind? We have kids in this house."

"You don't care about the kids we have in this house. You come in this house at three or four o'clock in the morning nearly every night and claim you were working out or working an event. Detroit doesn't have that much going on. You think your kids don't notice how late you come in here?"

He stood up from the table and walked out of the kitchen.

"Where are you going? I want you to answer my question. Did I pick a man just like my father? Is that it?"

Marvin stopped in his tracks and turned to face her. "No, baby, you didn't pick a man like your father. I have been working. And I'll try to stop working as much."

"What about the earring, Marvin? Are you cheating on me?"

"I don't know about the earring. Maybe it's Cammy's or one of the women at the station. The car is a demo; I toss the keys to people all the time. I'm not cheating on you, baby. If you're listening to the radio, you know that's Marvelous talking and not me. It's all for ratings."

"I'm tired of hearing that. Marvelous and Marvin are the same . . . one and the same."

"Forget it. You want to rant and rave and act a fool this late with the kids upstairs probably listening to every word."

"Rant and rave, Marvin? What are you talking about?"

"I don't have anything else to say." He retreated to the bedroom and locked the door. She turned the knob, banged on the door a few times and kicked once. "You're an asshole. You know that?"

The lock on the door was his DO NOT DISTURB sign.

Georgia went upstairs and checked on Chloe, who wasn't sleeping like Georgia had assumed. Rather, Chloe was stretched across their leather sofa in the game room, talking on Georgia's cell phone.

"Is that my phone?" Georgia asked as she stood in front of Chloe who ignored her question. "I see you and your father have something in common. Neither one of you knows how to answer a question." Georgia cleared her throat. "I believe you're talking on my phone, and it's too late to be on the phone."

"Hold on, Byron. Oh, yeah, I just grabbed it off the table over there. Can you add me to your family plan so I can have my own since I *am* part of the family now?"

"I'm so glad you mentioned being a part of the family. That means tomorrow night you can help me cook dinner and wash the dishes like my sons do."

"That's okay. Then I'll just keep on using your phone."

"Oh, no, you won't," Georgia snatched the cell phone from Chloe's hand. "Byron, you will have to call Chloe back at a decent hour."

"Man, what you do that for? You illin'."

"Illin'? I don't have a problem with you using the phone, but not at three o'clock in the morning when you should be asleep."

"Marvelous Marvin finally made it home, huh? He cheatin'. He says so right on the radio every morning, and I wouldn't take that shit off of him if I was you."

"You're not me. And you won't be using profanity in this house. And you will learn to speak properly. All that slang and splitting verbs really irritates me." Georgia turned to leave the room.

"But cheatin' don't, huh?"

Georgia stopped on the second step and looked over her shoulder. "If you're going to stay here with us, you will need to enroll in school because you will not be able to go back to your old one. It's too far away."

Chloe shrugged, "I don't care about school—my old school or a new one."

Georgia walked back up the stairs. "There are some really good schools in this area. Even the public schools are top rated. So I'll do some checking around, and hopefully we'll get you in a new school by early next week."

Chloe shrugged again.

"Because education is the key."

"The key to what?" Chloe asked.

"To a brighter future."

"You sound like one of them UNCF commercials."

"Those commercials," Georgia said, correcting Chloe, "not them commercials." Chloe shrugged. "You keep shrugging like nothing matters to you. But let me tell you that the Grosse Pointe schools rank among the highest in the nation, and they were in the top ten percent in their English scores on standardized tests. You will only embarrass yourself if you go into a class splitting your verbs and speaking Ebonics. There aren't many blacks who live in this area, which means you could very well be the only black girl in your class."

"So I got to behave for the white folks? Is that what you're saying?"

"No, you're behaving for yourself and for your father."

"Psssh. Please . . . my father? Not-So-Marvelous Marvin. Whatever."

"Good night, Chloe. I'm taking you to school tomorrow."

"Whatever."

That night, Georgia slept in one of the guest bedrooms.

The next morning, she dropped off the boys at their private middle school and tried to enroll Chloe. Georgia wasn't sure how this arrangement with Chloe would work. She had her own kids to worry about. It didn't seem fair she now had to add a teenager—who was a fast girl at that—to the mix. But the child needed a stable environment.

Georgia clutched her hobo Coach purse as she sat on the edge of her seat in the principal's office. Chloe studied her long nails, which didn't curve like her mother's but were painted up just as fancy. She would have been popping her gum if Georgia hadn't made her spit it out in the garbage can. That, and take out her gold grill before they entered the building.

"Perception is everything," Georgia told Chloe. "Don't have these people perceive you as being ghetto."

"I am ghetto," Chloe said, "and proud of it."

The principal was perched at her desk. So young, Georgia felt, for such an important position, but Georgia's best friend, Claudette, had become a principal when she was in her late twenties.

"While we're waiting on Chloe's school records to be faxed over," the principal said, "can you tell me why you felt it necessary to change schools?"

"It's very simple," Georgia said as the fax came through, the pages spilling onto the principal's desk while a few fell to the floor. "She was living with her mother, but now she's living with her father and me."

"Really? Well, that's interesting," the principal said as she looked at the cover page of the fax along with the next page and then picked up the pages from the floor. "Really?" she said as she placed one of the pages in front of Georgia. "Are you sure about that?"

Georgia stopped and turned to face Chloe who took her time walking to the car.

"Why didn't you tell me you were expelled from school?" Georgia asked. She pounded her pumps against the pavement like she did with her Nikes while walking around the neighborhood with Art. "I could have stayed in my sweats for that embarrassment."

"You didn't ask me if I was kicked out. You just asked me if I had a problem with going to a different school, and I said I don't, and I don't. Can I have my grill back?"

Georgia ignored Chloe's question. "What were you doing with a gun in your possession anyway?"

"Well, this nigga I was kickin' it with—"

"A who you were doing what with? Do not use that word. Ever. Start over."

"This boy I was kickin' it with. You know, chillin', spending a little time, kickin' it. He's not my man, I'm not his woman, we're just kickin' it. He was the one who brought the gun to school. He wanted me to hold it for him so I did, but around third period I started thinking, 'How am I gonna get through the metal detector when I leave?' So I turned it in to my teacher, and she took me to the principal's office. Because I wouldn't tell them where

I got the piece from, they said they had to assume it was mine, and so they kicked me out. I had to go to court behind that and everything."

"Why didn't you tell them where you got the gun from?"

"Because I ain't no snitch, you crazy. I'm like Lil' Kim—I'll take a fall for my peeps."

"Lesson number one: Don't ever hold anything for anyone, especially something that's illegal. And as far as being a snitch, it's either you or them. You better start picking yourself, because your *peeps* aren't thinking about you. You see what happened to Lil' Kim—her *peeps* ended up snitching on her and she ended up in prison."

"Okay, whatever," Chloe said.

"Why is it always, 'Okay, whatever'?"

"Because okay, whatever. I hear what you sayin'. But do you? If you really feel that way, why are you with a man who goes on the air and talks about you, admits to cheating and all of that? Why can't you start picking yourself over him?"

"That's different because I don't believe he is cheating on me. He loves me."

"Are you serious? Forget it. Can I have my grill back?"

"So many women have served time for holding their men's drugs and served long sentences. With that on your record, it's going to be hard to get you into another school, Chloe."

She shrugged. "I was kicked out. No school is going to have me. I don't need school, no way. Can I have my grill back?"

"Oh, yes, you do need school. Don't ever say you don't. There are alternative schools you can go to. Don't worry, I'll find one. My best friend is a principal, and she knows all there is to know about the educational system in Detroit. You're going to get into a school. Trust me."

"I just want my grill back."

"You're not getting it back, so get used to your own teeth." Georgia studied Chloe's teeth every time she spoke. "I think I'm going to take you to the dentist for a cleaning." In the car on the drive back to the house, Georgia asked, "Do you mind if I ask you a personal question?"

Chloe shrugged. "I ain't answering no questions until I get my grill back."

Georgia reluctantly handed Chloe her gold grill. "I'm not answering any," Georgia said, continuing to correct Chloe.

"Whatever. What's your question? Go 'head with it."

"Have you already been sexually active?"

"Yeah. Why?"

"Because you're only thirteen."

"And?" Chloe shrugged again.

"Just once, I hope," Georgia said as she rode down Lake Shore toward her home. "And that would be one time too many."

"Nah, it's been a whole lot more than once."

"A whole lot more than once?" Georgia's heart sank. As the conversation continued, Georgia learned that Chloe had been with more sexual partners than she had—so many Chole lost count. The youngest had been her age, the oldest forty-four.

Georgia literally became sick to her stomach. "Forty-four? Your dad is forty-four." Georgia's mouth watered, and she felt like she was going to throw up.

Chloe didn't understand what the big deal was, because her mother knew she was sexually active with grown men and never seemed to care. She was the one who took her to the clinic and signed so she could get birth control.

"Well, I can't ever condone a thirteen-year-old having sex. And as for those grown men messing with you, they need to go to jail for what they did."

"For having sex?" she asked, squinting, her face displaying obvious confusion.

"Yes, for having sex with a minor." Georgia pulled into the driveway and remained in the car for several minutes talking to Chloe. "Don't you understand that's not right? A young girl your age shouldn't have sex at all. Do you ever watch *Dateline*'s 'To Catch a Predator'?"

"What's that?"

"It's a television show that sets up men who prey on young girls online. They go to jail for it."

"For having sex?"

"For having sex with minors. You are thirteen years old, and these are grown men."

"But I don't look my age."

"I don't care what age you look; I'm talking about your actual age."

"My momma don't care, so why should you?"

"Don't you want a different life? Don't you want to grow up and become a doctor or a lawyer?"

"A doctor or a lawyer? Be for real."

"I am being for real. Don't you want to be successful?"

"Yeah, sure I do, but I can't grow up and be no doctor or no lawyer. Marvin ain't no doctor or no lawyer, and he's doing just fine. You ain't no doctor or no lawyer either. In fact, you ain't nothin'. I mean, you don't work and you living good off him."

"So what do you want to be when you grow up?" Georgia asked her.

"A rapper."

"Oh, not another rapper." Georgia caught herself. It was never her intention to crush anyone's dreams, especially a child's. "Well, if that's what you want to be, at least become an educated one so your rhymes make sense and flow nicely."

"My rhymes will flow and so will my dough."

Georgia shook her head as she pulled her SUV into the garage.

With her eyes closed and hand clasping her son's, Corliss took a deep breath as she stood in her tiny foyer.

Corliss dreaded *it*. The *it* was work.

The very thought of going made her nauseous. There were times when she would be on her way and would suddenly turn around to go back home—not that home was any better, but at least she could sleep. Sometimes, she would drive as much as a mile before reason and her responsibility toward Jelani set in, causing her to make another U-turn toward work. But today, just making her way to the car was difficult.

She felt a light tug.

"Mommy," Jelani said, looking up at his mother with endearing eyes. "Let's go."

Corliss slowly lifted her eyelids and looked down at her son. "How does Mommy look?" she asked as she straightened her tight skirt.

"You look sexy, Mommy."

Corliss frowned. "Sexy? Where did you get that word from, little man?"

"Daddy."

Her right eyebrow rose. "Who was Daddy calling sexy?"

Jelani shrugged.

"Oh, yes, you do know." Corliss attempted to bend down to her son's level, but her tight skirt prevented much movement. So instead she walked him over to the sofa in the living room and sat beside him. "Now, tell me. Who did Daddy call sexy?"

Jelani covered his eyes and shrugged again.

"Is he dating someone?"

Jelani nodded.

"Is it serious?"

Jelani continued to nod.

"Did he tell her he loved her?"

Jelani nodded. "And he gave her a ring."

"He gave her a ring?" Corliss shouted.

Jelani nodded. "Yes, from the Cracker Jack box."

"From the what? Did Daddy give some woman a ring or not?"

He nodded again. "From the Cracker Jack box. I told you."

"Oh, forget it, Jelani. I thought you were being serious. Let's go to school, baby. Are you ready?"

"I'm ready. You ready for work, Mommy?"

The very word *work* hit the pit of her stomach. "As ready as I'll ever be."

In the car, after she dropped Jelani off at nursery school, Corliss was laughing so hard that she almost ran into the car in front of her at the red light. At least Marvelous Marvin had a way of getting Corliss's mind off her misery. He was on the air discussing church and his beliefs.

"Why should I give to a church building fund that hasn't built a damn thing in the ten years since I've been giving? But that's what my wife does, tithing twenty percent of *my* income into her bishop's pocket."

"Twenty percent, Marvin?" Cammy said. "That seems kind of high."

"Exactly. I had to ask her, 'Did your bishop specifically say he was building a church?' Because the only thing I've seen him build is a mansion around the corner from ours. And how can he afford to live behind the gate when we can't? I guess that's because we're too busy tithing."

"Amen," Corliss said as she sped through the light after it turned green. She was late for work again, and this time she had run out of excuses. She'd overslept like all the other times, but that didn't prevent her from stopping at Bob Evans to get a carry-out breakfast.

Instead of saving time by taking the stairs to her floor, she waited for the elevator. Once the doors opened to her floor, she walked confidently to her cubicle, even with all eyes on her and her revealing outfit that broke every dress code rule—the V-neck was too low, the sweater too tight, the skirt too short, *and* she didn't appear to be wearing a bra.

Before turning on her computer and logging in, she switched on the radio already tuned to the *Marvelous Marvin Morning Show*, and put in her earplugs to continue listening.

"No, that fool didn't," Corliss said trying to hold back her laughter. "Ooh, he needs to quit dogging Georgia like that." She could feel her three cubicle desk mates staring in her direction, which caused her to laugh even louder. Someone had already complained to the group leader that she blasted her radio, a move that made Corliss immediately invest in some stereo earplugs, because *The Marvelous Marvin Morning Show* was one radio program she refused to miss.

If Corliss had to work—and she did in order to raise her son—then she was going to be comfortable while doing so, and both the radio and music relaxed her, as did eating breakfast at her desk.

"I'm giving away four tickets to see John Legend in concert at the State Theatre. All you have to do is be my tenth caller."

Corliss quickly picked up her cell phone from her desk and pressed TWO, which had the radio station's number programmed. She held it to her ear while dousing her omelet with two tiny salt packets and pulled a bottle of ketchup from her oversized leather Coach handbag. She kicked off her stilettos, wiggled her toes, and started singing John Legend's "Ordinary People." Seconds later, she got the loud busy signal.

"Damn, I can't ever get through." She narrowed her eyes at Vanessa, who was scowling in her direction. "Good morn*ing*," she said, imitating the character Madea while making repeated attempts to contact the radio station. Vanessa rolled her eyes and picked up her phone's receiver. "Yeah, heifer, do some work for a change," Corliss said under her breath.

"You're our tenth caller. Your name?" the young woman asked.

"Oh my God! I'm the tenth caller, for real? I love John Legend." Corliss began singing "Ordinary People."

"Miss, may I have your name?"

"Oh. My name is Corliss Riggs and I am Marvelous Marvin's number-one fan. I've been listening to him from the time he first went on the air, before his show even went into syndication. I was the very first fan club member to sign up. Do I win a prize for that?"

"Do you want your tickets mailed?" the young woman asked.

"No. I will come down to the radio station and pick them up, because the last time I won some tickets from your station, I never got them in the mail and you're not about to say my John Legend tickets were lost. Not the way I love John Legend." She continued to sing "Ordinary People."

"Corliss, do you have a few minutes?" Trish, the group leader, asked.

Corliss nodded and held up a finger. "Give me one minute. I'm trying to make a doctor's appointment, and I need to take care of this because it is extremely important."

"Dr. Marvelous Marvin," Vanessa said, snickering.

Trish snatched a sticky from Corliss's desk and wrote, "In the conference room now," and posted it on Corliss's computer. "I need you in the conference room now, and bring your earplugs and breakfast with you."

Corliss took a deep breath before examining her heavily made-up complexion in the portable mirror resting on her desk while she raked her fingers through her long, straight auburn weave. She was so tired of Trish and her communication via Post-it notes. She stood, slid her feet into her sandals, and pulled down her tight miniskirt.

"I'll be back," Corliss said, imitating Arnold Schwarzenegger, as she looked over at Vanessa, who had a smirk on her face while she stared at her computer monitor.

"Hopefully not," Vanessa mumbled.

The gossip mill quickly began churning as Corliss headed toward the conference room. *Haters,* Corliss thought. When Corliss walked in, she saw Trish sitting at the far end of the conference table with a manila folder in front of her.

"Have a seat," Trish said as she moved her seat closer to Corliss. "What's going on with you?"

"What do you mean what's going on with me?"

"You're the best collector in here, and by right you should be a team leader. But your attitude and the fact you don't have a degree holds you back. Many of your coworkers are intimidated by you. They say you walk by them in the morning and don't speak—"

"Is it in my job description to speak?"

"Corliss, you're missing my point. Your actions only hurt yourself. You always want to know why you don't get any of the jobs you post for, and I'm trying to tell you why."

"You don't have to tell me why. I already know why. That posting system is a joke. They already know who they want, and they're just going through all the necessary channels to make it appear like they're being fair."

"You're the one who'll either stay sitting in that seat as a collector or tossed out the door without a job. And with the way the job market is right now in Detroit, I'm sure you don't want that to happen, do you?"

"Are you threatening my job?"

"I'm the reason you're still here, because you are my best collector. But don't get on my bad side. The main reason I called you in here this morning is because you're violating the dress code policy and I'll need to send you home to change."

"How am I violating the dress code policy?" Corliss asked as she stretched her arms out and twirled them. "This is Donna Karan."

"Well, you might need to go up a size or two because that's too tight, and you're not wearing a bra."

"I do have on a bra."

"I can see your nipples."

"I can't help that I have big nipples."

"Just choose your outfits a little more wisely, okay?"

"I live almost an hour away. If I leave to go home, I'm staying there."

"And if you stay there, you won't be paid for the day."

"How can you not pay me for the day? Is my outfit that bad?"

"It's too revealing."

"I can't help the way I'm built."

"But you can help the way you dress."

Corliss stood and pushed her chair in. "I can't get back in an hour," she said.

"Just get back as soon as you can."

"What do you mean you don't see my name on your call-in sheet? I'm not in the mood for games. I *was* the tenth caller."

"Were you the tenth caller this morning or another morning?" asked the young woman sitting behind a desk piled with papers. She flipped through her clipboard.

"Weren't you the one I talked to this morning?" Corliss asked. "You sound like her."

"I'm the one who answers the phone and writes down all the names and addresses for the winners."

"You need to get organized. Look at all this shit on your desk." Corliss picked up a pile of papers and tossed them back down. "All I know is that I was the tenth caller and I told you I was coming down to pick up my four tickets. If you need to get Marvelous Marvin out here, then go on and do that because I'm not leaving without my John Legend tickets."

Corliss paced for a few minutes, plopped down on the leather sofa and folded her arms. She watched as people walked in and out of the station. Then she began studying the framed pictures of the morning show team—Marvin, along with Big Fella Mike, Milt Merlin, and Cammy.

At that moment, the studio door opened, and Marvelous Marvin strolled out followed by two members of his morning team.

"Mr. Marvelous," Corliss said, leaping from the sofa. "I was the tenth caller this morning for the John Legend tickets and I came all the way here to pick up them up, but Miss Secretary over there is saying she doesn't have a record of it."

"Mr. Marvelous. I like that." He looked Corliss up and down. "Give the young lady her tickets, Frances."

"Yeah, Frances," Corliss said as she stomped over to the woman and stuck out her hand. "Give me my tickets."

"And while you're at it, you can give me your number," Marvelous said as he stood beside Corliss and placed his hand on her behind.

Corliss pushed his hand away. "Uh-uh. Don't be coming over here touching my ass. Just because you're a radio host, and I'm a big fan, doesn't mean you can disrespect me the way you disrespect your wife. I don't want you. I want these John Legend tickets." She snatched the tickets from the receptionist's hand, rolled her eyes, threw her shoulders back, and marched out of the radio station.

At work, everyone was abuzz about some recent promotions, threat of a union, the possibility of a merger, and a class-action lawsuit involving six women and the center manager. As usual, Corliss tried to ignore the watercooler gossipers—or rather, they ignored her. She focused on what she hated most—collecting—while counting down the minutes until her one-hour lunch break. But she couldn't help but wonder if there was any truth to the sexual harassment lawsuit.

In the afternoon, as she left the lunchroom with Sharon, they passed the center manager, who was taking the home-office executives around the building. Corliss and the center manager made brief eye contact and Corliss smiled.

She recalled going several months ago to his office, where he had an open-door policy, to discuss the lack of job opportunities for someone like her—someone without a college degree. Instead, they had spent too much time flirting, and never got around to the topic at hand. Corliss didn't know why she bothered flirting with him, whether she felt deep down it would help her get promoted. He had picutes of his wife and children displayed on his desk, and if there was one thing Corliss wouldn't do, it was get involved with a married man. She may have cheated on her man, but that was different. She and Jermaine weren't married.

"What was all that about?" Sharon asked, looking over at Corliss who was sucking air through the straw in her thirty-two-ounce Styrofoam cup.

"What was what?" Corliss asked as she jabbed the straw up and down in the cup, hitting clumps of ice. She shrugged. "Nothing."

"Is that who's been sending you the roses?"

"Girl, please. No."

"Are you sure he's not the one sending you those damn flowers every week? He certainly can afford to, and I saw the way the two of you looked at each other."

"It was probably just your imagination. The man is too short, too old, and too married."

"But he ain't too broke," Sharon said, making Corliss laugh. "That's enough to make all those other toos not too important. And if you join along in that class-action law-suit, you won't be too broke for too long either."

There was a deliveryman in the reception area, hold-ing a dozen sunset yellow and orange roses.

"Corliss, I already know those are for you. It's the nine-teenth. So who is your secret admirer if it's not the big boss?"

"Somebody who really loves me."

It was Saturday, and Georgia and Chloe had hair appointments.

"I'm not getting my hair cut," Chloe said as Georgia pulled into the tiny parking lot situated near the barred beauty salon. Chloe eyed the building. "Why do you come here? I thought you would go somewhere a little more upscale with all your money."

"I've been going to Millie ever since I was your age."

"Ever since *you* were *my* age? Well, how old is the woman? Ninety?"

"She's in her fifties."

"I don't want no old lady doing my hair."

Georgia shot a look at Chloe, who quickly corrected her speech.

"I mean, I don't want an old woman doing my hair."

"She's good. Trust me. And for the record, fifty isn't old. It's the new forty."

"Forty is old."

"It's the new thirty."

"Thirty is old."

"It's the new twenty."

"Well, twenty isn't really old."

"Yes, twenty, thirty, forty, and fifty are all too old for you. So the next time you meet a man who tells you he's any one of those ages, tell him he's too old, will you?"

When Georgia and Chloe walked through the door of the salon, Millie's eyes lit up. "Oh, come here, child, let me take a look at you!"

"Why is she talking like that?" Chloe asked.

"She's from Jamaica."

"So this is Marvin's baby?"

"I'm not a baby."

"Yes, Millie, this is Marvin's daughter."

"Well, you're a baby to me. Take a seat." Millie patted her stylist chair while she briefly studied herself in the mirror, fingering through her gray hair that she kept feathered to perfection.

Georgia walked toward the back of the shop to use the restroom.

"I need a perm. Do you have Mizani?" asked Chloe.

"Chil', you don't need any chemical in your hair. It's the chemical that's causing all this breakage." She lifted sections of Chloe's wavy hair to reveal the shorter layers underneath. "Your hair wasn't cut this way, it fell out. Why would someone put chemical on a hair texture that doesn't require it?"

"Old lady, I know what I need, 'cause I know how I like my hair to look."

"Old lady?" Millie said, placing her hand on her hip. "What you need is some respect for your elders."

"All I'm saying is, you're so old, you might not be up on the styles and what girls my age do. We like our hair straight."

"I know when hair is in need of repair. You have a naturally wavy texture. If you want your hair straight, all I have to do is flat-iron it, but not before your hair is back healthy. In the meantime, you need to stick to roller sets, but I'm not doing anything for you now, chil'. Move out of my chair."

Georgia rushed from the back of the salon. "What's wrong? What happened?"

"This chil' right here is rude. I will not lift one finger to do anything with her hair."

"Please, Millie, if she apologizes, will you do her hair?" Georgia asked.

"I don't need my hair done. I can keep wearing a ponytail."

"Well, you heard the chil'," Millie said with attitude. "She doesn't need her hair done. Let it fall out for all I care."

"Millie, please, will you do it for me?"

"I will do it for you, but it has to get cut. A lot of it."

"I ain't gonna be bald like you."

"That's it, I'm not doing it."

"I will," Velvet, another hairdresser, said as she raised her shears and simulated a cutting motion with them. "Chop chop."

"Y'all some weave-wearing haters up in here," Chloe exclaimed.

"Chloe, you do need your hair cut. I'm sure it will grow back quickly and what I need are braids. Go sit at the shampoo bowl so Millie's assistant can wash your hair."

Chloe walked to the shampoo area, dragging her feet.

"Did you just say braids?" Malik, one of the barbers, asked. "You're getting braids after the way Marvelous Marvin went on air dogging women who wore them, calling it the lazy woman's hairstyle?"

"Yes. That's why I would like to have them."

"As much as you want to get even with Marvin, and as much as I would like for you to, I refuse to braid your hair."

"So you agree with him?"

"No, I don't ever agree with what that man says. I'm too busy today to spend five hours braiding your hair."

Georgia threw her hands up, "I'll tip you a hundred dollars."

"I just don't have the time, sweetie."

Sassy, one of Millie's clients whose husband was a doctor at an inner-city clinic, walked in.

"I listened for your husband on the radio yesterday, but I didn't hear him," Georgia said. "Friday was the day, right?"

"It was supposed to be the day," Sassy said.

"So what happened? Marvin said he'd put him on during rush hour, which is the only reason I even listened."

"He may have said that, Miss Georgia, but he didn't do it."

"What do you mean, he didn't do it?"

"I'm not surprised," Millie said. "What can you expect from a man who calls himself Marvelous?"

"Marvin does some messed-up things, but I've never known him to promise something and not carry through with it."

"He promised to love, honor, and cherish you, didn't he?" Millie said. "Is he carrying through with it?"

"You can talk to my husband if you like," Sassy said. "He wasn't put on the air, and he was very upset at the treatment he received. First, they kept him waiting. They asked him several times who he confirmed his appearance with, and when he said you, some woman on his show said, 'She doesn't count; she doesn't work here. She doesn't call any shots.' Then he told the woman that he had spoken to the show's producer, and she said he was lying, because their show doesn't even have a producer. He said he also talked to Marvin, and again, she told my husband he was lying."

"It wasn't Cammy, was it? She's usually not like that."

"No, I asked him if it was Cammy and he said it wasn't. It's sad, because all he wanted to do was use the radio as a format to spread awareness about free AIDS testing at inner-city clinics, to urge everybody to get out there and know their status. There was no reason to treat him like he was trying to steal something. People just don't care about others. Especially your husband. I hate to talk about him—"

"Why not talk about him?" Velvet asked from across the room. "He talks about her."

"Don't worry—I'll make sure your husband gets on the air to spread his message."

"I'm not sure my husband wants to go back on your husband's show."

"I understand."

"Do you still want braids?" Velvet asked.

"Yes, I still want my braids. And I'm tipping big."

Velvet raised her rat-tail comb. "I can make it happen. And let him get on the air and say something about it. I'll be his first caller greeting him with all kinds of four-letter words."

"Do you need me to run out and get the hair?" Georgia asked as she walked from Millie's station over to Velvet's.

Velvet reached underneath her station and removed two bags of strawberry-blond hair. "This is Detroit. You can't be a hairdresser in this city without hair on hand. Let's really shock him. Not only will you have a hairstyle he hates, you'll also be rocking a color he can't stand. Lord help me, that's ugly."

Later that afternoon, Georgia and Chloe returned home with new hairstyles—Chloe had a shoulder-length bob that she was in love with and Georgia had her braids. Marvin didn't immediately notice as he talked on the phone in the great room.

"Do you like my braids?"

Marvin didn't even look up. Instead, he continued talking on his cell phone.

"Who are you taking to?"

"No one."

"You're on the phone, Marvin. Who are you talking to?"

"I'll talk to you later." He removed his earpiece from his left ear and tossed it on the stone coffee table.

"Who was that?"

"I was talking to one of the producers of the show."

"One of the producers of the show? That's funny—I thought you didn't have producers on your show."

"What are you talking about? You know we have producers."

"Well, someone told Dr. Greene that I was a nobody and that your show didn't have producers."

"Who is Dr. Greene?"

"Dr. Greene is a young doctor trying to do some good in an impoverished neighborhood. He's a Harvard graduate working in the inner city when he could be at Johns Hopkins or any leading hospital making major money. His salary is paid for by a government grant and it's not much at all, but he loves helping people. You treated that man like he was nothing." Georgia used the back of her hand to wipe away some tears. "After you told me you would put him on the air."

"I did?"

"Yes, you did. But you also told me you would love me. And you obviously don't."

"Are you okay?"

"Not really."

"Are the braids in too tight?"

Georgia rolled her eyes. "Everything's a joke, but not everything's a joke."

"Tell him to come back to the station Monday morning. I'll make sure he gets on the air this time."

Georgia walked out of the room, stopping at the entranceway. "Just because he doesn't make a seven-figure income doesn't give you the right to waste his time. I wouldn't insult him by asking him to return." She turned to walk away. "You're not the only radio host in town."

"I'm the best one in town."

"That's your biased opinion."

"Everybody hates Marvin, is that it? I'm not a bad guy. A lot of women would love to be in your shoes."

Georgia threw her pair of pink fluffy house shoes into the room. One landed in front of Marvin and the other hit him on the head.

"There they go," Georgia yelled.

When Georgia answered her home phone, she wasn't expecting to hear her brother's voice.

He sounded rushed and anxious.

He asked her to meet him at the White Castle on Woodward. She knew which one, because it had been there forever—for as long as Georgia could remember—long before she started high school. Her brother said she wouldn't recognize the place, because it had been remodeled from the inside out.

She took Chloe and the boys with her, because she wanted them to see a different side of the world—the side often forgotten unless you lived on it. Georgia had read in the paper that 9500 people slept on the streets of Detroit every night, her brother among them. But when she arrived and saw him, and could tell he was sick, she regretted bringing the children.

He stood on the corner in front of the White Castle, rocking on the edge of the curb.

When Georgia saw him, her heart broke in pieces. He was not the Peter she had known—not the Peter she had called her brother. He seemed to be a shell of a man. When people saw him, they wouldn't think survivor, but he was one. They would forget he was once a child with parents of his own. No one could have guessed how clear his skin had been before the jaundice had set in. They wouldn't know he once had shiny, curly hair where he now wore his filthy wool cap. They wouldn't know how straight and white his teeth had been before they started decaying and falling out. No, they'd only see a dirty, unshaven man with yellowing eyes and skin, and dismiss him as one of Detroit's homeless. They would never know he had an engineering degree and three children, and had one time been a homeowner and husband.

He had been living a hard life for almost ten years, and she wasn't sure what to expect. The last time she had seen him, a little over a year before at the community support group, he had worn clean clothes and was freshly shaven. He had said things were looking up. She wanted to know if that meant he was ready to leave the streets.

"Things can look up from the streets, too."

Although Georgia could understand the plight of the homeless—that many were veterans or people who had lost their jobs—she couldn't understand her brother who chose to live that way. She would sometimes rely on Kendra's assumptions that he was crazy or on drugs—but he wasn't. At least he hadn't been.

"Why is your phone number listed?" he asked after they had all gone inside the White Castle, ordered, and sat down with their sacks of small, palm-sized burgers.

"So you'll always have a way to reach me. I can't have my privacy until you get off these streets." She looked at her two sons and Chloe to see their reactions.

Peter hadn't even acknowledged the children, who sat with them at the table near the window, munching on little square burgers and onion chips while slurping their frozen Cokes.

Peter was in his own world today.

He stretched his arms in front of him while trying to keep his hands steady and at eye level. But his swollen hands shook.

"You have an MBA and an engineering degree."

"And? That was a long time ago in a world so very far away now."

"You can get off the streets if you want to."

"I don't want to. These streets are my friends. Woodward Avenue has been here for me and will be here. So will Cass and Forest and Warren. I know them all better than I know most people. I've spent plenty of nights with them, talking and telling them about my life. No one knows me the way the streets do."

"I brought my kids along—"

"So they could see who not to be like, right?"

He was right, but hearing him say it made it suddenly sound so wrong.

"Yeah, kids, don't be like me. You definitely don't want to be like me. I'm a loser, someone who couldn't hang. What society refers to as a reject. I guess I didn't try hard enough. Maybe if the engineering department would have provided some of the same training seminars they had given to their sales and marketing folks . . . maybe I'd be out selling and marketing myself. Yeah, that's it. I can blame it on corporate America."

"Next month, I'm going to take you to see *The Pursuit of Happyness* as soon as it comes out. It's a true story about Chris Gardner, a homeless man who turned his life around and became a multimillionaire."

"*The Pursuit of Happyness?* And what will seeing that do?"

"Inspire you, maybe."

"If it were that easy. Only if it were that easy."

"I'm tired of worrying about you day in and day out."

"Don't worry about me at all. I've told you that a hundred times before. I'm not a person you need to worry over. But there is someone I'm worried about, and that's why I called you."

"Who?"

"Look," he said, dropping his hands. "I don't ever ask for anything for myself. But there's a lady . . . a friend of mine. Just a friend. She's a single mother, and she and her son are living on the street. The shelters are too full. She's near the top of most of the waiting lists, but you know how that goes. I need you to do me a favor and rent her an apartment."

"Rent who an apartment?"

"Leslie and Ian—a mother and son. You would quickly do it for me, so why not do it for them?"

"Would you live there with them?"

"No."

"I'm sorry but, Peter, I can't rent an apartment for a stranger while my brother is still homeless."

"Your brother?" He shook his head. "That's such a joke. *Your* brother?" He looked at the faces of the children and stopped himself. "So you can't help a stranger? You have to know the people you help?"

"That's not what I'm saying."

"So what are you saying?"

"Where is her family?"

"People are never with you when you're down. Don't you know that?"

The sack of burgers was gone, and Chloe and the boys were starting to fidget. Chloe had brought her backpack with her and used that moment to pull out her science book.

"Science was one of my favorite subjects," Peter said to Chloe.

"Mine too."

"Don't worry, just because we have something in common doesn't mean you'll end up like me."

Chloe shrugged. "You haven't ended up any kind of way yet. We're all just a work in progress."

"I guess I have a lot of work in progress then."

"Little bit," Chloe said.

"Can you help my friends?" Peter said to Georgia.

"I'd have to ask Marvin."

"You know what he'll say—he's not Goodwill."

"I can't sign a lease or anything, but I can pay for a cheap furnished apartment—one of those month-to-month deals—only if you agree that you'll live there also."

"Why does everything have to have a string attached? If you don't want to do it, just say no."

It was hard for Georgia to just say no. No meant she didn't want to help. No meant she had access to money, but would rather keep it than help a single mother and her young son get off the street. It would be like attending Sunday service every week having done no good. She wanted to help—felt compelled to.

"I'll get you the apartment—month to month—and whatever you do with it is your business."

"I got you. So if you get it for me and I give it to her, then you don't care."

"Then I don't know."

"Then let's do that."

"Do you have a place in mind?" Georgia asked.

"Maybe someplace like the Milner Arms or The Park Apartments."

"Whichever one is nicer," Georgia said as she stood. "If we're going to do this thing, we may as well do it right. How old is the son?"

"Five."

"No, I won't have them in a dump and I won't have you on the street either."

After they left White Castle, they rode with the windows partially cracked to help dispel the odor of Peter's unwashed body. Georgia drove to West Adams and rented a furnished apartment for two months.

"It's yours now," Georgia said, handing him the key. "But before the two months are over, I expect to hear from you so I can pay for the next two months. At least that way, I'll hear from you every two months."

She prayed he would stay in the apartment at least one night before handing it over, but she doubted it. She was thankful for so much—thankful that her and Marvin's financial situation had turned around for the better, grateful that she no longer had to live in his parents' home, but also thankful that his parents had allowed her family to live there for those years.

Georgia was at a very big turning point. She had her sons and Marvin's daughter and a life of her own. But there was something inside her—a feeling that she needed to prepare for something big, because something was brewing.

The sun had just started to rise when Marvin finally made it home. To Georgia, he looked worn and smelled like an ashtray and Jack Daniels.

He collapsed on the bed without taking off his clothes or shoes.

"Long night?"

"Very."

"Mmm. I'm taking Chloe shopping today. You can watch the boys."

He didn't respond.

"Marvin," Georgia shouted. "Did you hear me?"

"Huh? What did you say?" He had wrapped himself under their one-hundred-percent Egyptian cotton comforter and immediately fallen into a deep sleep.

"Forget it. I'll take the boys, because you probably won't wake up anytime soon."

Georgia drove to the Prime Outlets in Birch Run, Michigan, and shopped for several hours before taking a break for lunch. They made it home close to eight o'clock.

"You mean he's home on a Saturday night?" Chloe asked. "He must have had a rough night." She turned to face Georgia. "I wish you'd leave him. Even if you don't divorce him, you still need to leave. He's getting away with too much. And it's weird, but I see his car here and I actually wish it weren't here. I wish it were gone like it usually is."

"Don't say that, Chloe."

"Well, I do. Life is so nice when it's just you and me and my brothers."

In the few weeks that Chloe had been living with them, Georgia felt that she and Chloe were starting to bond. Chloe and the boys got along. They understood she was their sister and Georgia wasn't her mother, and that's when Georgia realized kids today were much more grown-up than back in her time.

"Marvin's my husband. And we've shared a life together. I can't leave him. We made a promise to stay together and that's exactly what we're going to do."

Chloe couldn't believe how naïve Georgia was. "If Juanita can leave Michael Jordan, you definitely can give Marvin the boot. He *ain't* all that. And that's the way I meant to say it, so please don't correct my verb usage."

* * *

Georgia and Chloe pulled several dozen bags filled with clothes, shoes, and Coach bags from the back of the SUV. Now Chloe had enough to last at least through the school year. After everything was put away, Georgia made a cup of coffee and sat in the kitchen, her mind racing. Around eleven, she decided to put her thoughts to rest and try to get some sleep.

"So you took her shopping?" Marvin asked as he sat in bed flipping through the channels on their plasma television.

Georgia stood in the bathroom brushing her teeth. "I bought her a few things. Why? I know you don't mind."

"I'm sure it was more than a few things. No, I don't mind you taking her shopping, but I do mind that she stays up all night yapping on our damn phone. That I do mind. Why would she do that unless she's trying to play somebody? Are you going to nip that or do I have to?"

"How do you know she's on the phone all night?" Georgia asked as she walked into the bedroom, her braids pulled back into a long ponytail.

"This is how I know," Marvin said as he pressed the speaker button.

"And I want you to keep having that fat bitch buy you things," Bernadette said.

"Don't worry, Momma, I will. And I'm actin' like I'm so grateful for everything that fat bitch has done for me. She took me to an outlet mall, as much money as they got."

"Took you to a damn outlet? The bitch could have at

least taken you to Somerset to Neiman's. I bet she don't take her own kids to no damn outlet."

Georgia had heard enough. She pressed the speaker button. "I'll be right back," she told Marvin as she walked out of the bedroom and upstairs where she found Chloe lying across the leather sofa.

"I can see why her husband dogs her so bad with her fat weak ass."

"Is that right?" Georgia asked as she walked into Chloe's view and snatched the phone away, holding it to her ear. "What kind of mother would teach her daughter to disrespect the adult who is taking care of her?"

"Who the hell do you think you're talking to? All y'all are doing is shit y'all should have been doing years ago."

"Here's your daughter." Georgia threw the phone on the sofa.

"I gotta go," Chloe said to her mother while Georgia walked away.

Georgia couldn't find the strength to get out of bed in the morning. Not even for church. And Georgia never missed her weekly dose of encouragement from Bishop L. T. Anderson and First Lady Thelma Anderson of Greater Everlasting Faith. But today she had to pass.

Marvin rose early and told her he would be out all day with his trainer. As he left the bedroom, a weary Georgia, who lay snug underneath the sheets, turned to him and said, "Nice guys don't always have to finish last."

"What is that supposed to mean?" he asked.

"Even the nicest person in the world can get tired. It doesn't mean they have to stop being nice, but it does mean they have to stop being nice to certain people. Do you understand me?"

"I agree," Marvin said. "I tried to warn you about that girl."

"But *that* girl isn't my problem," she said after he left the room. An hour later, Georgia knew she needed to get up. It was noon, and she heard Chloe trying to quiet down her sons as they ran through the house.

"Your mom isn't feeling well, so you snotty-nose brats need to shut up."

Georgia sprang from the bed. She threw open the door and yelled, "Don't tell *my* children to shut up, and don't you ever call them snotty-nose brats again! There's only one snotty-nosed brat in this house and she sure in hell isn't one of my kids. This is their house and they can make as much noise as they please. Edrik and Haden, tear up the joint." She heard them cheer, and then a crashing sound. Georgia realized she might have lost it, because she didn't even care what they destroyed.

Shortly after, Chloe knocked on Georgia's bedroom door before opening it. A look of sheer panic was in her eyes. "Do you mind if I come in?" Chloe asked.

"Yes, I mind."

Chloe started to close the door.

"What do you want?" Georgia sat on the edge of her bed as Chloe cautiously entered.

"I'm sorry," she whispered.

"What was that? I didn't hear you. Speak up."

"I said I'm sorry for what I said about you. I didn't mean that stuff. I know you don't believe me, but I really didn't.

When I talk to my mother, that's how I have to talk. I can't tell her that I like being here, that I like you, and that I love my little brothers. I can't tell her any of that, because it would hurt her, and I don't want to hurt her. You've done more for me than she has in thirteen years, but I have to lie and make you out to be a monster, make you out to be someone who I can't stand," she said as a single tear dropped from her right eye. "I say all that instead of telling her the truth . . . that I love you."

Georgia straightened her back and applauded. "Have you ever considered becoming an actress instead of a rapper? Because that right there was an Oscar-winning performance."

"I'm not acting. I'm for real. I do love you."

"Love is as love does. And I heard you last night." Georgia walked into her bathroom and shut the door.

Priscilla sat confidently behind the wheel. Her spruce-colored Bentley Continental GTC with the personalized 1FM California plate emerged from the Lodge expressway onto Jefferson Avenue. Her gloved hand lowered the volume on the radio as she stopped for a red light. She pressed the phone button on her steering wheel and voice-dialed Lisa Hernadez. *It's worth a shot*, Priscilla thought as she phoned the shock jock out of the Tampa Bay area with over ten years of radio broadcasting experience. Priscilla was willing to try anything at this point to find a female host. If she were looking for a man, her search would have been long over.

Leslie had worked for Priscilla's dad in the past, but had moved on to a different station for more money and a better spot—the afternoon drive. But what Priscilla could offer was even better than that—the best time slot—her own morning show from six to ten a.m.

"Hey, Leslie. It's Priscilla Pusey, Thomas's daughter."

"There's only one Priscilla Pusey."

"Hey, girl. How are you doing?"

"Great! Loving Florida," she said.

"Really? Well, how would you feel about coming to Detroit as the radio personality for our new morning show?"

"Detroit?" Leslie laughed. "You want me to leave the Tampa Bay area and all of these beautiful beaches for Detroit? Let me ask you something—what's the temperature there today?"

"I don't know. Maybe thirty-five."

"It's sunny and eighty-six here today, so I think I might have to pass."

"You're going to turn down an opportunity to have your own nationally syndicated morning show because of a measly fifty-one degrees? Is that what you're telling me? You would be heard throughout several U.S. markets!"

"Do you want to know where I am right now? I am on Clearwater Beach, gazing out at the *clear* blue water and strolling along Pier 60 about to prance through white sand, and you want to know if I want to come where?"

"I want you to come to Detroit."

"I can't wear my bikinis there."

"You can wear 'em. You'll just freeze your ass off, but I'm sure the Detroit men would love to see a few bikinis this time of year."

"Sweetie, I would love to do it for you. Not for your dad, but for you. But why Detroit? It's a national show; you can broadcast from anywhere. You can broadcast from Florida. How about Miami? I'll do it there."

"I bet you would, but Dad wants to open back up in Detroit."

"Let me guess—the target is Marvelous Marvin."

"Yep."

"I don't know. He's got some pretty loyal listeners. You've seen the Arbitron ratings."

"He's doing well, but the host we find is going to do even better. She'll have to."

"She? So you definitely want a female? I'm surprised your dad is going for that. You know his philosophy on women and radio—the two don't equate, which is why I had to leave."

"Well, I'm in charge now while Dad expands our company into satellite. I'm trying to change those old views he has."

"As tempting as the offer is, I want to stay in Florida, work four hours a day, and pretend I'm retired."

"Just think about it. Right now, I'm so desperate I might do it myself, but whoever I choose won't have long to step up. I want to know you'll consider taking the spot if the money's right."

"If the money's right, anything's possible."

The next call Priscilla made was to her father.

"Tommy," Priscilla said into her speakerphone. "I feel like we've got a major Motor City problem."

"No problems, just creative solutions. Put that Columbia degree to use."

"Believe me, I have been. But my degree isn't helping me find a host. I've talked to everyone who claims to be someone in this city, which has done me absolutely no good. I've gone to modeling and casting agencies. I'm out every night partying and trying to stay connected, but so far nothing. How are we going to open up this market by the beginning of the year when it's right around the corner? I've been here for months. It's cold and the skies are gray. I miss Cali. This is so damn frustrating."

"I'm in Detroit next week. If you still haven't found a host, I'll have to stay and help you."

"We've been trying to find a host for months. I doubt if I'll find one by next week. I'm thinking about auditioning for one."

"Auditioning? Are you serious?"

"Yes, very. Why not audition?"

"Because that's not how hosts are selected. But again, I want you to do what makes you comfortable. I'll make a few calls, take out a two-page spread in *Essence* about the casting and try to get an article in the magazine. Maybe that will lead to something. Call your friends over at *Vibe Vixen* and see if they can put something in there."

"You know I don't call in favors."

"Well, you better start. This is a favor-run business. And also, why don't you reconsider the female host angle? Men do much better in radio than women."

"I have to disagree."

"Disagree with what? The facts? I've been in radio longer than you've been alive. You want a woman to go up against Tom Joyner, Steve Harvey, Rickey Smiley, even Marvelous Marvin, as much as I can't stand him? Let's be real."

"The right woman can."

"That would be quite a woman, but still keep in mind that the most successful radio hosts have always been men."

"Well, the host of *our* morning show is going to be a woman. And she's out there somewhere. I know she is."

"Am I going to find her today or not?" Priscilla asked as she peeked around her office door in the Guardian Building, and surveyed the crowded reception area. She closed the door and turned to face her father who had flown in to offer emotional support since the ordeal of finding a host seemed to be getting to her. He folded his *Wall Street Journal* and placed it in his lap.

"Do you need me in the room with you during the interviews or do you think you can handle it?"

"I can handle it so don't you worry. Kevin, Monique, Rick, and I will put this thing together."

He nodded. "I know you will. There's nothing to it but to do it." He stood to embrace his daughter and then walked out of the office toward the elevators in the hallway.

She sighed when her father left. She had really wanted him there. He had a knack for air talent. Most of the ones he picked had established long, successful radio careers.

By late morning, they had gone through two dozen interviews, and as usual, Kevin was ready to cut the day short.

"A few more," Priscilla insisted.

"One more," Kevin demanded.

A tall, slender woman dressed in all black walked in clutching a large portfolio.

"Let me guess, another model," Rick whispered as the woman approached their table and passed out headshots before taking the seat across from them.

"Hey, you look great," Priscilla said. "Tell us a little about yourself."

"I'm from Atlanta, but I missed your Atlanta auditions so I flew here. And well, in case you haven't figured it out, I'm a model and an actress."

Kevin started laughing uncontrollably. It seemed as if every woman and even many of the men who had auditioned so far were all models and actors. "What have you been in?" Kevin asked.

"I auditioned for *Flavor of Luv* season one and two, but I wasn't selected. Then I tried for *The Apprentice*, but I didn't make that either. I was on *American Idol*, season four."

"You went to Hollywood?" Kevin asked.

"No, I didn't make it that far, but my audition was televised, and Randy told me I had a unique voice like something he had never, ever, ever heard before. He stressed the ever."

"Oh, my God," Kevin mumbled. "Where do these people come from?"

"So now you're ready to become a radio host of your own nationally syndicated show?" Priscilla asked.

"Yes, I would love that."

"Do you have radio experience?" Monique asked.

"No, but I love to talk, so I really don't see where I'd have a problem."

"What would be your hook?" Kevin asked.

"My hook?"

"Why would I want to listen to you every morning? What would you discuss? What would your format be? What would you bring to the show?"

"Why do you want to be in radio?" Priscilla asked, after noticing the young woman's blank expression toward Kevin's questions.

"Don't those morning show hosts make a lot of money?"

"Next," Kevin said, turning over her picture.

"Well, don't they? I mean, I know for a fact Frank Ski makes a lot of money. Somebody e-mailed me pictures of his house. I want a house that looks like that."

"Next. Thank you. Next," Kevin said again.

"What? You asked me why I wanted to be in radio," the young lady said, still planted firmly in her seat. "I'm just being honest. What's wrong with me making lots of money if I'm making the radio station lots of money also?"

"And we appreciate your honesty," Priscilla said. "Perhaps we're just looking for something with a little more—"

"Substance," Kevin said.

"I can give you substance. I mean money isn't the only reason. I feel like I could get a lot of listeners, because basically, what is there really to it but talking and playing music, and I can talk nonstop and I'm into music. I would love to interview Ludacris and Usher and Chris Brown. Jay-Z. Oh, he's my favorite."

"Would you ever interview any women?" Kevin asked.

"Of course, I'm just thinking about my personal favorites right now."

"Can we please get rid of her?" Kevin mumbled to Priscilla as he turned in her direction. "Paula Abdul, you're the nice one. Tell her again how pretty she looks, and then in the nicest way, ask her to leave."

"So you came here all the way from Atlanta?" Priscilla asked.

"Okay, you just want to torture me," Kevin mumbled, "because I really don't care where she came all the way from. She can be from the moon for all I care."

"And I'm so glad that you're not broadcasting from Atlanta, because I'm ready for a change. I mean, I'm single and I want to be married one day, but it really is true what I've heard. There are a lot of gay men there, no offense," she said as she looked over at Kevin.

"Why would I take offense?"

"Oh, I thought . . . never mind, sorry."

Priscilla squeezed Kevin's thigh to calm him down. "Oh, you thought I was gay? Not a chance, baby. Please."

"I'm sorry. I didn't mean to offend you."

Priscilla stood. "It was nice talking to you, and we'll definitely keep you in mind."

Kevin gathered up the young lady's pictures from the

other three and handed all four back to her. "Yeah, we'll keep you in mind, but we'd hate for you to waste these."

They watched the young lady prance through the door. "Let's get something to eat and clear our minds. I don't want to see anybody else. I need a drink."

"I need a host," Priscilla said, ready to pull her naturally curly locks out.

Georgia yanked the plug to her Hoover upright out of the wall at precisely 3:15 P.M. Forty-five minutes. That would have been just enough time to quiet down Edrik and Haden, who were playing in the game room above her; weigh herself; take her afternoon snack of blueberries, walnuts, and parmesan cheese out of the fridge; and then snuggle in front of the flat-screen TV mounted over the fireplace in the great room to watch *Oprah* in comfort. But today there was a slight change in her usual routine. She had invited Art over to vent about Chloe and the things she'd overheard.

"So where is the bastard?"

"Art," Georgia said, her eyes widening, "she's still at school. Her father is picking her up today, because I refuse to ever speak to her again. But what if she had been here and heard you?"

"I wasn't talking about Chloe. I was referring to your husband. Doesn't he get off at ten? Does he ever come straight home?"

"Oh," she said, waving her hand. "Rarely."

"And you accept that from him, and the way he talks about you on the air? He's your husband, yet you can't forgive a child who probably doesn't know any better?" Art asked as he set his cup of coffee down.

"She knows better."

"But your husband doesn't?"

"It's not the same."

"I know. It's worse for your husband to do it. He took a vow to love, honor, and cherish. Chloe is just a misguided kid, and you have the opportunity to provide her with some stability. You told me you always wanted a daughter."

"I did."

"Well, now you have one."

"I thought she liked me, until I heard her call me a fat bitch."

"I don't believe kids today. No respect," Art said, shaking his head.

"She apologized for it, but you know how that is. Sorry just doesn't make it right."

"In her defense, if there is one to offer, she is very misdirected. You are the adult, so you're the one who needs to work on the relationship and trust. Don't give up on her. If you can hang in with Marvin all this time, you can at least give the girl one more chance."

"I don't know, Art. I'll do my best."

Whenever Georgia picked Chloe up from the school, she had noticed Chloe leaving the building alone with her head down, far away from the others. Georgia wondered if Chloe had a self-esteem problem or trouble socializing. She came across as so bossy and confident at home, but at school, she seemed meek and quiet as a mouse.

Georgia walked Art to the door. When she returned she stood on the last step of the spiral staircase and yelled, "Edrik and Haden, quiet down up there! You know what time it almost is. Boys, you're so loud I can't even hear myself think."

"But it's game time and we're in the fourth quarter," Edrik yelled. "If we win this game, Denver's going to the playoffs."

"Well, we're in Detroit and the Lions aren't going anywhere, so hurry up and shut it down. And your game better not go into overtime!"

"Whatever it takes to win, Mom," Edrik yelled right before she heard a crash.

"What was that?" Georgia yelled back. "Don't be up there tackling and knocking over the wrong things."

"But the other day you told us we could tear up the place," Edrik yelled back.

"Today is a new day. I better not hear a single crash."

She knew her sons loved playing football. They were both on little league teams, but it was her oldest son, Edrik, who couldn't get enough of the sport. Denver was his favorite team, and Champ Bailey and Darrent Williams were his favorite players. Georgia had even surprised the boys by remodeling their bedroom with football helmets on the headboards, and Berber carpeting that resembled a football field.

"Should we stop our game until *Oprah* goes off?" Edrik asked.

"Yes," Georgia yelled. "Great idea."

"They can't do that in real football, Mom."

"Okay, well, when you start playing real football, Mom won't expect you to do it either, but in the meantime, put that on pause." She headed for the master bathroom to step out of her clothes and onto the scale. Even with two days of fasting and her daily walks, she had somehow managed to gain two pounds, bringing her weight to a whopping one hundred and eighty-nine pounds—just eleven away from her worst nightmare.

She slowly turned to face the full-length mirror and her naked body for the first time in months. The sight of her flab and bulging stomach frightened her and nearly brought her to tears. Georgia couldn't believe she was a perfect size eight when she married Marvin, and now, eleven years later, she wore a size 16–18.

Georgia was a long way from her personal goal of one hundred and fifty pounds, and even with the Dove real-beauty campaign, it was difficult for Georgia to look at her body and be satisfied. She wasn't happy with the skin she was in—not with it sagging, not with the cellulite. But how could she even complain when she didn't want for anything materialistically?

Georgia sat on the closed toilet lid in a daze. Suddenly, watching Oprah wasn't as important as it had been just fifteen minutes earlier. As much as Georgia loved Oprah, sometimes it became a love-hate relationship. Oprah already had it all—money, fame, power, and beauty. And even though Oprah was once heavy herself—*if I had a chef and a personal trainer and billions of dollars with access to the very best doctors, and Dr. Robin to help overcome my emotional problems, I'd be thin, too*, she thought—but then again, why couldn't she have all that? Maybe not the billion dollars, but surely a personal trainer and a maid. She didn't need a chef, because she took too much pride in preparing meals for her family.

Marvelous Marvin's morning show had been in syndication for several years, and even though she didn't know exactly how much her husband's salary had increased, she knew it had to be significantly higher. Most likely seven figures, she assumed.

The tears just wouldn't stop falling.

She was miserable with her life.

And something had to change soon.

"**H**ey, bitch, somebody said your daddy is Marvelous Marvin," the young boy said to Chloe as she walked by. He stood in the hallway with his backpack swung over his left shoulder while he bounced a basketball between his legs. "Is that true? Is your daddy Marvelous Marvin? 'Cause if so, I want you to bring me his autograph. That's my man. He be puttin' you hoes on blast."

"What did you call me? Bitch? Ho? Boy, you better learn to have some respect for me."

"Have some respect for a chick? Your daddy don't have respect for your momma. So what do I need to have some for?"

"First of all, Marvelous Marvin ain't none of my daddy. I mean, Marvelous Marvin isn't my father. My mother don't . . . doesn't have a man and doesn't need one. We live in a big house that overlooks Lake Saint Clair, we got . . . we have three fly cars . . . me and . . . my two brothers and I are well taken care of without a man."

"Oh, really, what your momma do?"

"My mother . . . um . . . well . . . she's a . . . a doctor."

"Okay, that's cool. I'm sorry. That's just what somebody around here said. So your momma is the one who be driving up in that sweet Cayenne when she comes to pick you up."

"That's right. That's my mother."

"And she's a doctor. Where is she a doctor at?"

"At a hospital, fool. Where do you think?"

"I mean what hospital?"

"Harper, Grace, Henry Ford, Detroit Medical Center. Take your pick. She's a specialist, so she travels all around."

"My name is Marquis," the young man said.

"Did I ask you for your name? Who cares?" Chloe rushed through the door after looking at the wall clock in the hallway, realizing Georgia was probably outside waiting for her. But there was a different car in the space Georgia usually occupied—a Mercedes instead of a Porsche. Marvin instead of Georgia.

"I'd rather fuckin' hitchhike," she said under her breath as she stormed toward the car. "And who is that trick he got with him?" She jumped in the backseat.

"Hey, girlfriend," Destiny said.

"Girlfriend? Who are you talking to?" Chloe had her arms folded tightly across her chest.

"You're so pretty. You look just like your daddy."

"I don't look like him. You better put on your glasses."

"See, Marvin, if we had babies, they would look like her with that wavy jet black hair."

"Babies?" Chloe spit. "How is he going to have babies with you when he's married and already has babies with his wife? Are you crazy? Who are you anyway?"

"She works at the station," Marvin said. "She's a part of the morning team and she's just acting silly."

"The only woman on your team is Cammy, and she doesn't sound like Cammy or look like her, because Cammy has come up to my old school before."

"Oh, no, sweetie, Cammy isn't going to be at the station for much longer. I'm her replacement."

"Ratings drop," Chloe said, "if you're her replacement."

"We won't have to worry about ratings dropping, because your father is so far ahead of all the rest."

Chloe rolled her eyes and turned her head toward the window. She couldn't wait to get home to tell on Marvin. This time she would snitch. For someone like Marvin, she could make an exception.

"Oh, Chloe, I have a little something for you," Marvin said as he handed her the Motorola cell phone box. "I'm always getting things at the station. Unlimited airtime. You can talk anytime you want for as long as you want."

"Just as long as I don't talk to Georgia about Miss Thang, is that it?"

"No, that's not it. Why would you talk to Georgia about Destiny when Destiny just works for the radio station? I was just giving you a phone because I knew you wanted one. And there's more where that came from."

It was Monday morning. Cammy walked into the studio eating a bag of Frito's from the vending machine. Marvin tried to figure out how to tell her she had been replaced. Though Cammy was a producer, Marvin had pleaded his case to the station owner about needing to move in a new direction, and won support. Marvelous Marvin's number one rating spoke loudly, and he normally got what he wanted.

"Damn, it's too early in the morning for this room to smell like funky toes. Get rid of that shit," Marvin said.

Cammy crumpled up the bag and tossed it into the small garbage can. She looked over at the tall, slender woman standing beside Marvin. "Who's she? A listener?"

"No, this is Destiny, the latest addition to the morning team."

"I thought you always said you would never have more than one female on your team."

"I did. And I won't." He noticed Cammy's expression change. Her smile quickly dropped, and he knew she understood. "We've decided to move in a different direction."

She stood stiffly, her eyes circling the room, looking for something to throw in his path. "So you replaced me? Just like that? After five fucking years of being on the air with your boring ass, you replace me with one of your whores?"

"What did she just call me?" Destiny asked.

"A whore. Do you need me to spell it? I know it's a big word for your limited vocabulary."

Destiny dismissed her with a flick of her backhand and placed her headphones on.

"We're about to go on air," Marvin told Cammy, "so you better go. Management is here and is waiting to talk to you."

"Bruce and Bill are here, you mean. I was here before you—back when Curly Smith was on the air. We built this to the number-one radio station in Detroit, not you."

"If you're going to speak, at least state the facts—the station was not number one when Curly Smith was on the air." Marvin placed his headphones on and went live.

"You don't give a shit about anybody but yourself, do you?" Cammy asked as she snatched the microphone away from Destiny. "Let the listeners know you fired me, Marvin."

"I was going to let them know, but you just took care of that for me."

"I know this is the best move for me because I am so tired of listening to your lame jokes. You're always talking about people—mainly your wife, who is a better woman than you know. She puts up with your lying, cheating, conniving ass. I hated your damn show, and I can't believe listeners are letting someone like you rise to the number-one ranking—*if* those numbers are even accurate. You know damn well you don't have higher ratings than Tom Joyner."

"Are you finished?" Marvin asked. The microphone had long since been turned off and commercials played instead. What was going on in the studio could be heard only by those inside it.

"I know so much about you," Cammy said, glaring coldly at Marvin. "All I'd have to do is make one phone call to Georgia, and your world would come crashing down."

He picked up his cell phone to speed dial his home number. "Be my guest." He held the phone toward her after Georgia answered. Georgia's voice could be heard saying, "Hello."

"Go ahead. If you have something to say to her, say it." Cammy wouldn't take the phone away from him, and he ended the call.

"Fuck you, Marvin."

"Nah, I'll pass. Once is too much with you."

"You wish," Cammy said as she stormed out of the station.

"No, you wished, remember?" He took a deep breath. "Everyone's okay?" He surveyed the rest of his morning team who all nodded, glaring wide-eyed. "Terminations are never easy. But if you gotta go, you gotta go." He took another deep breath. "Okay, we're on again. Good morning, listeners. Are y'all waiting for this morning's topic? Before we get to that, you may have heard a little commotion in the station. Unfortunately, Cammy had a little outburst and has left the building. She was going to announce later in the week that she was moving on anyway. We have a new team member here and ready to step in for her. Please welcome Destiny to the air. And now, moving on to our most popular topic—infidelity. You know how I like to talk about cheating. And I'm going to have some real insight into this topic as a man who himself has cheated."

"Does your wife know you cheated?" Destiny asked.

"If she listens to my show, she knows."

"But she's never caught you in the act?"

"That might explain why she hasn't left me. No, she has never caught me in the act. She did find a diamond earring in my car, but I was able to lie my way out of that one."

"You're not worried that your wife will leave you one of these days?" Destiny asked.

"My wife isn't going anywhere—that much I do know."

"You're that confident?"

"Yes. We've been through too much, and she knows I may not be the best husband, but I'd never leave her. That's the promise I made her, and I keep my promises."

"Do you really?"

"Yes, I really do."

"So what about the promise you made me?" Destiny asked with attitude.

"What promise was that?"

She leaned into the microphone and spoke very clearly. "The promise you made that you would leave your wife so we would be together. What about all those things you told me while we were making love, and you were telling me how good I made you feel? And how you never had any woman give you head as good as me?"

"I think you have me confused. You and I haven't been together. I love my wife."

"How the hell can you say you love your wife when you're supposed to love me?"

"Destiny, you're tripping. Are you on something?"

"I bet you'd like for me to be on top of something right about now. No, you're the one tripping. You keep telling me you're going to leave her, and you don't. The only thing you've done for me is put me on your show and I don't even want to be on the radio. Besides, I'm too fine for radio; I need to be on TV."

"Oh, *you're* too fine for radio?" Marvin asked. "Let me tell you something before you let the lies go to your head. If *I'm* not too fine for radio, you're definitely not too fine for radio."

"The only reason I asked you to kick Cammy off and put me on was to tell all of your listeners that Marvelous Marvin is a lying, cheating bastard—and the dick ain't even all that good."

He laughed. "We're going to come back and take some callers. You're listening to Marvelous Marvin in the morning. Hit me up and tell me what's on your mind or just call to cuss me out. My tenth caller will be entered in my dream-a-day sweepstakes, where you can win ten thousand dollars and a dream-filled day of fun. Some restrictions do apply and as usual, you must be eighteen to enter."

"**C**ongratulations, you're my tenth caller," Marvin said. "Tell me your name and where you're calling from."

"My name, Marvin, is Georgia Brown, and you know where I'm calling from. Our damn house, and I am mad as hell. Mad as hell, Marvin! You have the nerve to put your other woman on the air! What kind of example do you think you're setting for your children? For your two sons about being men, or your daughter about what type of man to allow into her life? How could you do this to me? I've put up with your disrespect for far too long, but what you just did defies all reasonable judgment. You have lost your damn mind. I hope you know that I believe in karma. What goes around, baby, *will* come back around. You better know it."

"First of all, my sons are too young to listen to the radio. And as for my daughter, she's going to be just like her mother anyway—running from man to man—and there's nothing I can do to stop it."

"See, that's where you're wrong. There's nothing you're willing to do to stop it, but there's much you could do."

"You've tuned into the *Marvelous Marvin Morning Show*. I have the tenth caller on the line—my wife. Georgia, I hope you know you're excluded from the dream-a-day sweepstakes."

"What? Do you honestly think I called your station to be entered into your sweepstakes? All I have to do is withdraw money from our bank account."

"Yeah, my money."

"You know what? I'm wasting my breath. You can continue dogging me out and disrespecting me, and your listeners can keep laughing about it, but don't bother coming home."

"Well, Georgia, I hate to cut you off."

"And you won't." She hung up.

And Marvin's phone lines immediately lit up.

"Caller, you're on the air."

"Marvin, I listen to your show every morning. I've been married to my husband the same length of time you've been married to Georgia. I don't know if that new woman you have on the air is one of your pranks, but I believe you need to invite your wife in so the two of you can sit down and talk it out. We always hear your side. Let's hear hers."

The next caller said, "You a dog, Marvin. A real dog. Georgia needs to have her own show."

"Yeah, right," Marvin said, "and talk about what? The laundry?"

"That's right. Her dirty laundry—you."

After taking several more calls—all from women, all desiring to hear more from Georgia—he agreed to invite his wife on as a guest.

"Let me call her back and see if she'll come in tomorrow."

He called her cell phone first and when it went to voice mail, he called the house.

"What?" Georgia asked irately.

"My listeners want to hear from you. They want to know your side."

"After all of these years, they finally want to hear me?"

"Can you do it tomorrow?"

"I don't know, Marvin. Let me check my Franklin Planner."

"If I don't hear from you, I'll see you tonight."

"Not tonight, Marvin. Do not show your face in our home tonight. That shouldn't be too difficult for you since you don't normally come home."

The on-air sign flashed. An anxious Georgia sat nervously at the controls with headphones on and a microphone extended in front of her.

"How do you feel, baby? We're getting ready to go live," Marvin said.

"Oh, suddenly I'm your baby and not a cow?"

"You've always been my baby," he said with a wink.

"Listeners, don't I always give you what you ask for? You wanted to hear my wife's side of the story, and guess who I have with me this morning? You've heard me talk about her for years now, and she's finally here, she says, to set the record straight. What would you like to say, Mrs. Brown?"

She leaned toward the microphone and said, "I'd prefer to be called Georgia."

Marvin laughed. "Feisty this morning. Okay, Georgia. Even though you are still Mrs. Brown."

"For now."

"For eleven years you've been Mrs. Brown, and that won't change."

"Never say never, Marvin."

"Well, I'm saying never. We will never split up. Just like I will never be broke again."

"Never say never."

"What do you want to say besides, 'Never say never'?"

Georgia sat quietly for a few seconds and composed her thoughts. Finally, she exhaled slowly. "If you are the most popular radio host in the morning, what does that say about our society? That we would cheer for a man who puts down his wife, brags about cheating, and so on and so on? Why can't we cheer for what's good and right? Why is there always a scandal attached? What about love and commitment? You promised to love, honor, and cherish me. What happened to all of that?"

"I do love you. Do you love me?"

"Of course I love you—not the person you've turned into, but the old Marvin. We've shared a lot together. We went from middle-class to no class to upper-class, and now we're raising three kids together. Well, I'm raising three kids."

"And I'm the moneymaker who works to make it easier for you to raise those three kids. Who said we both can't work?"

"We both do. I have several jobs, actually. I stay at home to raise the kids, cook, and clean every day. Marvin, you have it made."

"Do I really?"

"Absolutely. You work four hours a day, and when you come home, you don't have to do anything."

"You keep a clean house, I will give you that. And you are a wonderful cook. You could try being a little more exciting in the bedroom."

"You should try being a loving husband." She took several deep breaths to calm herself. "Look, I really didn't come here to argue."

"Well, what did you come here for?"

"I came here because you invited me, and because I wanted to tell my side."

"So tell it. Why did you agree to come on the show?"

"I came on here to give a voice to women who are a lot like me."

"Are there a lot of women out there like you? Are there a lot of women out there who are able to stay home even after the kids are old enough to go to school, who don't have to do anything other than clean a few rooms, cook a few meals, and spend their husband's money, drive around in Porsches and jet-set?"

"Jet-set? Be for real, Marvin. The only one jet-setting is you. Our house stays immaculate. I cook a different meal every day. Women want to be loved and not torn apart and criticized. It's sad to me that you couldn't love me as the woman who gave birth to your two sons and is raising them along with your daughter, my stepdaughter, as if she is mine. As the woman who stood by you and your dream and lost a job behind it."

"How did you lose a job behind my dream?"

"I can't believe you are asking me that question. How could you forget? I stuck by you, but back then it wasn't hard to, because I knew you loved me."

"And I still love you. What do I need to do to prove that to you?"

"It would be nice to start with an apology."

"Okay, I'm sorry."

"Sorry for what?"

"I don't know, but you want an apology, so I gave you one. Let's take a caller. Caller one, you're on the air. Do you have something to say to Georgia?"

"Yes, Georgia, honey, it's time for you to tell your man farewell. He's not all that. Leave him and take half, and get you another man who's going to give you what you want, because Marvin's too busy spreading himself all around the city to have any left when he comes home to you. Don't you ever think about diseases, Marvin?"

"As much as the next man, which is never. Next caller, what do you have to say?"

"Hey, man, my name is Michael. I go to Greater Everlasting, which is your wife's church."

"Hello, Michael," Georgia interjected.

"Hello, Georgia. All I want to say is your husband is doing you wrong. He has his listeners thinking you're unattractive and big as a whale and Marvin, man, if you don't know it, let me just say you have a beautiful wife. You better watch out, man. I'm a single man who knows how to fill a void. *And* I'm a Christian."

"You don't sound like one, trying to take another man's wife. Get off my line with that."

"Georgia, I'll see you on Sunday," Michael said. "You be blessed."

"Oh, I will."

Marvin said, "Okay, no more callers. Unless some of y'all call up here and show me love. What about Marvin? No one loves Marvin. Millions of you must. . . . Otherwise, I wouldn't be the number-one morning show host. Well, Georgia, thank you so much for stopping by. It was nice to get your side."

"I haven't even told my side, but I'd like to. I do have a side and maybe one day I'll be able to share it . . . and help others do the same."

"Caller, you're on the air. What do you have to say to me or my wife?"

"This is to Georgia. Georgia, my name is Priscilla Pusey. You mentioned you have a side you want to share. How about sharing it on WFOR, The Force, as our new morning show host?"

Marvin started laughing uncontrollably. "Do you honestly think my wife would accept your offer? Please." He glanced over at Georgia. "Here, it's for you," he said mockingly and then transferred the call to the red line in the station. Georgia removed her headphones, feeling she had to take the call. It could just be a crazy person, but she had to find out.

"Georgia, I'm offering you a morning show spot on a nationally syndicated show that will broadcast from the Guardian Building downtown. I've been looking and searching, and then I turned on the radio and heard your voice . . . a voice that others need to hear. Thousands have tried out for this and I'm willing to hand it to you."

Georgia looked over at Marvin who was still in stitches over the idea.

"Could I have your number to discuss it further?" Georgia asked.

"Do you have something to write with?"

Georgia grabbed a pen from her purse and one of the station's business cards that was lying around.

"Yes, I have something to write with." Marvin snatched the pen out of Georgia's hand. "Stop, Marvin."

"Are you ready?"

"Yes. I'm more than ready."

"The meeting will be at Seldom Blues this Friday at six o'clock."

"Okay," Georgia said. She didn't want to write down the

information, because Seldom Blues was a sophisticated jazz supper club located on the lower level of the GM Renaissance Center, home to Marvin's radio station. She knew if he saw where they were meeting, he'd show up, so she simply said, "Sounds good."

Marvin sat at the dining room table ready to feast on a home-cooked meal when Georgia placed a Hungry-Man TV dinner in front of him, and said, "I'm rushing, so here."

He pushed the plastic container to the side.

"What the hell is this?" Marvin asked. He had been looking forward to Georgia's cooking after spending all week treating Destiny to expensive meals at downtown restaurants.

"What does it look like?" Georgia asked sarcastically. "You're a hungry man, aren't you? So eat."

"I know what it is, Georgia, and I know damn well this isn't our dinner tonight."

"Of course this isn't our dinner."

"I was about to say."

"But it is *your* dinner. I have a dinner meeting tonight."

"A dinner what?"

"A dinner meeting, Marvin." She hesitated for a moment. "I've been offered a job."

"You're getting a job?" he asked, stunned.

"Remember the woman who called the station?"

"That wasn't serious."

"I'm having a meeting with her tonight."

"You don't need to work."

"I want to work."

"Doing what?"

"Doing something I never would have imagined I'd do—hosting a radio show."

"Wait a minute," he said, following behind her. "Are you serious? You can't be on the radio."

"Why can't I?"

"Because you wouldn't make it. Stop tripping."

"I'm not tripping, Marvin."

"I'm sure they'll offer you a receptionist position or something like that—not an actual on-air personality job. Hell, I can get you something like that at my station if you want."

"I'll be home in a couple hours."

The introductions flew around the table. It was beautifully adorned with cobalt blue water glasses and a little domed cover for the butter that resembled a bell. Within the hour, Georgia and the 1FM management team were nibbling on popsicle lamb chops drizzled with mustard and thyme.

The waiter brought small scoops of sorbet with champagne to cleanse the palate before the entrees were served.

After dinner, Georgia, Priscilla, Thomas, and three other 1FM employees sat in the private River Room of Seldom Blues. Georgia occasionally glanced out the giant windows to take in the handsome views of the Detroit River, the waterfront, and the Ambassador Bridge.

She couldn't remember the last time she had dined in a restaurant of such stature—several years at least. After Marvin's million dollar win in Los Angeles, he treated the family to dinner at a five-star restaurant in Beverly Hills, but Marvin had never taken her to Seldom Blues. She had cooked her family's meals nearly every day of their married life, even when they lived with his parents. After they had their own home, she took gourmet cooking classes so her meals complemented the beautiful and spacious kitchen, even though Marvin was rarely there to enjoy them.

Thomas refilled Georgia's empty wineglass. He rarely spoke, allowing his daughter to handle most of the negotiations with Georgia. Priscilla explained the show's New Year's Day launch, which was just a few weeks away.

"Do you have any questions for us?"

"Are you sure about having me as the host? I am Marvin's wife, and I wonder how listeners will take that. After all, he is the number one radio host in the urban market."

Thomas cleared his throat. "We are well aware of his ranking," he said. He took a sip of 1961 Petrus. "And I'd be lying if I said reclaiming the number one spot in this market is not a personal goal of mine. With that said, my daughter believes she has found someone who can help us accomplish that—you. And you just so happen to be Marvin's wife. I didn't hear you on the radio, but I do have to agree with my daughter that you have a beautiful voice. But, then, it simply goes along with the entire package."

Georgia sucked in her stomach and sat up straighter in her chair.

"Now, all of that said, I must admit I am a little uneasy about having Marvin's wife as the host of our new show. I can only imagine the jokes he'll make as a result."

"You don't have to worry about any jokes. If I become a radio host, he will not make a joke about it. The one thing he doesn't do is discuss other on-air personalities."

"He'll make you the exception, because to him, you're not an on-air personality—you're his wife. And he always dogs his wife. That's what he's famous for. Now, my question to you is, what will you be famous for?"

"For not dogging my husband." Georgia added, "I would like for my morning show to empower and uplift people. Educate them. Teach them about taking control of their finances, their health, and beauty, all of that."

"That's what we have Oprah for," Priscilla said. "This is radio and our format is to basically entertain. That's why, when you actually start firing back at Marvin, listeners will surely tune in."

"You mean talk about him," Georgia clarified.

"Isn't that what he's been doing to you?"

"Yes, but that's definitely not my style."

"Your style? You've never been on the radio before so

you don't have a style yet. Make it your style," Priscilla said as she picked her wineglass up and started sipping. "Create a persona. It doesn't have to be who you really are. It's acting."

"My persona is going to be the real me—sweet Georgia Brown. I'm not stooping to his level."

"What is your goal with your show?" Priscilla asked.

"To become a household name."

"And the only way you're going to do that," Priscilla said, "is if you give your listeners something to talk about."

"I'm going to give them plenty to talk about. I just won't be talking about my husband."

"We'll discuss this later. I'm sure you'll see my point of view. This is entertainment. We're not trying to save the world over the airwaves. We want advertisers, and advertisers are only concerned about one thing—ratings. The way we'll get huge ratings is by fighting fire with fire."

"I can't do that. As mad as Marvin makes me sometimes, I can't blast him. But I would still like the opportunity."

"Let's toast," Thomas said, raising his glass, "to all that's new—a new year, a new show . . . and a whole new you, the one that will be on blast."

Georgia raised her glass.

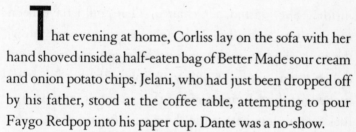

That evening at home, Corliss lay on the sofa with her hand shoved inside a half-eaten bag of Better Made sour cream and onion potato chips. Jelani, who had just been dropped off by his father, stood at the coffee table, attempting to pour Faygo Redpop into his paper cup. Dante was a no-show.

"Be careful with that, little man. If you get that red shit—stuff, I mean—on the carpet, it isn't coming out."

They were watching their favorite show, *Deal or No Deal*. She loved that game show more than any other, because winning involved one-hundred-percent luck. The hardest thing about the game was getting on, which she knew all about because she had sent in her videotape months ago with no reply. Corliss was screaming at the TV when the phone rang.

"Hello?" Corliss asked, her eyes glued to the television. The contestant had just turned down a deal from the banker for $202,000 after the last case she picked had only five dollars inside. This was up from the previous offer of $107,000. "Fool, you should have taken it! Do you know what I could do with $202,000?" The only high number left was the million dollars, which the contestant continued to say was in her case.

"Corliss!" Dante shouted.

"Hold on a second." The woman only needed to open one case. "Don't pick number seven. That's the case with the million dollars in it. Don't pick it," she told the woman. She obviously couldn't hear Corliss, because she picked seven, and it did, in fact, have the million dollars inside. "She wasted her chance. That could have been me up there, and I would have taken that money. Now, the most she can go home with is twenty-five thousand dollars, and you can't quit your job with that." Corliss turned off the television, upset that a contestant who was lucky enough to get on the show was too stupid to know when it was time to cash out. "Greed," she sighed. "Okay, Dante, I'm back. Where are you? With your so-called cousin?"

"I'm at work."

"Work? You didn't even come home last night."

"Yeah, baby, I was working. I pulled a double. Trying to make that money."

"When you make it, what do you plan to do with it? Because you haven't been contributing here. You've lived here several months rent free. You can at least pay half. That was the deal."

"I will."

"With all this so-called overtime you're working, paying rent shouldn't be a problem."

"You're right. It's not."

"Okay, then, when you get paid, I want my half of the rent."

"You'll have it. I was just calling to say hey during my break."

"Hey," Corliss said dryly.

"All right, I'll let you go."

As soon as she hung up the phone, it rang again. "Hello?"

"Let me tell little man good-night," Jermaine said.

"Hello?" she emphasized.

He laughed. "Hello. How are you?"

"I'm fine. You just dropped him off and said good night."

"Okay, can I say it again?"

"Little man, Papa's on the phone for you."

His eyes lit up. "Papa's on the phone!" Jelani ran and snatched the phone from Corliss and hopped in her lap. "Hi, Papa."

"Hey, little man." Corliss could hear Jermaine's every word. "I love you, little man."

"I love you, too, Papa."

"We're gonna spend this weekend together and go to Chuck E. Cheese."

"Chuck E. Cheese!"

"Don't give your momma a hard time getting you in bed. I don't want to hear any stories about you getting up in the middle of the night like a crying baby. You gotta be a little man, okay?"

Jelani started nodding.

"He can't hear you," Corliss said to Jelani who continued to nod. Corliss took the phone from Jelani. "He's nodding like you can see him."

"Oh, really?"

"I think you're scaring him. He probably thinks you're mad at him."

"He knows better. Give him a kiss for me."

"I will."

"This ain't right."

"What?"

"Nothing."

"What? Say it?"

"Nothing."

"What's not right?" Corliss prodded.

"Us being apart. I wish I could trust your ass."

"You wish you could trust my ass?"

"Yeah, I do, but I can't. I gotta go."

Jermaine hung up and Corliss sat still for a moment with the receiver still in her hand. There was no use trying to figure Jermaine out. The best thing for her to do was decide what movie to watch before bed. She studied her massive collection—it was a toss between *Lady Sings the Blues* and *Jason's Lyric,* but also *Ali.* Then, impulsively, she decided on *Bird,* because it had been a good six months since she had last watched it.

"**G**eorgia!" Marvin yelled, slamming the door leading from the kitchen to the garage. "This shit just can't be true."

"What, Marvin?" she asked as she rushed out of the bedroom. "What can't be true?"

He held up a copy of the *Detroit Free Press* and turned to the front page of the entertainment section.

"That's me," she said excitedly. The photo shoot had been exciting, and the prints had turned out great, even though she had to force herself to smile.

"Oh, Mom, you look good," Chloe said. Georgia and Chloe had decided on a fresh start, and Georgia had been touched when Chloe asked if she could call her "Mom."

"Oh, so she gets her own radio show and now she's your mom?"

"No," Chloe said, narrowing her eyes at Marvin. "I have been calling her that—you just haven't been around to hear it."

"Is there something you want to tell me?" Marvin asked. " 'Irate housewife determined to become a household name,' " he said, reading the headline.

She had no idea she would make the front page of the Sunday entertainment section.

" ' "Expect billboards to be plastered throughout the city by New Year's," Priscilla Pusey of 1FM says.' I thought you told me you weren't going to do it."

"I don't remember telling you that, Marvin. In fact, just the other week, I told you I was going to do it. The night I went for the dinner meeting."

"Oh, that night? The night you left me with your kids and a TV dinner?"

"*My* kids. Are they just my kids?"

He continued reading. " 'Sweet Georgia Brown's morning show will be the best thing listeners have heard in a while.' "

"Marvin," Georgia said, trying to stop him from reading the article.

"Wait, there's more. 'This former housewife turned morning show host is best known as the *ex*-wife of Detroit radio host Marvelous Marvin, who spent many days on his number-one-rated morning show dishing out insults about his plus-size bombshell wife. Prospective listeners are already buzzing, hopeful Georgia Brown will use her show to do the same to him.' So you're my ex-wife now? Is there something you forgot to tell me?"

"That was a misprint. I'll ask Priscilla for a correction to be printed."

"No one reads the corrections, Georgia. And besides, I doubt it was a misprint, because you've been keeping me in the dark about a lot of things lately."

"I'm on the air tomorrow morning. Six a.m. Be sure to check me out."

"Georgia, please don't go on-air and try to compete with me. You're out of your league. In fact, you're not in any league—not when it comes to radio. That would be like me trying to win the U.S. Open against Tiger Woods. It can't happen."

Marvin had an insatiable urge—not for another woman, though Destiny was with him for the ride, but for the lure of fast money, free drinks, and flashing lights. He needed to get to a casino fast. He rode through the high-energy historic Greektown district, Georgia and 1FM on his mind, and passed Nikki's pizza and other landmarks as he headed for the next casino. *The nerve of them to call my radio station and offer my wife a job*, he thought. He felt it was a cheap marketing ploy—another opportunity for their call letters to be heard over the number one urban radio station in the country. And for them to actually assume that his loyal wife would betray him in such a way? At the time it seemed ridiculous. Georgia wasn't a traitor. But now, the reality was sinking in and Georgia was drifting away, doing her own thing, and he wasn't used to that.

He entered the Greektown Casino and headed for the poker room. It was the largest in town with twenty-one tables, several plasma screens, and convenient bar service.

While he waited for Destiny to come out of the restroom, most likely taking a cocaine break in one of the stalls, a lovely young woman in a black dress and high heels distracted him. She sat at a dollar slot machine, seemingly distraught for having lost so much.

"Try your luck at something else," Marvin suggested.

"What?" She glanced up and pulled the handle. One seven. Two sevens. Three sevens. She had three sevens! Her machine lit up and a loud siren sounded. Coins started pouring from her machine. One bucket wasn't enough for them all and Marvin quickly grabbed three from a hostess who walked by. He helped the woman gather up her winnings. "Don't take any of my money."

"I won't. I have plenty of my own."

"I don't need to be distracted by a good-looking man trying to rob me."

"I'm not trying to rob you. I'm trying to help you."

"Well, you look at the chart and tell me how much it is."

"Twelve thousand five hundred."

"For two dollars?"

"So double that to twenty-five thousand. It won't all come out of the machine. Someone will come over." He stood to walk away.

"Hey, are you my good-luck charm? I wasn't having any until you showed up."

"I don't know. I was wondering if you might be mine. There's only one way to find out."

"How's that?"

"Stand next to me in the poker room to see if I win."

"Just as soon as I collect all of my money, I'll meet you. But I don't play poker, so don't expect me to put my winnings on the table."

"I'll handle the betting."

He put his skills to work at the seven-card stud table where players won by having the best hand or by betting high and forcing the others to fold before the showdown.

As Marvin puffed on a Cuban cigar, he examined the seven cards he had just been dealt, selecting the best five to make a high hand. He had too much on his mind to focus on much of anything so he folded, and then his next urge kicked in.

"Let's get out of here," he told the woman.

"Get out of here? Get out of here and go where? When I leave, I'm going home . . . to my husband."

"And when I leave, I'm going home . . . to my wife. Let's leave the casino and go somewhere intimate where we can talk and get to know each other."

"There you are," Destiny said as she walked up to Marvin and stood by his side. "And who's your pretty friend?"

"I'm sorry," Marvin said, turning to the woman. "I don't even know your name."

"Heather."

"Heather was going to join us this evening."

"Mmm, three's company," Destiny said.

Marvin was slouched in one of the accent chairs in the bedroom of the suite at the Atheneum Hotel with a glass in his hand and a bottle of rum and a can of Coke on the end table beside him, pretending to enjoy the show the women were performing.

They were naked and standing on their knees on the king-sized bed, kissing each other and feeling on each other's naked bodies. More into each other than they would probably ever be into him, he assumed.

His mind was buzzing about so many things, especially about the money he owed, but also about Georgia. *Will she leave me?* he wondered.

He glanced over at the women, whom he no longer found the least bit entertaining. Money, and how he was going to get ahold of some, became the focal point. He needed to come up with a scheme, a way to get some fast money.

What to do? he wondered, taking a few more sips of his rum and turning back to the ladies' show.

PART THREE

Who's Zoomin' Who?

Chloe, Edrik, and Haden sat in the studio around Georgia who was beaming from excitement. Her sons would be back in school tomorrow, but Georgia had to go to Chloe's school on the eighth concerning a fight Chloe had gotten into trying to protect her best friend Vernita from some cruel remarks.

"Good morning to my listeners. I'm your host Sweet Georgia Brown, and welcome to our first day on the air. I have two lovely morning team co-hosts who many of you already know. Ladies, will you introduce yourself?"

"Hey, I'm not mad at you, but I am mad with you," Cammy said. It had been her signature line on Marvin's show. "It's me, Cammy from that other man's show, the man whose name I refuse to say. Y'all, I'm back. That other station may have fired me—wrongfully by the way—and then tried to disguise it, but that man's better half, Georgia, saw my true talent and personally asked for me. I'm so glad to be here with you, Georgia."

"And I'm glad to have you here."

"And hey, I'm crazy Tonya Aires, taking a break from The Divine Divas Comedy tour. Make some noise for a new year and a whole new station with three fly women behind the mic. And we keep it kronk."

"Today our very first guest of the brand-new year is Dr. Marshall Greene. He'll be with us after the commercial break to talk about a very serious topic in the African-American community—HIV/AIDS. He has information everyone needs to hear, so please don't turn that dial."

Dr. Greene, the young doctor whom Marvin had shunned from his show, wanted to discuss the upcoming National Black HIV/AIDS Awareness Day. He and his guest settled into chairs near Georgia and placed headphones over their ears.

"I want to thank you both for coming on the show."

"Thank you, Georgia, for having us," Dr. Greene said.

A producer yelled, "And we're back on in five, four, three . . ."

"Welcome back. You're listening to the *Sweet Georgia Brown Morning Show*. Now, when I say our first guest is a man on a mission, I mean just that . . . and I want our listeners to hear what Dr. Marshall Greene says, giving him the same respect you would Kanye West or Fantasia. Please don't turn the station just because the content may be hard to listen to. Believe me, I'm sure it's even harder to live with. Doctor, what do you have to say?"

"I want to thank you for having us on to discuss a topic most people don't want to hear about—not only first thing in the morning, but ever. And the more we openly discuss it, the faster we can plan for a change. Your husband wouldn't put me on his show to talk about HIV/AIDS. He's not trying to educate or enlighten anyone. Just entertain. And it's hard to entertain when you're six feet under. It's hard to laugh when you're in the hospital dying from a host of diseases you can contract because of a low immune system. By having me on your show, you're saving lives."

Georgia looked over at Priscilla, who beamed as she nodded.

"Thank you for coming on," Georgia said. "I tried to get you on his show before, because I know how important this topic is, and you went all the way to the station and waited. But I'm not going to keep my listeners waiting, because they need to know this."

"HIV/AIDS is destroying our community. African Americans make up 12.3% of the U.S. population, yet account for fifty percent of new diagnoses each year. Young black women especially need to be concerned, because it's the number one killer among black women ages twenty-five to thirty-four."

"That's startling," Georgia said. "The number-one killer."

"It's also a fact that the mode of transmission for black men is sex with other men, while the primary mode for women is sex with men."

"Which means men have sex with men and then pass the disease to women," Georgia said, shaking her head as she looked at the woman Dr. Greene had brought with him.

"We don't want to leave our other guest out this morning. Would you like to introduce yourself?"

"Yes, I sure would," the young woman said proudly. "My name is Winona Fairchild, and I am HIV-positive."

Georgia appeared stunned.

"Are you okay?" Winona asked her. "You look like you've seen a ghost."

"Yes, I'm fine," Georgia said, "but I have to admit I just assumed you were another doctor. I feel a little embarrassed, because I don't want to say what I'm thinking, but I should, because many people probably think the same way."

"That she doesn't look like someone who would be HIV-positive?" Dr. Greene guessed.

"Exactly, and I'm sure you get that a lot. How did you find out you were infected with the disease?"

"Through an illness I assumed was the flu. I got sick. I went to the doctor, got tested, and was told I was HIV-positive. The man who was in my life at the time, who was also my daughter's father, knew he was HIV-positive. He knew he was gay, and I say gay because I don't believe in the term bisexual. He didn't tell me until he had no other choice, waiting until the moment before my results came back.

"I hid my status from everyone for many years, because

I didn't even want to admit it to myself. I didn't tell my children or my parents. The only person who knew—besides my doctor—was the man who had infected me."

"Is this man still in your life?" Georgia asked.

"No, he's dead. He was killed in a car accident."

"Did you run him over?" Tonya asked. "I wouldn't blame you if you did."

"I should have, but no. What goes around comes around—I truly believe that. But I fault myself for trusting a man I didn't know with something as important as my life. Sex should not be casual. I didn't know him that well. I met him at the mall, and then the next thing I knew, we were living together. I had a dangerous need to be loved at any cost. I was young at the time. All this nonsense about when to discuss sex is also dangerous. I don't believe there is a right age. I have a daughter around the same age as yours, and when she leaves the house, those men trying to pick her up have a whole lot more in mind."

Georgia looked over at Chloe, who seemed to be really listening to Winona.

"Winona, what would you say to a young girl, thirteen or so, who has been sexually active?"

Winona shook her head. "Just stop. Don't do that to yourself . . . to your body. Don't give any more of yourself away. These boys—"

"And men," Georgia interjected, "because in some cases, these young girls mess around with grown men."

"Sadly, that's true," Winona said. "No, they don't care about you—they don't love you. They're searching for a feeling, and they don't care where it comes from. And for those young girls and boys who haven't had sex, don't be pressured into doing something that you have so many years left to do. Concentrate on your education—it can't be said often enough. Sisters Living Positively is a support group that educates young women about sex and using protection."

"What do you tell them?"

"We'd love to say abstain, but we try to be as realistic as possible. Many people won't practice abstinence, even though they should consider it. There's nothing wrong with using a toy."

"You're not lying there, girlfriend," Cammy said. "Believe me when I say there is nothing wrong with using a toy."

Winona continued. "On November seventh, 1991, after Magic announced he was HIV-positive, I remember women saying how men wouldn't be so promiscuous now, but nothing changed. If it had, we wouldn't be faced with this current crisis. Listen, sex is great when you're with someone who loves you and it's monogamous. But it's nothing when you're just another piece. And believe me, people don't tell you the whole truth of what they've done or who they've been with. Protect yourself. You don't want to be lying in a hospital bed with sores over ninety percent of your body, blind, and ravished from AIDS. The last thing on your mind then would be how good the sex was. You're going to be fighting for your life, so fight for it right now."

"Where can our listeners get tested?"

"There's a Web site, HIVtest.org. Put in your zip code to find the testing site nearest you."

"I can't help but stare at the rather large rock on your finger," Tonya said.

"Are you married?" Cammy asked.

"Well, I'm engaged to a wonderful man, Porter Washington."

"Porter Washington?" Georgia asked excitedly. "The jazz musician? I can't wait to get his new CD next month. I have to get him on this show. Will you let him know he has an open invitation? He's your man?"

"That's my man. He accepted my status, accepted me and my illness. We love each other, and we've tried not to let this disease stop us from living."

"That's wonderful. He has to be a very special man."

"He is," Winona said. "And there are more special men out there."

"So when is the wedding?" Georgia asked.

"Oh, boy. We've put it off a couple times. There's so much going on in our lives. But we might marry this fall during the grand opening of our jazz club, The Blue Room. I'll definitely invite you guys."

"I'm going to hold you to that. Please, you and Dr. Greene must come back next month on February seventh, National Black HIV/AIDS Awareness Day, to enlighten our listeners even more."

"**M**om, now that you're on the air, are you going to stay with Not-So-Marvelous Marvin?"

"What do you mean, stay with him? Where else would I go?" Georgia and Chloe had just arrived home for the day—Georgia's first on air.

"Anywhere else. He's cheating on you. How can you stay with a man who's a cheat?"

"I don't think he's cheating on me."

"Where is he right now?"

"Your dad is very popular."

"Tell me about it, especially among the ladies. So where is he? How can you think he's not cheating when he says he is on air?"

"That's all part of his act."

"What about Destiny?"

"How do you know about that?" Georgia asked.

"I heard about it."

"That was all part of a prank on me."

"Is that what he told you? That Destiny was a prank?" Chloe shook her head. "She's no prank."

"It makes perfect sense."

"I guess to someone who wants to believe it, but not to me. He brought Destiny with him when he picked me up from school, and all she talked about was how their child's hair would turn out wavy like mine."

"Don't lie about your father. I know you don't like him, but please don't lie. Did he really bring that woman to the school to pick you up?"

"Yes, he really did." She took her Motorola cell phone out of her pocket and twirled it around. "And he gave me this so I'd keep quiet. You have to leave him. You just have to."

"I've been with your father for eleven years. We have two children together, and now you're a part of our lives. We have this home. I have a good life. A better life than I have ever had. It's not perfect, but it is so much better than what I am used to. He has never ever hit me. And he's here—he's with me—with our children being a father."

"So all I have to do is find a man who won't hit me, and will only be around whenever he feels like coming around?"

"No, I'm not saying that."

"So what are you saying?"

"I don't believe your father is cheating on me," Georgia said, flipping through the television channels.

"Oh, I get it. You're one of those women who has to see it to believe it. Well, there are plenty of private detectives in the yellow pages. Why don't you hire one? You've got money," Chloe told her. "Hire someone and let them show you what I've just told you—the truth."

Georgia stopped on CNN.

"Denver Broncos' cornerback Darrent Williams was shot and killed early this morning in a drive-by shooting after a dispute at a nightclub," the reporter said.

The shocking news forced Georgia to sit upright. Her eyes fell from the screen as images flashed of the Broncos' final game of the season. "We just watched him play yesterday," Georgia said to Chloe, who sat on the opposite side of the large leather sectional.

"Is that the game Edrik wanted to watch so badly?" Chloe asked as she glanced at the television. "That's not who he said was his favorite player, is it?"

Georgia nodded. "Yes, he's the one. I don't know how I'm going to tell him." When the reporter mentioned Darrent's two children, Georgia became overwhelmed with grief as tears began to surface.

The phone rang.

"How are we going to tell them?" asked Marvin on the other end. "Especially Edrik?"

"Telling him will break my heart. How long will it take you to get home?"

*   *   *

Marvin arrived within the hour.

Edrik and Haden were upstairs playing video games as Chloe watched over them to make sure they didn't inadvertently switch on the television. This sort of news needed to be broken to them very gently.

"Boys," Georgia said, "your father is downstairs and we need the two of you to come to the living room."

"But Mom, I'm kicking his butt," Edrik said.

"Please, boys. It's important. You can finish your game later."

Edrik and Haden ran downstairs. Georgia and Marvin sat beside each other on the sofa with the boys directly across from them. Finally, Georgia started.

"Boys, come over here," Georgia said, patting the empty space beside her. "We have some sad news," she said as tears began forming. She looked into Edrik's innocent eyes. "About one of the Broncos."

Edrik's smile vanished.

Georgia sighed. "I'm sorry, baby."

"Sorry about what, Mom? What about one of the Broncos?"

"I'm sorry, baby."

"Nothing happened to Darrent or Champ, did it?"

"Darrent—"

"What happened to Dee Will?"

"I'm sorry," Georgia said, her words choking.

"Son," Marvin said, taking over. "Darrent Williams was hurt badly."

"But he's going to be all right. Right? By next season? He's going to play next season, right?"

"No, son. He won't be playing next season."

"Why? What happened to Dee Will?" Edrik asked again, but this time he stood looking up to his father.

Marvin placed his hand on his son's shoulder. "Some bad people . . . took his life early this morning."

"His life?" Edrik said, his voice quivering. "His life?" He momentarily looked away from his father as his mind searched to understand. "What do you mean his life?"

"Son, let me explain."

"What do you mean, Dad, by his life? Why would someone take his life? Everybody loved Dee Will. I don't think you know what you're talking about. You never know what you're talking about. All you do is say things that aren't true about other people, like the way you talk about Mom."

Marvin appeared stunned.

"Now, you're trying to hurt me the same way you hurt Mom."

"No, son," Georgia said. "Dee Will was at a party, and some gang members started arguing with people. Dee Will got into his limo and left with his friends, but the limo was shot and he was hit by a bullet."

Edrik's eyes filled with tears. "Lies," he said as he ran out of the living room, slamming one of the French doors so hard it shattered the glass. Marvin rushed after him while Georgia remained seated on the sofa with Haden.

"Are you okay?" Georgia asked, wiping away her tears.

"I'm okay. Are you okay?"

"I'll be okay. It's just so sad."

"I'm confused, Mom."

"I know. So am I. None of this makes sense."

"Isn't Dee Will in heaven?"

"Yes."

"Isn't heaven someplace everyone wants to go?"

Georgia was surprised by Haden's reaction. He had gone to church with her since he was a baby, and she had always noticed him listening attentively to Bishop Anderson's sermon.

"Yes, but Dee Will was so young. It would have been nice to have him here a while longer before he went to heaven."

"Do you think heaven has a football team?" Before Georgia had a chance to respond, he nodded and said, "Of course they have one. Dee Will got drafted. Denver had to give him up, because he was traded to a much better team. That's what happened."

"Well, yes, son, those on God's team are on a much better team than anything man could put together."

"I gotta go tell Edrik." When Haden rushed out of the room to tell his brother, Chloe walked in and sat beside Georgia.

"I've been watching the news, and I went on the Internet to read more about what happened." Chloe shook her head. "A man who used to be in a gang, but now is a community activist, said that witnesses who have information probably won't come forward for fear of becoming targets.

And he talked about the street code of not snitching. I can't believe I used to think like that. To see Edrik hurt like that, and to think about Darrent's own kids and his family—a person's life is not worth a code."

Georgia put her arm around Chloe as Chloe leaned her head on Georgia's shoulder. "I know, baby. It certainly isn't."

"Good morning, everybody. Thank you for tuning in to the *Sweet Georgia Brown Morning Show* on this second day of January." She paused and took a deep breath, searching for the right words. "I am saddened this morning by a devastating tragedy. For those of you who may not have heard, Darrent Williams, a starting cornerback with the Denver Broncos, was slain on New Year's. He was shot and killed in a limo after leaving a Denver nightclub at two in the morning.

"Words can not express the sorrow I feel. While I did not know him personally, I had seen him play many times, and his positive attitude and big smile were infectious. As a mother myself, I cannot help but think of his mother. My condolences go out to Miss Rosalind and the entire Williams family. We lost a bright young star in Darrent Williams, affectionately known as Dee Will."

Georgia's throat tightened and her eyes began to tear. "Please stop the violence. This was so senseless. Many details haven't been released yet, but whatever the motive was, it certainly wasn't worth a life. I have peace knowing Darrent Williams is in a better place. While he only lived twenty-four years, to quote his mother Rosalind, 'Maybe that's why he did so much, because he knew his time on earth was limited.'

"Now, I am asking for the public's help. If there is anyone who may know something that could help the police apprehend the suspects, please call the Denver police. If you want to remain anonymous, please call Crime Stoppers. Let's start this New Year off by doing what's right. If we could just do that, we'd live in a much better world. My son loved Dee Will, and I had to tell him his hero would no longer be on the playing field." Georgia choked back tears as she momentarily covered her mouth with one hand and the microphone with the other.

She fanned her face with her hand to calm down, and then composed herself. "I had to tell my son that the young man we had just watched play on New Year's Eve had been killed. Now, as hard as that conversation was, just imagine how Darrent Williams's two children felt when they learned they would never see their father again."

Georgia queued up ten inspirational songs, starting with "Millions." The music filled her spirit. She lifted her arms to the Lord. "Millions may not have made it, but he was one who did." She followed with "Heaven" by Bebe and CeCe Winans. "We must not despair, because Darrent is in heaven right now." Next came "I'll Take You There." "I know this isn't hip-hop, but can't you still feel it?" The songs continued with "Ain't No Need to Worry," "Up Where We Belong," "The Question Is," "Tomorrow," "A Friend," "Don't Cry," finishing with CeCe Winans' "Pray."

"Do you know what I think of when a promising young man's life is cut short? I think how short life truly is. And for those of you listening, you need to think about your lives. Are you doing everything you want to do? Are you proud of what you've accomplished? If you don't see tomorrow, are you confident you'd be in heaven? Tomorrow? Forget about tomorrow. 'Whoever promised you tomorrow better choose the Lord today, for tomorrow very well might be too late.'"

Corliss couldn't believe that of all the people in attendance at John Legend's concert, he would be one of them.

Jermaine had claimed he would be working and couldn't watch Jelani. The woman he was with wore her hair in a curly fro and had an eclectic style—not the type of woman Corliss would expect him to be with. Although, as the two strutted past her row toward the front of the auditorium, Corliss knew one thing about the woman that Jermaine was attracted to—she had a big behind.

She couldn't believe that Jermaine was out on a date. Sure, she assumed he dated, but to see his arm around the tiny waist of the woman and notice their smiles—*she must have been the sexy one he was referring to*. If she didn't know any better, she'd swear he was there to make her jealous; if so, he had succeeded. But Jermaine had no idea Corliss was at the concert. She had lied and told him she had to work late and would need him to babysit. Now, Corliss knew he was lying, too, when he said he had to work, but it wasn't as if she could call him out on it.

"Take Jelani to your mom's," he had told her, though he knew how Corliss felt about her mother—the two had never gotten along. She was a halfway decent grandmother, but a terrible mother, and it wouldn't bother her one bit if she never had to see her again. But she had no choice about taking Jelani there—not that she doubted her mother would take good care of him—but it meant she would have to see her mother twice and listen to that raspy smoker's voice spout advice, which had come a little too late.

As the concert got under way and the lights dimmed, Corliss's heart sank as John Legend began playing her favorite song on the piano. She wondered if Jermaine thought about her while John Legend performed "Ordinary People." That was their song. There had been so many times they had made love while it played in the background. She reached over to touch Dante's hand even though she would have preferred holding Jermaine's.

As the song continued to play, so did her memories. The pain hit close to her heart and tears streamed down her cheeks. She moved her hand away from Dante and wiped her tears as she continued to sing along.

The final straw was when Marvin didn't come home all night . . . and pictures didn't lie.

The ones Georgia had in her hands screamed the truth.

It had been Chloe's idea to hire a private investigator to follow Marvin around. Only a child could be so adventurous.

Georgia planned to catch Marvin red-handed and confront him with the incriminating evidence. She crept down the busy street, keeping her eyes focused on the Everest green metallic Mercedes-Benz in front of her. Marvin had a woman sitting comfortably in the passenger seat, and they seemed to be headed toward the Greektown Casino.

She was stopped by a red light on Beaubian Street.

"Shit," she exclaimed, banging her gloved fist on the

steering wheel after slamming on the brakes. She narrowly escaped hitting the bumper in front of hers and lost sight of Marvin after he made a right onto St. Antoine Street.

Georgia turned into the casino's valet entrance—no doubt the service Marvin used—and pulled up to an attendant who rushed to open her door. She remained seated.

"Did a man in a green Mercedes pull up here not too long ago?" she asked.

The attendant hesitated. "I'm not sure."

"You couldn't have missed his custom green Mercedes with the Marv102 plate on it." She took a fifty dollar bill from her wallet. "Is he here or not?"

"I really couldn't say."

"Yeah, I guess after he comes out, he'll give you a hundred dollars for keeping quiet after you tell him his wife came looking for him. And please be sure to tell him that I did."

Georgia arrived home just after midnight. Chloe was in the great room watching television, and, Georgia assumed, talking on the phone. But Georgia was shocked when she didn't see a phone glued to Chloe's ear.

"Let me ask you a question," Georgia said. "How did Destiny look?" She had gotten a few quick glances of the woman's curly reddish-brown shoulder-length hair.

"Dark-skinned with a long, straight, black weave—jet-black."

"Really?"

"Why? You saw him or something?" Chloe looked over at Georgia who stood clutching her handbag in the entrance to the great room. "The woman you saw him with didn't look like that, did she? I'm not surprised. No telling how many women Not-So-Marvelous Marvin has."

Chloe noticed Georgia tightly clinch her purse strap. "I'm sorry. I guess I shouldn't have said that."

Georgia shook her head. "It's okay."

Chloe moved cautiously on the sofa, reaching for the remote to mute the television. She was too young to give advice, she thought, but that had never stopped her from doling it out to Bernadette. She had always been the one to tell her biological mother when to end toxic relationships, which was often, because all of Bernadette's relationships were—whether they were with men, or the brief affair with a woman.

Chloe stood for a moment, with one leg still bent beneath her, and then sat back down. She bounced up and down, trying to decide what to do. She was nervous for Georgia— nervous for the woman whom she wished were her mother.

"Mom, are you okay?"

"No." Georgia smiled when Chloe said "Mom." It was her favorite title—not missus, not wife—just Mom. And she felt even more privileged that someone who wasn't her daughter had chosen to say it.

Chloe walked over to Georgia and helped her over to the sofa. They sat near each other in silence. Chloe's mind raced with thoughts of what to say.

She couldn't say the things she said to Bernadette:

"He's a junkie, and I'm tired of being around him when he shoots up."

"He put his hand up my skirt and wiggled his nasty finger you know where."

"Why do you let that man hit you?"

She was getting closer.

Finally, she said to Georgia, "Why do you let that man hurt you? You don't think you could make it out there without him or something?"

Georgia was quiet for what seemed like forever, but Chloe was willing to be patient and let her question linger.

"You'll never be able to function in the present as long as you're stuck in the past. Last year, I got chlamydia. Have you ever heard of that?"

"It's an STD, isn't it?" Georgia asked.

Chloe nodded. "And the doctor told me and my mother that I probably would never have kids. I didn't care, because I never wanted any—not before I came here anyway and saw how good you are with your kids, how much they brighten your life, and how much they love you. It feels good to be a kid in your house. So I've changed my mind about kids. I do want them, but I don't want a husband."

"Don't say that."

"Not after seeing the way Marvin treats you, and all the mess you put up with. It makes me feel like that's the best I could ever hope for. Is it? It's not too late to change my mind."

"What could I do to change your mind?"

"I don't know. What could you do? What do you want to do?"

Georgia stopped in the middle of packing. Her last suitcase was too full to close.

Am I doing the right thing? she wondered. *Of course, I am*, she reassured herself.

Once again, Marvin hadn't come home the night before—only this time, Georgia had seen him with the other woman. The other times, she knew what he was up to, but wanted so badly to believe it wasn't true. She had thought the realization would hurt more than it did, but she didn't even cry. He wasn't the man she had fallen in love with. That Marvin left five years ago on the stage at the Shrine Auditorium.

She sat on the suitcase while Chloe attempted to close the bag, but the zipper split open and looked like a train off-track. "That's okay," she said to Chloe, pulling several sweaters out and fixing the zipper so the bag would close.

"I can't leave," she said, coming to a sudden halt, her large Samsonite behind her. "What would his parents think?" Her marriage was ending—the life she had known for eleven years was suddenly about to change. She would be lying if she said she wasn't scared.

"His parents? Didn't you tell me you haven't seen them in years?"

"I haven't."

"Then who cares what they think? Are you happy?" Chloe asked.

Georgia didn't want to admit she was miserable, but she didn't want to lie either. "Happiness is a state of mind," she said.

"Is your mind in that state?" Chloe asked.

"My mind isn't in any state right now."

"You should be excited. You accomplished a goal."

"Did I? I don't ever remember setting my sights on becoming a radio host. I think I became one because I'm married to Marvin—not because of me. I want my own identity."

"Well, it's still a great opportunity with more to come. I think Marvin thought he could change your mind."

"Don't call him Marvin. He's your father."

"I don't know that man, and he's not trying to get to know me. At least you've been concerned since I got here—and after what you overheard me say about you, you really didn't have to be. Why were you so concerned?"

"I can understand why you may have resented me for having this life with your father while you and your mother struggled."

"I don't feel resentment toward you. Maybe I did in the very beginning, but not anymore, because you really are a nice person."

"Well, thank you."

They were both surprised to hear the garage door open.

Georgia had wanted to have their bags packed and in the trunk before Marvin arrived. Actually, she wanted to have already been gone when he did.

Marvin opened the garage door and spotted the bags. "What's going on? Why the bags? Are you leaving me?"

"Yes," Chloe said. "She's leaving you."

"Leaving me?" he asked. "You're leaving me?"

"Chloe," Georgia said, shaking her head. "That wasn't nice."

"And neither is he."

"Stay out of our business, little girl. You're leaving me?" Marvin followed Georgia into the garage and watched as she lifted her bag and placed it in the back of the SUV.

"Chloe, hand me your bag."

"Are you seriously leaving me?" he asked, grabbing her arm. "After all we've been through? All the struggle? Two kids? Now we've made it, and you're leaving?"

"No." Georgia snatched her arm away. "You've made it. And now it's my turn."

"Well, go on, then. Leave. I don't need you. And take that devil girl with you. But my boys are staying with me."

"Edrik and Haden are coming with me, Marvin. You don't have the time to raise children."

"If he did have the time, he wouldn't even know how," Chloe said.

"Chloe, enough. Get in the car and wait for me."

Chloe climbed into Georgia's Cayenne and sat in the passenger seat with her arms crossed.

"Are you leaving me, baby? Please, let's think about this. Don't go." He ran his fingers through her hair. "I like your new hairstyle. You got a perm. So now that you're leaving me, you go and get a perm? That's all I ever wanted was for you to get a perm."

"So a perm would have made it all better?" She shook her head. "Who would have guessed that?" Georgia walked back into the house to get the boys. "Edrik, Haden, come on." They ran down the stairs with their backpacks strapped on.

"Where are you going to stay?" he asked.

"I have a place."

"Your own place? How long have you been planning this?"

"Remember, I told you the station has provided me with a place."

"I bet they have."

"Boys, go out to the car," she said.

"Are you sleeping with Thomas? He's just trying to get even."

"No, I'm not sleeping with Thomas. I'm not like you. How long have you been cheating on me?"

"What are you talking about? I'm not cheating on you."

"Her name is Destiny. She was on the air, remember?"

"I told you that woman has a mental problem."

"No, what you actually told me was that you were pulling a prank on me."

"That's right."

"You can't even keep your lies straight. If I were the same woman I used to be, I'd keep believing your lies, but I'm no longer a fool. Our relationship is over now, Marvin.

And here is your parting gift." She handed him the manila folder filled with photos before she walked toward the garage. "Didn't know I had it in me, did you?" she asked as he followed her. "I didn't either."

She slammed the car door. "Good-bye, Marvin."

"You'll be off the air in six months! You can't hang with me!"

She honked the horn as the kids waved good-bye.

"**G**et down here now!" Marvin shouted to Chloe. Georgia was at another dinner meeting, this one at Opus One restaurant, and she had dropped the kids off for Marvin to watch.

She turned up Bow Wow's "Price of Fame" to block out Marvin's voice.

"Don't make me come up there!" He stood at the base of the stairs, one foot resting on the first step. "Don't make me come up there!" He walked up a few more and then stopped. "Don't make me come up there!" he yelled at the top of his lungs.

"I ain't making you come up here. Stay down there. Shoot, I don't care."

He wanted to burst into his daughter's room, but she

had locked the door. Then he remembered Chloe had company. Her best friend, Vernita, was spending the night.

"Open the door, Cleo."

"My name is Chloe, *Martin*."

"Just open the door." He began to pound.

She turned the music down. "Why? I don't have to do what you say."

"As long as you're living under my roof, you do, young lady. Why are you acting out in front of your friend?"

Chloe pulled the door open and held the edge of it. "Because I can. She's my best friend, and I can be myself around her."

"I just wanted to make sure you ladies would be okay while I step out for an hour or so."

"I'm sure it won't be an hour. We'll be fine. We're not little kids. We're thirteen."

"Well, watch your brothers, also. When my wife gets in, tell her I went to a function and to call me on my cell if she needs me."

"Your wife doesn't get in for another couple of hours. I thought you said you'd be back in an hour."

"Here," Marvin said, taking out two twenty-dollar bills and setting them on the dresser. "If you girls want to order a pizza."

"Mom would never want us to order pizza without an adult in the house."

"We live in Grosse Pointe Farms. Not Detroit. You girls will be fine. Just don't tell the delivery boy you're home alone."

After Marvin left, they placed their order for two large pan pizzas from Pizza Hut and waited downstairs for the delivery person who came within the hour. The boys grabbed their box and ran back upstairs to their Xbox while Chloe and Vernita retreated to the twin beds in Chloe's bedroom for some girl talk.

"All the boys in school think you're so fine," Vernita said.

"No, *all* the boys don't."

"Yes, they do. They have never been as nice to me as they are now, because they know we're best friends. Even the boy I have a crush on has a crush on you."

"Use it to your advantage. . . . Get to know him."

"He likes you, Chloe, which means he won't like me."

"What's that supposed to mean?"

"We don't look anything alike. You have pretty, light brown skin."

"Light? I'm not light. I'm very brown."

"Compared to me, you're light. And you have pretty, long wavy hair. The boys at school just love the way you look."

"The boys at our school are a bunch of knuckleheads. We're all in that school because we were kicked out of regular school, so the last boy I want is one who goes there."

"That's not right. We're there."

"Yeah. I've been scared to ask you this before, but why did you get kicked out?" Chloe asked. "You seem so straightlaced."

"I got tired of people talking about me. Calling me names."

"Calling you names for what?"

"Don't be so nice. You know for what."

"No, I don't. For what?"

"Because I'm dark, and because I got a big nose and big lips. One time, this boy at my school brought a spray can of white paint and sprayed it on my face saying he was lightening me up. So I stabbed him in the eye with my pen."

"Oh, God." Chloe used her hands to cover her eyes. "That is so nasty."

"I know, but that's what happened. That's why I got kicked out."

"Did he lose his eye?"

"Well, I was aiming for his eye, but everything happened so quickly that I jabbed him in the corner of it, so he just had to get stitches. He still has both eyes. I prayed after that, and I swore I'd never fight again. Never try to harm someone for just name-calling."

"Shoot, I don't blame you for going for his eye. Just name-calling? I don't care for that mess. I have a name, so call me by it. And definitely don't come to school with a can of paint and spray it on me."

"I'm not a violent person, but I don't like being teased. It hurts. Just be glad you're pretty. That's all I can say, because it truly is a privilege."

"I don't want a boy who's just interested in me for the way I look. What about being interested in me for who I am?"

"You are a pretty girl—that is who you are."

"I'm much more than just a pretty girl. I'm thinking about becoming a scientist."

"A scientist? What, you're going to discover a formula for rapping?"

Chloe fell out in laughter. "That was a good one. No, I just want to be intelligent. My mom taught me to strive for more, just like she's doing now. She's on the radio, competing against her own husband. She's taking us to the science center tomorrow."

"The science center? Please be joking. I thought we would go to the movies."

"And see what?"

Vernita shrugged. "*Unaccompanied Minors*."

"That movie looks so lame."

"Can't nothing be lamer than the doggone science center—the science center, Chloe?"

"It'll probably be some cute boys there—cute, smart boys who go to regular school."

"And they'll be looking at *you,* not me."

"No, they'll be looking at the exhibits."

"No, they'll be looking at you like you are an exhibit."

"Whatever, girl," Chloe said. "Just eat your pizza and chill tonight, because tomorrow, you're going to learn a little something. My pretend momma already ordered our tickets to the 'Our Body: the Universe Within' online after I asked her to."

"What is 'Our Body: the Universe Within'?"

Chloe jumped off her bed, hurried over to the computer

desk, and logged on to the Internet on her laptop. The Detroit Science Center was saved in her favorites.

Vernita stood behind Chloe and read the text as she navigated through the science center's Web site. "I don't want to see no actual human specimens. Since when did you get all smart and interested in that stuff? What happened to your rapping?"

"I still love hip-hop, but don't you think the world has enough rappers?"

"No, not female rappers," Vernita said.

"Well, one day, I just asked myself what else I like doing. Science is my favorite class."

"I can't stand science."

"I'm getting an A."

"Good for you."

"I wasn't bragging. I was just saying I'm getting an A because I love it. I just soak that stuff up. History, on the other hand—that's probably my worst subject."

"I like history and math, but I can't stand science. But I'll go to the science center if I must, and it's only because you're my best friend."

"Thank you, best friend," Chloe said, putting on the biggest grin.

"Oh, and I never said thank you for taking up for me in school. Thank you, but I'm sorry you got in trouble."

"That's okay. I don't regret it, but I will be glad when Monday gets here and I can go back to school. I just hate Marvin has to come there."

"Why? Don't you love that you have a famous dad?"

"Famous? He's not Will Smith."

"But most people know who he is."

"Just like most people will know who my mom is in a minute—Sweet Georgia Brown."

Marvin felt like he had nothing else to lose.

He took a checker cab downtown. He had to get away.

"No one loves me," Marvin said, holding a paper bag with a bottle in it. The cabdriver ignored him. "This ain't nothing like *Taxicab Confessions*."

"You want ride to casino," the man said in an Aramaic accent. "That's where I'm taking you. If nobody loves you, that's your own personal problem."

"What's your name? I want to be sure to blast you on my radio show. I'm Marvelous Marvin, if you didn't know."

"Sure you are. And I'm the mayor of Detroit. Can't you tell?" he asked as he looked at Marvin in his rearview mirror.

"I never knew the mayor was Chaldean."

"Well, I always knew Marvelous Marvin was an asshole. Maybe that's why no one loves you."

"Okay." Marvin leaned his head back. "I would say something, but maybe you're right. I am an asshole. My sweet wife is on the verge of divorcing me now that she has her own show. It's too bad, because I hate to take the mother of my children down, but no one is going to show me out."

Twenty minutes later, the cab arrived in front of the Motor City Casino.

"Twenty-five fifty."

Marvin paid the man the exact amount. "I guess you're looking for a tip. Well, here it goes: Next time, don't insult your passenger."

"Do you want to hear my tip for you? Don't be such an asshole, and maybe your next wife won't leave you," the cab driver yelled as he pulled away.

Once inside the casino, Marvin checked his coat and got a drink to take with him to the poker room. He moved to a table in the smoking section and lit one of his expensive Cuban cigars.

The dealer dealt, and the betting began.

Marvin looked at his two cards—a seven and a two off-suit—the worst starting hand in Texas Hold 'Em.

He slid a stack of chips forward, and raised the bet.

One person folded and the betting continued around the table.

Three flop cards were dealt face-up—a jack of spades, ten of diamonds, and king of hearts.

When the betting came around to Marvin, he raised the bet again.

The fourth card—the ace of hearts—was dealt faceup and Marvin raised the bet.

The final card—the ace of clubs—was dealt faceup. Marvin pushed all his chips—fifty thousand dollars' worth—in front of him. The remaining players folded except for one man who matched Marvin's bet, laying down two aces.

"You thought you were going to call a bluff," the man said. "Well, you just lost fifty thousand."

"Fifty thousand?" Marvin said, finishing his third drink. "Oh, I've lost a lot more than that."

"Marvin, my friend," a short man said as he approached the table. He was with two very tall and burly men. "Let's talk. I'm surprised to see you here losing fifty thousand when you owe me over four hundred."

Marvin walked with the men outside to the parking structure.

"You changed your cell phone number. As if you think we can't get the new one."

"Man, I've just been having personal problems. My wife left me. My son is distraught over Darrent Williams's murder . . ."

"Enough with the sad stories. You're talking to someone who really doesn't care; you owe me too much money. But you have an important resource—national airtime. And I'm going to start slicing up some of that airtime and selling it. I'm going to tell you what to say, and you're going to be my puppet until you're all paid up."

Marvin shook his head. "I can't do that, man. The FCC is cracking down on that. I can't get busted. I'm working on some things to get you your money."

The man took a revolver from the holster concealed by his suit jacket and removed a silencer from his pants pocket.

"You're going to kill me over some money?"

"Some money? A lot of money. People have killed for less."

"Look, I'm on my knees," Marvin said as he dropped to the floor, clasping his hands in prayer. "I'm begging you." Tears fell. "I'm not ready to die. You can sell the airtime until I come up with the money on my own."

"You can start with my nephew. He just released a CD." He handed Marvin a copy. "With your help, he's going to be larger than Justin Timberlake." The man's two goons helped Marvin up from the ground. "When I turn the radio on in the morning, I expect to hear it playing every hour."

"What label brought it out?"

"I funded the project. My brother started an independent label for his son."

"That won't fly. I could possibly give it to our producer, but we don't play independents on-air. It'll look funny to them if I tell them to start playing this."

"I don't give a damn how it looks. Just make it happen."

Georgia smiled nearly the entire day. And a long day it was. She, Chloe, and Vernita arrived at the New Detroit Science Center as soon as it opened to see "Our Body: The Universe Within," showcasing twenty actual bodies and one hundred and thirty-five anatomical displays.

They ate a light lunch in the science café and shopped for souvenirs at the science store. Chloe bought a telescope while Vernita opted for a T-shirt. And if it hadn't been for Chloe's last-minute desire to see the IMAX showing of *The Human Body*, Vernita would have made it to her grandmother's home on time.

Georgia observed Vernita in the rearview mirror.

She could tell something was bothering her.

The girl chewed on her short nails and stared nervously out the window.

"How much longer before we get there?" Vernita asked.

"About ten minutes," Georgia said. "Is everything okay?"

"My granny's going to go off. It's almost ten and she's been up all day. She told me to be home by eight."

"I'll go in and explain to her if you like," Georgia said.

"No, please don't. She'll just embarrass me. I'd much rather take my cursing out in private."

"I'm sure your grandmother won't curse you out. Not for being at the science center with your friend."

"You don't know my granny. She's cursed me out for waking up in the morning."

"I'm sorry," Chloe said. "I'll go in and personally apologize to your grandmother. I'll let her know it was my fault we spent all day at the center. I guess we shouldn't have gone to see the movie. You should have said something."

"I didn't want to ruin the day. I'd much rather take the cursing."

Georgia drove past the once thriving shopping areas near West Outer Drive with payday lenders and liquor stores having replaced the now defunct businesses. The area seemed to have drastically declined in just five years.

She pulled into Vernita's grandmother's driveway. It was a two-story beige brick colonial in the 5100 block of West Outer Drive. Georgia couldn't help but notice the growing number of for sale signs in the front lawns, or the large red refuse bins planted outside several homes—all a sign of looming foreclosure, and a sight that brought back her own unpleasant memories. She was shocked by the changes in the area. It had always been a model for middle-class home ownership—an area where Aretha Franklin, Marvin Gaye, and Berry Gordy had all once lived.

Vernita's grandmother's home was in good shape, offering a pleasant exterior.

Vernita hopped out of the backseat.

"I hope she doesn't get in trouble," Chloe said.

"Let's go in. I'll talk to her grandmother," Georgia said.

They both exited the vehicle, and Vernita, who nervously waited for them at the side door, turned her key in the lock and shook her head again. "No, seriously, you all don't have to come in. Let me deal with it."

"Vernita, you were our guest, and you should not be fearful to come home because we kept you out late."

Vernita continued to struggle with the lock, then said, "She's probably not going to let me in."

"Where would you stay?"

Vernita shrugged.

"What's your grandmother's phone number?" Georgia asked as she took her cell phone out of her purse.

"No, she might be asleep and the phone will bother her," Vernita said, practically in tears.

"Vernita, we're not going to leave you out here. Do you want to come back home with us?"

"No." Vernita said, then quickly rattled off the number. Georgia proceeded to call.

"Hi, I'm Mrs. Brown. Your granddaughter stayed with us this weekend. We're at your side door. Her key isn't working."

"That's because I put a double lock on the door," the grandmother shouted. Her voice so loud Georgia had to hold her phone away from her ear. "I told her what time she needed to be here."

"It's not her fault, ma'am. It's ours. We were the ones who kept her out at the science center. We didn't think the movie would run so late. We really should have called."

"Exactly, you didn't think it would be a problem, because she didn't open her mouth up and tell y'all what time she needed to be home. If she would have, I'm sure you would have brought her, and then there wouldn't be a problem."

"Is it possible for you to open the door and let her in?"

Moments later, Georgia heard a lock being turned from the inside, and the door creaked open.

"Get your black ass in this house and go to bed," Vernita's grandmother, a fair-skinned woman who appeared to be in her early to midsixties, said as Vernita rushed through the opening and was greeted with a slap to the back of the head.

Georgia was stunned. "I hope she's not going to get in trouble."

The grandmother turned to face them and assumed an entirely different demeanor when she caught sight of

Chloe. A smile surfaced, and her eyes lit up. "Chloe, you are such a pretty young girl . . . and you're a friend of my granddaughter? You must feel sorry for her with her ugly little self."

Georgia was stunned again. "Vernita's a beautiful young girl."

Chloe was bouncing. "I have to use the bathroom," she whispered to Georgia.

"Okay, we're going. We'll stop along the way."

"Did you want to come in? I have a bathroom she can use. It's clean."

Reluctantly, Georgia and Chloe entered the woman's house. She showed Chloe to the bathroom and then sat in the dining room while Georgia stood. "Did you want to sit down?"

"No, thank you." She needed to break the uncomfortable silence. "A lot of your neighbors are selling."

"Selling? Hmm. They don't have a choice. It's a shame what those crooked mortgage companies like Worldwide Financial did to my friends, convincing them they needed to take out a second mortgage on a paid-for home. Now some of them have lost everything they had—their dreams gone. They're my age and moving to apartments. We've been living here for thirty years. One of those men in suits came to my door and I answered it holding my shotgun. You can't fool me, no, sir, I told him."

Georgia noticed Vernita peek around her bedroom door at the same time Chloe walked out of the bathroom.

"Get your ugly black ass back to bed. Don't come looking out at grown folks talking. I'll deal with your ass in the morning."

"Maybe you shouldn't play with Vernita in that way by continuing to call her ugly. She might believe it."

"She should because she is. Ain't nobody playing. That's why her momma left her for me to raise. I raised my kids—beautiful girls, and every last one of them ended up with some lazy ass, ugly bums who knocked them up and produced ugly kids. Got to be careful who you lay with," the grandmother said to Chloe. "Men gonna be coming after you because you're pretty. My granddaughter will be lucky if she ever gets a boyfriend."

"Are you being serious?" Georgia asked, determined to defend the child from the same mental abuse she had suffered as a child—not being considered as pretty, because she was darker than the rest of her family. Being left out of games with her cousins or always tagged as "it" and then made fun of. "Don't do that to a child."

"Can we go?" Chloe asked. "I don't want to get her in more trouble."

"Yes, we can go, and again, your granddaughter did nothing wrong."

"She knows the damn rules." Vernita's grandmother showed them to the door, and they could hear her yelling as soon as she slammed it.

Chloe walked to the SUV with her head down. "I feel bad for getting her in trouble."

"You didn't get her in trouble. It's just like she said, she gets cursed out for waking up in the morning—and after meeting that woman, I believe her."

Before driving home, Georgia drove Chloe by Marvin's parents' home, and sat outside. It was too late to go to the door. "This is where your grandparents live. And this is where we lived for a few years while we tried to get everything together."

"You mean y'all weren't always rich?"

"No, we struggled for several years before your dad won that money. Did you see your dad on *The Last Laugh*?"

"No, I didn't see Marvin on television. I didn't even know who he was back then. I didn't find out about him until my mother and I got into the cab that afternoon and headed for your house. She told me on the way I was going to stay with my dad."

"Because of the house fire?"

"What house fire? What house? It was because my momma had a man, and her man didn't want any kids around, and that was fine with me, because I didn't want to be around any more of my momma's men. She's had some who only wanted to be around kids, if you know what I mean."

"Unfortunately, I think that I do."

"You do."

"One day, I'll bring you over to your grandparents' house so you can meet them."

"I don't want to meet them," Chloe said.

"They're very nice people. And you would like them. Besides, it's been far too long since I've paid a visit."

"**H**ey, it's Marvelous Marvin, and I'm about to play a new artist who is about to explode onto the scene. He's a little hip-hop, a little R and B. He looks like Robin Thicke and sounds like Kanye West—I'm going to open up my lines, and I want you to buzz me your thoughts on Fabio Ferrari."

The track began to play, and he prepared himself for a lot of flack before the day was over. He hadn't mentioned the new record to his production team, who seemed confused at the sudden change.

"Caller one, you're on the air. What did you think of Fabio?"

"I can't believe you played that shit," the woman said. The ten-second delay allowed the producer to edit the profanity. "It was terrible, and I just don't understand. I'm a local artist from Detroit and I have sent you my CD so many times, but you haven't once given me airtime, yet you play that shit. This is obviously pay-for-play. It's okay, though, because your wife, Sweet Georgia Brown, played my song on Friday."

"I don't see how that's going to help you when no one listens to her show. Next caller."

"What happened to your prank calls?" the woman asked.

"Today is Talkback Monday."

"Talkback Monday? I thought it's usually Talkback Tuesday?"

"Oh, Jesus, I would hate to be your man. I can already tell how you interrogate. Sometimes things change. Now, do you want to talkback or waste five more minutes of my time?"

A loud dial tone was heard.

"I'll pray for you," Marvin said. "It's Talkback *Monday*. Tell us your name and where you're calling from."

"Yo, what's up, Marvin?" an energetic male voice asked. "This is Rick from Chi-town. I have a voice mail I want you to listen to. It's my woman leaving a message on my other woman's cell phone, and it's so funny."

"Okay, let's hear it."

While the voicemail played, keeping the producer busy editing, Venice, the new female addition to the team— after Marvin ran out the last three—held up her portable radio so Marvin could hear if Georgia announced any big contest. He had to top her if she did.

* * *

Marvin arrived ten minutes late to the school. Georgia was just happy he came at all.

The eight o'clock morning meeting meant they would both miss two and a half hours of their four-hour shows.

The girl's father leaped from his seat in the reception area when Marvin, dressed in an eggshell suit with matching gaiter shoes, entered the office. "It's my man Marvelous Marvin," he said, shaking Marvin's hand. He turned to the principal, who had just walked out of his office. "Do you mind if I run out to my car to get my digital camera?"

"Yes, I do mind. We have more important things to deal with this morning."

"You mean Lavonne got into a fight with Marvelous Marvin's daughter? Girl, what were you thinking?" he asked, turning toward his daughter.

"She's the one who started in on me. I was talking to another girl."

Kids in the hallway peeked in to the office.

"See, I knew Marvelous Marvin was your daddy," Marquis shouted as he stuck his head in the doorway before edging his entire body inside. "Can I get your autograph?" Marvin scribbled his name in the boy's notebook.

"Marquis," the principal said, "go to class." The principal led both parties into his office, where everyone took their seats.

Marvin set his hat on the edge of the principal's desk and sat beside Georgia.

"Why don't you apologize to Chloe for what you said?" Lavonne's father asked.

"Apologize for what? I wasn't even talking to her, so she shouldn't have butt in."

"Oh, yeah, I should have butted in, because Vernita is my best friend and she's too shy to take up for herself."

"Hold on," said the principal. "Let's stay calm. What did actually happen?" the principal asked, looking between Chloe and Lavonne.

"I'll tell you what happened, Mr. Armstrong," Chloe said as she sat on the edge of her seat. "She called my best friend a 'black-ass monkey' and said Vernita was so black that she was blue. She wants to talk about somebody's skin color and call her names? Ignorant."

"Who are you calling ignorant?" Lavonne asked, nearly leaping from her seat.

"Then you started talking about her nose and hair, making Vernita cry. What was I supposed to do but whoop her ass?"

"Chloe, watch your mouth," Georgia said, firmly.

"Well, if I'm a friend, I'm a friend for life—a ride-or-die type of woman."

"Chloe," Georgia said, tapping Chloe's leg to calm her.

"Is this true, Lavonne?" asked the principal. "Did you say those things?"

Lavonne sat mute.

"Answer the question, girl," Lavonne's mother said.

"Yeah, I said it."

"Say you're sorry," Lavonne's father said. "Where do you get off talking about people like that?"

"That's how y'all talk around the house."

"We're adults. Don't do as we do. Half the time, we're just joking."

"Well, maybe you should refrain from joking in that manner," Georgia said. "As much as I don't want my child fighting, I understand why she would want to protect her close friend and shield her from such ignorance."

"Now you're calling us ignorant, too?" Lavonne's mother asked.

"From what I'm hearing today, I don't feel Chloe was at fault, but I don't like how she responded. The best course of action would have been to report Lavonne to the office." The principal decided to give both girls one week of after-school detention.

After the meeting, Chloe went to class, while Marvin and Georgia left the building for their cars.

"Why would our child have the same punishment as that other girl?" Georgia vented. "I don't like that at all. Did that make sense to you?"

"Our child?" Marvin snickered. "That's cute."

"What do you mean by, 'That's cute'?"

"I guess you want a daughter so badly that you overlook certain things like when you were played by a thirteen-year-old."

Georgia stopped in her tracks. "Chloe isn't playing me anymore. I truly believe God brought your child into my life for a reason."

"Are you hungry?" asked Marvin. "Let's eat at the Detroit Breakfast Club. You've always wanted to go there. My treat, even though you're all big-time now."

"No, Marvin. Thank you for coming," Georgia said as she hopped inside her SUV.

He blocked Georgia from closing the driver's-side door as the cold wind whipped.

"I'm freezing, Marvin. I need to close the door."

"Don't forget about the dinner with Bill and Beverly this weekend."

Every year for the past three, Georgia had cooked a full-course gourmet meal to celebrate Marvin and Bill's birthdays. Bill was president, part owner, and program director for 102-HITZ.

"I forgot all about that. But okay, I'll get it done."

"**W**ell, look what the cat done drug in—this muthafucka. I know that ain't Marvin," Pookey said as Marvin walked through the front door of his cousin's modest duplex, following a black stray cat.

"What's up, Pook?"

Pookey sat on the living room floor between the shapely legs of a young woman who was braiding his hair. "You tell me, man. I'm the one who ain't seen you since you made it all big and shit. The last time I saw your ass was on TV—on *The Last Laugh*. I gotta listen to you on the radio like the rest of America. That ain't right."

The young woman continued braiding while she snickered at what Pookey said.

"Like we ain't even blood. Like I ain't even your first

cousin. Like my momma and your daddy ain't even siblings and shit—and they ain't no step, they ain't no half—they have the same momma and daddy. I talked to my uncle last week, in fact, and asked about you. He said my guess was as good as his as to how you're doing, because he ain't talked to you since you made like the Jeffersons and moved on up, living in Grosse Pointe. I can't even ride down Lake Shore Drive without a cop following me. And that's the last thing I need when I'm still on probation for another two years. No, thank you. Don't have to worry about me visiting. You bought in the right area if you didn't want the relatives dropping by."

"Man, it's not even like that."

"Well, you done fooled all of us."

"Do you have a few minutes? I wanted to talk to you about something."

"Talk to me about what?"

"If you don't mind"—he looked at the young woman—"in private."

"This my old lady right here. I don't be hiding shit from her."

"She ain't hardly old."

"Well, you know what I'm sayin'. This is my wife."

"A few minutes . . . please."

"You gonna put me on the radio? I promote parties on the weekend. I'd love to pump my parties up on the air."

"I can see about that."

"Baby," Pookey said as he bent his head back and looked up at her, "give us a few minutes."

The half-naked woman stood and left the room, and Marvin had to force himself not to follow her with his eyes to remain respectful to his cousin.

"So what's up?" Pookey asked. "What it be like?"

"I need your creativity. I need to come up with a lot of money quickly."

"You make a lot a money and you still need more?"

"Yeah, I still need more. And I know you of all people still knows how to stack paper."

"You know I'm out of that business. I don't hustle no more. I'm married. Got a baby. For the most part, I'm living right. I mean, everybody got a hustle, but mine isn't the dope game."

"I need to come up with some money or it could mean my life . . . seriously."

"Let me think about it. Give me a few days. Do you have a number I can take to call you? A cell or something?"

Marvin gave Pookey his cell number. "Please, man, think of something and put your cut in it. If you get me out of this bind, I'll owe you big-time."

Marvin's car slowed as he neared his parents' home. He was happy to see they'd done some repairs, having put in a new roof and front door. He was hesitant about going by, but he still pulled into the driveway. It had been a long time since he'd seen his folks—over three years, and he missed them, even his dad.

"Your son is at the door," Marvin's father said as he

walked away from the open door with Marvin standing on the porch.

"You weren't going to invite me in?" Marvin asked as he stepped inside.

"Invite you in for what? Hell, we haven't seen you since you hit it big."

"That's a lie. I invited you over for Christmas right after we moved into the new house."

"Oh, for your house tour," his father said while he sat on his leather sectional. "I felt like I was in a damn museum. You didn't want us to touch anything. Couldn't go in certain rooms. You should have just roped them off."

"I guess I got that from you and all those years you put plastic over all the sitting furniture in the living room. But I see you replaced everything now. Did some upgrades?"

"You damn right. And guess what? I didn't win any money and didn't put it on my credit. Me and your momma did it the good old-fashioned way—we saved."

"I would have bought it for you. All you had to do was ask."

"That's the problem. I shouldn't have to ask. I let you and your family stay here rent free. When you won the million dollars, did I see any of that money?"

"Charles, we didn't need any of it," Marvin's mother said as she walked in from the kitchen drying her hands on a hand towel. She gave Marvin a long embrace. "It's so good to see my handsome man. Don't let your father fool you. He was just telling one of his friends how proud he was of you."

"Don't lie to that boy."

"When have I ever lied to you?" Marvin's mother asked. "He is proud of you."

"I'm proud you finally gave your family the life they deserved. I don't like what you say about your wife on the radio. Sometimes I turn away. It's not funny. I guess it's because I know what you're saying isn't true. And I don't understand how you could joke about that woman, as good as she's been to you."

"It's just for the radio. Nothing real."

"Your father's right, son. I don't like that either."

"Other than that, I have to admit I am proud," Marvin's father said. "I didn't know you had it in you. And those pranks? Man, those pranks are funny as hell. I do tune in for those. That's the kind of stuff I like."

"You do us real proud, son," his mother said as she gave him a pat on the back. "You do us real proud."

He stayed longer than he had expected to, staying for dinner and talking afterward. He caught up on what the rest of the family was up to, including his sister, who he learned was expecting her first child—he was going to be an uncle. He couldn't dare tell Georgia where he had gone. She'd curse him for sure, as many times as she'd begged him to take her because she was afraid to go alone—afraid they were mad at them for staying away so long, even though it was none of Georgia's doing. It was all Marvin.

When it was time for Marvin to leave, he stood at the doorway with his hands inside his pants pockets. "Thank you," he said.

"For what?" his mother asked.

He shook his head. "When we lived here, I was real angry at myself and my situation and never took the time to just be thankful. Georgia has a brother living on the street right now. It could have easily happened to us, too, but you all looked out. I should have bought you all that living room furniture. That was the least I could do."

"We need a dining room," Marvin's father said. "You can go right to Art Van, and they can deliver it any day of the week, because I'm retired."

"Retired? When did that happen?"

"Last year. The factory has seen all it's going to see of me."

"I'll buy you a new dining room set."

His parents eyed him strangely. "How's Georgia? You still haven't told us," Marvin's mother said. "While we were eating, you kept changing the subject."

"She's doing good, I guess. She's on the radio, too."

"On the radio doing what?" his father asked.

"Doing what I do, only for another station."

"What? We didn't know she was on the air," his father said.

"Yep," Marvin said, nodding. "Since the beginning of the year. She left me, took the kids, and now lives downtown."

"I knew all those jokes about Georgia were going to backfire."

"I would take every last one of them back if she would come home, but she seems to like the separation."

"If you want her back, get her back. Do the same things you did to get her," his mother said.

"I didn't do anything."

"You had to do something."

"She just fell in love with who I was."

"Then go back to being you."

Marvin left his parents' house with a lot on his mind. It wasn't easy going back to the person he was, because being Marvelous Marvin had made him rich. He was where so many others wanted to be—heard by millions on a number-one-rated show. Regular Marvin was the one who kept them struggling. As much as he wanted Georgia to return, he just couldn't get her back by being what he considered a failure.

Georgia felt a sense of well-being every time Chloe smiled, revealing her nice white teeth—free of the gold grill—which had recently been cleaned by the dentist. The two of them were sitting in the living room of Georgia's corporate condo.

"How is school going?"

"It's going."

"What's wrong?"

Chloe shrugged. "Girls don't like me because they think their boyfriends do, and the boys just want to get some and then go on about their business. I hate it when people stare at me, and I hear them whisper, 'Ooh, she's so pretty.' "

"Those are compliments."

"Yeah, I'm so pretty, but I don't have any real friends."

"Vernita's your friend."

"Vernita was my friend. I kicked that other girl's butt for her and got in trouble for it, and she had the nerve to tell me that standing next to me made her feel uglier. She doesn't want to be my friend anymore. What kind of crap is that? That really hurt. I want people to see me from the inside, and understand I have a big heart. I don't want girls to be jealous of me. What if something were to happen to my face? What if I were to get in a bad accident or something? It's not all about looks."

"You don't have to worry about that. Honey, I spent my entire childhood wanting to be beautiful. In my day, the boys were in love with Pam Grier, and that's who I wanted to look like. I didn't know how it would happen, but I prayed every night that I would wake up looking like Pam Grier. Then I wanted to look like Jayne Kennedy. But I still woke up as the same old Georgia."

"Who are Pam Grier and Jayne Kennedy?"

"Beautiful black actresses whose posters were pinned up on the walls of most black male teenagers back then. When I was growing up, society wasn't really saying any black women were beautiful. Hell, it wasn't until 1984 that a black woman was crowned Miss America—a pageant that started way back in 1921. Don't feel ashamed because you're pretty. You have to learn to love and appreciate yourself just the way God made you. He made you naturally beautiful, so use it to your advantage. Don't hide it, and don't flaunt it either. Be proud of your beauty, because I know it comes from the inside all the way out."

"What was your mother like?"

"My mother?" Georgia asked, not quite knowing what to say. "I've never told anyone this."

"What?"

"Not even Marvin. But I will tell you."

"What?"

The images of Georgia's childhood flashed through her memory like a slideshow.

"What's wrong?" Chloe asked. She could tell Georgia had drifted. "What are you thinking about?"

"My mother."

"What about your mother?"

"Well, I was really raised by my grandparents, because the woman I thought was my sister was actually my mother. And I never knew my father. I always felt like he didn't want me. Whoever he was, he left us."

Chloe frowned. "But don't you only have one sister? Kendra, the one who comes by the house. Are you saying she's your mother?"

Georgia nodded. "She's my mother."

For years, Georgia had assumed she was adopted, because she didn't look like the others; her complexion was darker, her nose wider and her hair a little kinkier. Even at eight years old, she had already noticed it. It took an ignorant relative—a drunken uncle—to explain it in a way she finally understood, and he did so in front of the entire family on Thanksgiving.

Kendra had said something to make him angry.

"And that's why your stupid ass has a sister who's really your daughter."

Georgia, who was eight at the time, had been eating at the dinner table, and still heard everything her uncle said as he was pushed out the front door. "Got pregnant at twelve years old because you didn't know how to keep your legs closed. Then you want to act like I did something to you when I ain't never touched you. Don't need to. And if they believed I had done something to you, do you think they would have me over here for dinner? I know who that child's daddy is—we all do—and it sure in the hell ain't me."

Kendra ran up the stairs crying. Their mother, who Georgia had just learned was actually her grandmother, followed behind her. Georgia's father, who was actually her grandfather, stormed outside and argued with his brother. Those left at the table continued to eat in silence. There were no looks of confusion from anyone other than Georgia, no straining of faces to understand what they'd just heard—they all had already known the truth. Georgia was Kendra's daughter, but they'd been raised as sisters.

"Wow," Chloe said. "You never know about people's lives, do you?"

"No, you never do."

"And you've never told anyone? Not even Marvin?"

"Kendra is a great sister. And that's what she's going to stay. My parents are dead, and have been for many years now."

"I understand. I mean, just because a woman has a baby doesn't make her a mother. I wish I had a mother like you."

It hit Georgia like being poor had years ago. She realized Chloe was the daughter she had always wanted, the one she had tried to have, but never could. The pain of her two miscarriages had gradually slipped away and been replaced with the blessing of a teenager named Chloe. "You do have a mother like me, because you have me."

Chloe looked over at Georgia and her eyes started to water. "Now, that was profound."

The very sight of those Post-it notes made Corliss cringe. Only one person, Trish, her supervisor, put them on her desk, and it was always after Corliss had left for lunch, so the bright colors greeted her first thing upon her return. It happened nearly every day and addressed some annoying issue. The day before, the flaming pink sticky note had said, "Look up the Marshall Evans deal and tell me why you put repo on hold."

Today, the neon yellow Post-it note on her monitor read, "Please see me ASAP about hours." She immediately walked to Trish's desk, but was brushed off as Trish rushed into her daily collection management meeting.

As the hours passed, Corliss forgot about the note, focusing instead on obtaining information off of the computer program Fast Data.

Trish usually left for lunch around one thirty, right after the management meeting, but it wasn't until three that Corliss discovered Trish had worked through her lunch so she could leave by four.

Corliss paid extra attention to what Marvin said on the air that morning. All week, he advised women what to look for if they suspected their men were cheating, but he did it in the voice of a character named Fast-talking Freddy. He disguised his voice, but loyal listeners knew Fast-talking Freddy and Marvelous Marvin were one and the same.

"A cell phone bill will tell you the entire story. That's all you'll ever need to get your hands on. You'll never find your man's cell phone bill lying around, even if you live with him—not if he's a true cheater—he's no fool. So you have to get creative. If you're not on the account with him, which, if he's a cheater, you aren't, then you'll need to call his cell phone provider and claim to be his wife and get your address changed. Have the bill sent to one of your friend's homes.

"Find out the billing cycle. After the bill has been mailed, call and have the address changed back, because when his bill doesn't show up, he will call the cell phone provider and find out why. But by that time, it won't matter, because you'll have all you need.

"Now, after you have the bill, start looking for the numbers he calls late or while you're gone. For those women with men who don't work, look for the numbers he calls while you're at work. Highlight any numbers he calls frequently and talks to for over five minutes. Especially check numbers he calls after he checks his voice mail. It says right on the bill when he's called voice mail.

"Now, men, why am I telling all our business like this? Because the new way to cheat is with a computer phone—and with Skype and a laptop computer. I'd never use a cell phone to call my other woman, so don't be a fool like most men—do your cheating online. There's no bill to check—only a low monthly fee and unlimited long distance. As long as you have Internet and access to a computer, you can communicate worry free with your other woman, or, if you're on the down-low, your other man. And the best part is, you can be anywhere in the U.S. and that number goes with you. There's no better way to cheat."

Corliss now knew how to get the information she needed. Plus, she had access to tools like Fast Data, a mainframe system providing names and addresses. Fast-talking Freddy said it would be easier to find a man's Social Security number than his cell phone bill, and once you had his Social Security number, you could get his phone bill.

Corliss had both.

She watched Trish shut down her computer and log off her phone, then grab her coat and purse and walk away from her desk. Trish said good-bye to everyone on her team except Corliss.

Then, as she paraded by Corliss, she stopped and turned to face her. "I almost forgot. I need to talk to you. We have to adjust your schedule. We can no longer accommodate you taking a thirty-minute lunch and leaving thirty minutes early."

"But I have to do that because I need to pick up my son from latchkey by five or they'll charge me an extra twenty-five dollars for every fifteen minutes I'm late. I can't afford to pay an extra fifty dollars a day. Latchkey is high enough."

"I'm sorry, but the problem with bending the rules for one employee is others take notice, and it's not long before they're requesting the same thing. If we let one person adjust their schedule, we'll have to allow others to, and we can't run a business that way. So starting tomorrow, your hours will be eight to five. Please make other arrangements for your son."

"It's not that easy. Seriously, it's not. You'd have to be a parent to understand."

"No, I wouldn't. I do understand, but you need to be in management to understand my side that it can't work this way. Please make other arrangements."

As soon as Trish left, Corliss felt her eyes water, then rushed to the restroom so her coworkers wouldn't see her tears. Not that they would feel sympathetic.

Corliss was tired of leaning on Jermaine, even though she knew he would come through like he always did, but leaving his job every day to pick up Jelani, drop him off at Corliss's house, then go back to the dealership would be too much to ask. Corliss would have to depend on her mother, who was the one person she never could depend on.

She went back to her desk, and with anger in her heart, contemplated quitting the job she hated. She logged on to Fast Data and spent the final thirty minutes researching numbers from Dante's cell phone bill.

*   *   *

"What do you mean, you need me to pick Jelani up from school every day?" Corliss's mom asked. Corliss was on her cell phone with her mother while driving to Jelani's school.

"That's what I mean. They're changing my schedule."

"You better ask Jermaine. I love my grandson, but I can't do it. Maybe once a month—maybe—but not every day. Not even every week."

"Why not? You're retired."

"Exactly, and I'm going to enjoy it. Ask Jelani's other grandmother, the one who gets to see him more than I do. See if she can do it. She's retired, too."

"But she works part-time in the evenings."

"Well, you better get that extra money it's going to cost from Jermaine. He makes more money than you do, and Jelani's his son, too."

"Forget it," Corliss said, hanging up the phone. Getting off at five meant Corliss wouldn't arrive at Jelani's school until five thirty. It would cost her a thousand dollars a month in late fees, which was more than Jermaine currently paid for the entire after-school latchkey program. She'd have to talk to him, and she knew he would come through. He always worked things out and provided the best solutions, which was one of the things she liked so much about him.

She and Jelani made it home by five thirty, and found Dante collapsed on the sofa with his arm hanging off the side.

Jelani pouted. "I want to watch cartoons."

"You can watch them in Mommy's room."

"No, I want to watch them on the big television. Tell him to move. I . . . want . . . to . . . watch . . . cartoons," Jelani said in an escalating voice.

"Shut up, I'm trying to sleep," Dante shouted.

"Don't you ever tell *my* son to shut up!" Corliss shouted. "With your cheatin', lyin' ass," she mumbled as she took Jelani by the hand and led him into her bedroom. She looked Jelani in the eyes and said, "We'll watch them in here until he gets up, and then I promise we'll go back out there and watch them."

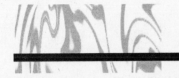

It was a perfect sunny Saturday.

Even though it was only the end of February, the temperatures had reached an unseasonable sixty-eight degrees. It was the kind of day Chloe felt would both start and end well—where nothing could go wrong. Georgia and the kids had dropped by the house to pick up some more belongings when Georgia and Chloe had decided to take a stroll with Art and his wife, Margaret, through the Patterson Park nature trails at the foot of Three Mile Drive.

Chloe was also happy because it wasn't a school day, so she didn't have to worry about any threats from girls regarding their boyfriends. They were just jealous, she thought, and she didn't need any of them—no friends, no boys. She had a new best friend in Georgia, so she didn't need Vernita either. She didn't need any girlfriends her own age, and preferred hanging around Georgia, and Georgia's best friend, Claudette. Georgia was a mother figure, also—the only one she had ever truly had.

"Mom, are you almost ready?" Chloe yelled from the top of the stairs before running down. Georgia walked out of her bedroom wearing her workout gear. "You look so cute."

"Do I?"

"Yeah, you've lost some weight."

"Did I?" Georgia said as she pepped up.

"Mmm-hmm. I can tell."

Marvin leaned back in the kitchen chair to check out his wife. She waved him off without commenting.

The doorbell rang.

Georgia answered in midconversation with Chloe.

"Maybe I'll make a batch of chocolate chip cookies— even though we are about to exercise, so I shouldn't even be thinking about cookies right now," she said as she flung the front door open, expecting to see Art on the other side. Georgia's expression immediately changed from that of excitement to immediate concern. "Bernadette?"

"Momma?" Chloe asked as she twisted her nose in disgust.

Bernadette strutted in with an older man following behind.

"Hey, baby, come give your momma a big hug and a kiss." Bernadette stretched her arms out toward Chloe, who hesitantly walked toward her mother.

"What are you doing here?" Chloe asked as she gave her mother a quick embrace.

"What do you mean what am I doing here? I can't come see my baby and introduce her to her new father?"

"My new what? He's not my new father. I already have a dad—Marvin is my father. I don't know this man."

Marvin leaned back in his chair again, and peered into the room for a brief moment, this time with a shocked expression.

"This *man*, baby girl, is my husband." Bernadette wrapped her arm inside of his. "See my ring."

Chloe lifted her mother's hand and squinted as she observed the tiny diamond. "It's the thought, baby, it's the thought."

"I guess."

"Bernadette, what are you doing here?" Georgia asked.

"I'm here to get my child." Bernadette looked over at Chloe and said, "You'll have a family now with brothers and sisters. It's going to be just like the Brady Bunch."

"I already have brothers—blood brothers."

"Half your blood."

"Better than none at all," Chloe said. She glanced at Georgia and could tell she was panicking ... as was she. "Mom, can I talk to you in private?" She pulled Bernadette outside the house, and walked her to the middle of the circular driveway.

"I told you I was coming back for you, baby. You didn't believe me?"

"You didn't tell me that. Not once did you say you were coming back."

"Well, if I didn't tell you, I should have. Aren't you happy to see me?"

"Look, I'm not trying to hurt your feelings, but it's time for me to get real with you. I like where I am. So why can't you give me a chance?"

"What do you mean by give you a chance? I'm trying to give you a chance—that's why we came here to get you."

"So that's Dexter?"

"No, Dexter and I aren't together anymore. That's Mr. Collins."

"Does Mr. Collins have a first name?"

"He does, but he prefers for everyone to call him Mr. Collins—especially children. That's the only name you need to know, and the only one you'll use."

Chloe shook her head. "For thirteen years, I've followed behind you and your men. I'm tired and too young to be tired, Momma. How long are you going to be with this one? A month, maybe two?"

"Didn't you hear me say I married this one?"

"You've been married before, Momma. Just give *me* a chance. For once, I feel like I have an opportunity—just let me have one."

"Well, I didn't even know you liked that fat bitch."

"Momma, don't call her that ugly b-word. She's smaller than you, and she's definitely not the b-word."

"The b-word? Like you don't know how to say bitch? Is she brainwashing you?"

"No, Momma. This is the person I want to be."

"What happened to your gold grill? And your hair? You don't even look like my Chloe."

"Good, I don't want to look like her."

"So you like being here? You like her?"

"How could I not like her? Think about it, Momma."

"Oh, why, because of the big house?"

"No, Momma, not because of the big house—because of her big heart. She has a big heart. She thinks about other people before she thinks about herself, Momma. Imagine that. Can you?"

"What are you trying to say? That I only think about myself?"

"Yourself and some man."

"That's not true."

"If it's not true, leave without me. You already said you have a Brady Bunch—minus me—minus Marsha."

"I don't want to leave without you—Momma needs her Marsha."

"There's no Marsha, Momma," she said walking away. "I'm not going with you. This is my home. Make yours without me."

"You wait right there, young lady," Bernadette said, switching to a stern voice. "You'll come when I tell you to. I'll take it to court if I have to. Just because he's current on all of his back child support don't mean a thing. I never gave up my custody."

Chloe whipped her neck around like a young girl possessed, and then turned the rest of her body toward her mother.

"I'm thirteen years old," she said through gritted teeth, "and I can make up my own mind. Let a judge ask me who I want to live with and I sure won't say you. I don't want to hurt you, Momma, but I'm not going to let you hurt me anymore either—or my chances for a better life. You've done things and allowed things to be done to me that could put you in jail. Now don't make me get ugly, Momma. Don't make me revert to the Chloe I can be. Just go on, Momma. Go on and leave me and my family alone. And if some adoption papers should come your way, you better sign them."

"Adoption papers? Why would he need adoption papers when he's your father? His name is already on your birth certificate."

"I'm not talking about Marvin."

"Who else would you be talking about? Her?"

"I'm just saying if they should."

"Oh, you think you gonna have another momma over me? Is that it? You're going to replace me? Is that what you mean? You're the only child I have—the only one I ever had. The only one I could have."

"I just said *if* . . . and if they should, you *are* going to sign them."

"Is that what she said? That she's going to adopt you? Why would she have to adopt you if she's married to your daddy? What's this really all about?"

"I just said if. I just took out my crystal ball and looked into the future, Momma. That's all I did and to be frank, you weren't in it."

Bernadette's large eyes narrowed. And then she cleared her throat. "Well, one less child might be a good thing." She removed her cell phone from her clutch purse. "Mr. Collins, I'm outside and I'm ready to go. No, I don't want to step another foot in that woman's home, so if you don't mind, please meet me outside at the car. No, Mr. Collins, Chloe has decided to forfeit my parental rights."

Georgia and the kids were living in a corporate apartment at Harbortown in downtown Detroit when she received a call from her brother. He called asking for money—not for him, because he never needed anything, never wanted to take anything. The money was for another friend, only this friend didn't need an apartment like the mother and her child had. This friend needed a bus ticket to Cleveland to get home for his mother's funeral. He told Georgia where he was living, which wasn't the Park Apartments, but the streets. Of which streets, he wasn't sure because he didn't always get things right anymore.

"Did you know I have AIDS? Did I tell you? Well, it's HIV or hepatitis. I think it's all the same thing."

"No, Peter, they're not at all the same. Which one do you have?"

"I know for a fact I have hepatitis. HIV, too, I think."

"Do you have HIV? Yes or no?" Georgia asked desperately.

"Yes."

Now Georgia had a connection to Winona—a strong one. She'd heard Winona's message loud and clear, but now she could relate.

"I want you off the streets, Peter. I'm not going to help another one of your friends until you get off the streets. How can I help strangers when my own brother won't accept my help?"

"Your own brother? My mind may be almost gone, but I'm not your own brother. I'm your own uncle. And I need you to help my friend. If you love me, that's what you'll do."

"Oh, God, help me," Georgia yelled out as she slid down the embankment. She took a moment to compose herself before crawling through the opening of the freeway overpass into one of the cells where she knew Peter had lived at one point and where he claimed she could find him.

It was a tight space for those living in it—thirty feet long, twelve feet wide, and six feet tall, but Georgia squeezed through, dragging her backpack with her.

"Yeah, what you want?" the weary woman with tattered clothing and dirty skin yelled as she stood with a broken broom stick in hand.

"I'm looking for my brother, Peter," Georgia said loudly

so her voice could be heard over the traffic. She passed a picture of Peter, taken before he had turned to the streets, to the woman. She prayed the woman would recognize him and know where he had been living, so she could take him away from this madness, drag him out if she had to—but this time, he was coming to live with her. Now that she had left Marvin, she could do what she wanted for a change, and helping her brother was her top priority.

"Yeah, I think I know him. He lives down on the other end. I don't know his name, but he kinda looks like that there. He's in and out. You wanna wait for him to come, that's fine."

Georgia inspected her surroundings of soiled mattresses, a few homeless zombies huddled in crevices, carpet remnants, and other odd fixtures. To her, it was a box, but to them, it was their home.

She couldn't imagine waiting for Peter. Not here, anyway. Maybe below.

"How long have you been living here?" Georgia asked the woman.

"Long time," she said, her hand shaking uncontrollably. The cell reeked of urine, and there was constant, deafeningly loud traffic whisking overhead.

"I have to go," Georgia said. "I really have to go now." She thought about her brother, who was actually her uncle, and how he had been homeless over ten years. Life had gotten the best of him. Too much had fallen on his shoulders at once, and he had caved—both parents passed within a month, his wife left and took the kids—one thing after another until he thought he had run out of good reasons to keep going.

When she climbed out of the overpass, she waited under the bridge. Her expensive lounge pants were dirty and wet. Some people passing by in cars took notice. Georgia thought she saw a few noses turn, or maybe she just imagined it. She leaned her back against the concrete, placed her backpack on the floor, and slid down until she sat on the concrete. She looked south toward Jefferson Avenue, where the traffic merged, and saw her billboard. But as excited as she was to embark on something new, the only thing that currently mattered was Peter.

After waiting and thinking for nearly an hour, she pulled herself up and dusted the back of her pants. She considered leaving, but couldn't. Another hour wouldn't hurt. She also considered driving back to the spot to park with the hazards on, but she felt she might miss him in the time it would take to get to her car and back.

Still, she was afraid a police officer would drive past, see her standing there, and accuse her of loitering, so she decided to take her chances and walk back to her car. She passed a man as she emerged from the walkway of the Lodge Freeway, a man she believed was Peter. She turned and called out his name, then watched as the pace of his stride slowed, but didn't stop.

"Peter, I know it's you," she said as she walked briskly to catch up with him. "Peter," she said, reaching out to touch his shoulder. "Peter, stop for me. I'm here to help."

"You don't understand," Peter said, shaking his head.

"Give me a chance to, Peter. I'm here. I'm your family. I want you to live with me and be a part of my family. You know I don't want you living on the street. How many times do I have to tell you that?"

She knew he wouldn't leave the streets he seemed to love so much—streets he referred to as if he were naming friends. He refused to abandon them the way his wife had done him. The day after she left, Peter walked out of his engineering job in downtown Detroit, and onto the streets where he'd been living ever since.

During their phone conversation, he admitted he had long replaced the medication he was taking to control his manic depression with drugs, and eventually began shooting up heroin. The only reason he put his name on a waiting list at the Wellness House, a Detroit-based housing project and food bank for homeless people living with HIV/AIDS, was because he knew there wasn't a chance he'd get in.

There were so many reasons Georgia felt her brother needed to come off the streets, and she hoped one day he would realize it was time to move on in the same way she had by leaving Marvin.

"This is my home. You don't understand."

"No, *you* don't understand. I bet you walked right past my billboard and didn't even notice. I'm on the radio with my own show and I have a place downtown, a four bedroom, and you can have your own room. Please come live with me."

"This is where I want to live. Help those who want to

be helped. I'm not one of those, so please stop wasting your time on me."

"I'm not wasting my time on you. You're my brother, and I love you."

"Stop saying I'm your damn brother. I'm *not* your brother—I'm your uncle. I didn't say that to hurt you. I'm just saying it, because your mother lives that charade, and I won't. And you don't have to, either. I love you, too, but if you really love me, let me live my life the way I want to. The way you can help me is by helping the kids, because there are a lot living on these streets. They're the ones who don't deserve to be here. I'm weak, and I'm not going to live too much longer. One day you're going to come looking for me, and you're not ever going to find me, because I'm going to be dead. I don't want you to waste your time looking for me. I'm gone," he said, tapping his forehead. "And I been gone for a long time."

She saw in his eyes he meant what he said, and there was no use in fighting. She handed him the backpack, with a care package inside with things she felt he could use—sardines, crackers, bottled water, antibacterial wipes, paper towels, and a portable radio with extra batteries, among other things. "Just do me a favor—keep the radio and listen to me from time to time . . . if you want to. Only if you want to."

Georgia walked away reciting the Serenity Prayer: "God grant me the serenity to accept the things I cannot change, courage to change the things I can, and the wisdom to know the difference."

Even though the birthday celebration was postponed by several weeks, Georgia couldn't say no. Not to Beverly and Bill, even if Bill owned her rival station. She had dedicated two years of her life and a small fortune to culinary classes and even received a certificate of completion. Georgia prided herself on her table and plate presentation. She had once envisioned being a black Martha Stewart, and had even contemplated opening a quaint downtown restaurant. But Marvin preferred she stay at home and just entertain family and friends. Besides, there was already a restaurant bearing her name.

This year, she invited Art and his wife Margaret to join the celebration. The three couples sat at the dining room table. They had just finished the crème brûlée and were sipping on cups of gourmet coffee.

"But what about her chocolate chip cookies?" Art asked. "I've never in my life tasted chocolate chip cookies that tasted so good, and also looked so perfect—big and perfectly round, not too soft and not too hard—and that gourmet chocolate syrup? Where do you get it from?"

"I'm not revealing my secrets," Georgia said, teasingly.

"You could sell those cookies and put Mrs. Fields out of business."

Georgia waved him off.

"It's a shame you can't legally protect a recipe. If you could, I'd get it done for you," Art said.

"Are you an attorney?" Bill asked.

"Used to be one, don't practice much anymore. I was a corporate attorney for ten years and specialized in contract negotiation. I worked for the UAW for a while, so I know how to play hardball."

"I need a good attorney. I'm always looking for one—that, and a good accountant. If you ever think about going back to work, let me know."

"I am considering starting my own practice from home."

Chloe was upstairs in the family room with Bill and Beverly's daughter, a freshman at Cass Tech High School with an interest in engineering, while Edrik and Haden played Xbox with the couple's young son.

"Georgia, let me help you clear off this table," Beverly said when Georgia stood and began picking up the plates.

"No, you're our guests. Don't worry. I can handle it."

Beverly insisted, but Georgia wouldn't let Margaret,

who was home only for the weekend, as her demanding executive job kept her away most weeks. She knew Margaret wanted to relax and love on Art when she was home, and not touch a single dish.

Marvin smiled as he watched his wife turn into superwoman. She cooked, she cleaned, and now she worked. *And pretty soon she'll be going at life completely on her own*, he thought. He expected the divorce papers to arrive any day. Not that Georgia mentioned anything about a divorce, but he was starting to see the writing on the walls. Nothing surprised Marvin anymore.

In the kitchen, Beverly stood near the entrance, observing Marvin. "He looks sad to me. Bill says he's not the same on air since the two of you separated."

"What does he mean, he's not the same?"

"Not the same Marvelous Marvin. Even some callers have mentioned it. He doesn't even do his prank calls anymore and rarely does any of his characters. I haven't told Bill this, but I listen to your show, and girl, I love it. You are a natural on the air. I never listened to Marvin's show anyway. He appeals to men, and he's negative about women. You and Cammy. You know I've always loved Cammy. And Tonya. The three of you ladies are a great combination."

"Thank you, Beverly."

"I'm just telling you the truth. And I rarely hear you and the ladies talk about Marvin, which I think is good. You don't have to do what he did to make a name for yourself in radio."

"I feel the same way. If only Thomas, the owner, did. Priscilla, his daughter, who runs the show, doesn't like how I deal with Marvin on the air."

"Oh, she's wants you to dog him, I bet. But, girl, you don't have to do that. Don't ever compromise you."

"I'm no Wendy Williams, and I think that's what they want—someone who can be controversial."

"Are you trying to be? I mean, is that what you want to be—a shock jock?"

"People know her. They know it's her just when they hear her voice or see her face. I want that. I want to be a household name."

"You will be. One thing's for sure—Georgia Brown definitely won't by marching to the beat of another person's drum. It's not who you are. India Arie never compromised herself or what she believes to sell records."

"Now that is so true. I've learned how to be me."

"Focus on the opportunities you have. And, honey, you have plenty." She peeked around the corner to make sure her husband was still seated at the table. "I love my husband and I'm proud of him and all he's done in radio, but I would love it if you became the number-one morning show host. Truth be told, Bill is ready to sell his share in the station anyway. It won't be long before we retire in Hawaii." Beverly reached for Georgia's hand and gave it a squeeze. "You motivate me, and now I'm trying to motivate you. Maybe you need to start listening to your own show," she said, laughing.

"I'm just getting on there being myself. I can't help

worrying, though, that I'm not as hip as the other radio personalities."

"Georgia, when that woman called your show and told you she was contemplating suicide because she and her husband had lost their jobs, their car was being repossessed, and their home being foreclosed, you told her about the time you had lost your house and your job and how, in spite of it all, you kept the faith. And because of you, she decided not to give up. Baby, there's nothing hipper than helping."

Georgia gave Beverly a big hug. "You are such a good friend and I appreciate you. If I want to be a household name, I can't focus on what my husband or the other radio personalities do. I just have to be me, because nobody can be me the way I can." A smile began to surface. "I wish I could get on the air right now, I'm so uplifted."

Marvin answered the phone on the third ring.

Pookey was on the line.

Georgia's eyes narrowed when Marvin excused himself, closing the den's French doors behind him.

"What did you come up with?" Marvin asked.

"I been thinking about this ever since you left. The money you need will come from the station."

"What?"

"You need to suggest a contest—a big contest—and get it sponsored. Instead of mailing checks to people, you're going to give away Visa debit cards—one thousand of them, each holding one thousand dollars."

"That's a million dollars."

"Bingo."

"Take what you need, and I'll sell them on the street for fifty cents on the dollar."

"How the hell do you think I could just take what I need? No one is going to give us a million dollars worth of debit cards to hold."

"If you're giving them away in one month, they will. One month, one million dollars—that's how you pitch it."

"One month, one million."

"Only it's going to be one month and five hundred thousand for them, and five hundred thousand for you. Well, more like two hundred and fifty thousand for you."

After ending the conversation with his cousin, he returned to the dining room. He was tempted to pitch the idea over dinner, but knew the best time to do it would be when Georgia was nowhere around.

Corliss and Dante had been arguing for nearly thirty minutes. At times, she got directly in his face and wouldn't back down.

"Jelani's father doesn't even hit him, and I'll be damned if I let you. They can put me in jail first."

"Woman, please," Dante said, trying to push by her, but Corliss stepped in his path. "All I did was grab his arm."

"You grabbed his arm and yanked him off the sofa. I saw your fingerprints on my baby's skin."

Dante waved her off. "I don't have time for this shit. I had just gotten home after putting in another double, and I didn't feel like hearing that cartoon shit. All he had to do was turn it off."

"First of all," she said, waving her finger around his face,

"I don't want to hear about you putting in another double. How is it you work all these doubles, yet never contribute to the bills? Secondly, this is my apartment. My name is on the lease—not yours. If my son wants to watch cartoons all day and night, he can. You're not his daddy, so you don't tell him what to do. As a matter of fact—get out!"

"What?"

"Out. You heard me. Leave."

"Girl, you trippin'. I ain't going nowhere but to bed." Dante pushed Corliss to the side and walked down the hallway.

There was a loud knock at the front door.

"Corliss, open the door!" Jermaine shouted. She rushed to the door to unlock it.

"Where is that fool who put his hands on my son?" Jermaine asked as he stepped inside the apartment followed by a man so large he had to stoop to get underneath the door.

"BG, what are you doing here?" Corliss asked. BG was Jermaine's half brother, and Jelani's only uncle. "How did you all find out about this?"

"Because Jelani called me. How do you think?"

Corliss searched the room for Jelani and found him cowered in the corner beside a kitchen bar stool, Corliss's cell phone in his hand.

"I pressed five. Remember, you said five is the number to Daddy?"

"That's right, baby. Five is the number to your daddy. Listen, I don't want y'all getting into trouble over that fool."

"What's this all about?" Dante asked as he walked back into the living room.

"You put your hands on my son."

"Man, all I did was ask him nicely to turn off his cartoon. He said, 'No, you ain't my daddy.' "

"That's right, you not his daddy," Corliss said.

"That's right," Jelani repeated, walking over to stand by his father.

Jermaine stooped down to Jelani's level. "Little man, go to your room. Your uncle and I need to take care of some business."

Corliss walked with Jelani to his bedroom and closed the door before returning.

"Listen, Corliss," Jermaine said, "what do you want us to do? Do you want us to leave? Are you okay? My son called saying this fool pushed him off the sofa and hurt his arm, and then I heard you screaming in the background telling him to get out. So what do you want?"

"I want him to get out."

"You heard the lady—leave," Jermaine said, turning to Dante.

"Leave and go where?"

"Leave and go anywhere," Jermaine said.

"Just get out of here," Corliss said, "because you will not lay one finger on our son. His father and I don't believe in that hitting, yelling, and yanking mess."

"I don't need this," Dante said, snatching his coat from the closet. "I'll get the rest of my shit later."

"It'll be waiting for you on the curb," Corliss said.

"Don't play just because you have your protection. I'm not in the mood. He isn't the only one who can bring his boy. I'm coming back for my shit, and it better not be on some curb."

"And if it is?" BG asked.

"It just better not be."

Georgia couldn't sleep, so she decided to make one of her many dessert specialties—large, round, one-inch-thick chocolate chip and walnut cookies—to take to work the next day. Her team gobbled them up within the first hour, and Cammy and Tonya raved about them on air.

And then a listener called in.

"I live in Detroit, and I own a bakery downtown. If it's not too much to ask, could you bake us a dozen of your cookies to sell out of our shop? We'll give the proceeds to the charity of your choice."

"I like your idea. Cookies for a Cause—can we call it that?" Georgia asked.

"We can call it whatever you want and donate to whatever cause you want."

"There are so many worthy causes, but the one nearest and dearest to my heart is homelessness."

Businesses started calling up offering baking supplies, flour, sugar, chocolate chips. An appliance store even offered a thirty-inch double oven.

Just after ten a.m. the next day, Georgia parked out front with four dozen cookies to hand-deliver. A small crowd had gathered outside to await her arrival. She signed autographs and took pictures before heading back to her corporate housing.

By noon, the owner of the bakery called, begging for more cookies for the next day. "We know you don't have time to do this with your radio show and all, but if we could come to some type of arrangement—maybe you can make the batter and we'll do the baking? We'll call them Georgia's Sweets. What else do you bake?"

"Anything and everything."

"We could dedicate our front display to your delicious treats."

"I get off work every day at ten a.m. I could bake after I get home. I would like to call it Cookies for a Cause . . . and you could call them Georgia's Sweets. It has a nice ring to it."

Listeners from Detroit started calling into the station raving about the cookies, which prompted bakeries from the suburbs of Michigan to ask to join the cause. Within a matter of weeks, bakeries from across the country were calling asking how they could contribute to Cookies for a Cause.

"This thing has exploded," Priscilla said as she paced her office. Georgia sat in the office with Cammy and Tonya while Thomas was on the speakerphone. "Cookies for a Cause is huge. We can make it even bigger."

"I don't want to commercialize it," Georgia said. "I don't want it to seem like an advertising ploy."

"You should want to commercialize it, because it could only lead to higher revenue for your cause."

"That's true."

"I would like for us to factory-produce her cookies and ship them out overnight. I envision paper sleeves with Georgia's face and the words—'Sweet Georgia Brown: Join us in the morning while you enjoy Cookies for a Cause.' It might need to be shortened, but you get the idea. Why didn't you tell us you could bake?"

"I can cook, also," Georgia said and shrugged. "I never thought to mention it."

"This is so perfect . . . just so right. The only way you can become a part of Cookies for a Cause is if we have an affiliate station in your city. So Chicago is asking for your cookies, but Chicago isn't getting any."

"I don't think I like that idea."

"I'm telling you this is a good way to expand the market. How can you promote your cookies and your cause if you are not being broadcast from that market? You can't. Dad, am I right?"

"All I'm hearing about are cookies, and I'm much more interested in ratings. Are people going to tune in because you can bake, or are they going to eat your cookies and listen to your husband's show? Your baking is not a substitute for your program."

"I agree," Georgia said.

"But, Dad, you have to admit, this is good publicity."

"Yes, it's good publicity, but as you know, publicity fades quickly. They'll be talking about something else next week. We have to keep the momentum going. You ladies are doing well. Don't let the baking become a distraction."

Corliss stood between a four door Wrangler and a Chrysler 300C SRT8 in the new car showroom of the Chrysler Jeep dealership where Jermaine worked as a new-car sales manager. She peeked through the driver's-side window of both. She wanted a new car, but she still couldn't afford one.

Jermaine was in his office with a family she assumed was closing a deal, so she waited and took a brochure from the stand to flip through.

Jermaine looked up and saw them, smiled and waved. He held up one finger for them to wait, which they did, and it didn't take too long.

He came out of his office smiling.

Jelani was excited and hugged his dad's leg.

"Hey, little man. I missed you."

"I missed you, too, Daddy."

He looked over at Corliss. "Thank you for bringing him by."

"That's no problem. Did you want to keep him tonight?"

"I don't know what time I'm getting off tonight. You know how my hours are. I'm here until the last customer leaves. I might be up here until ten or eleven. I'll just pick him up from school tomorrow and he can stay with me tomorrow night."

"Okay. Fine."

"Is there something wrong with that?" Jermaine asked as he followed Corliss out to her car with Jelani's hand locked inside of his.

"There's nothing wrong with that." Her voice dragged. "I'm just stressed out. I had to go to court over that Dante mess and get a restraining order. He had people call my phone and threaten me. The other week, all four of my tires were slashed, and I had to borrow my mother's credit card to get new ones. You know how I hate asking my mother for anything."

"You should have told me. I would have given it to you."

"No, I don't want to impose. I haven't had enough time to look for another place. It's time I moved out of that apartment anyway, and my lease is up at the end of the month."

"You and Jelani can come live with me."

"Live with you?"

"Yeah. I have a three-bedroom. Jelani already has his own bedroom, and you can have my other spare bedroom."

Corliss thought about it—as much as she didn't want to impose, it would save her a lot of money.

"If I did, it would just be temporary. Like a month, max. Just until I had time to look for a new place."

"You can take as long as you want. You don't even have to pay anything."

"Thanks, Jermaine."

"No problem." He held her stare for a moment. "I can't believe you're still driving that old-ass Sebring."

"Ooh, Daddy said a bad word."

"Yes, Daddy did, and Daddy knows better, too," Corliss said, rolling her eyes. "My car is only four years old and almost paid for, which is why I'm still driving it."

"And in my business, four years is ancient. People barely keep a car for four car payments nowadays."

"And that's why their credit is jacked up and mine isn't. I may not have much money, but I have one helleva FICO score."

"Which is why you should let me sell you a new car. With a good FICO, you can qualify for zero percent."

"Sell me a car?" Corliss said, squinting. She opened her backseat and fastened Jelani's seat belt. "Spoken like a true car salesman. I guess it's still in your blood."

"What was wrong with what I said?"

Corliss slid behind the wheel. "Oh, we need to discuss Jelani's birthday."

"My birthday," Jelani shouted from the back seat. "Chuck E. Cheese, yeah."

"I'll plan it," Jermaine said, "because I already know how you feel about Chuck E. Cheese."

Corliss didn't wait until the end of the month to move out. She picked the last Thursday of the month so Jermaine could help her on his day off.

They rented a U-Haul truck and Jermaine brought along a few friends to do the heavy lifting. While they hauled furniture, he pulled boxes from a storage closet beside the kitchen.

"What's in this box?" Jermaine asked. "It's kind of heavy." He set it on the kitchen table. "You wrote blockbuster across the front."

Corliss laughed. "Nothing. You can toss it."

"It's awfully heavy to be nothing." He took a knife from the kitchen drawer and cut through the tape, then pulled out one of the many black pressboard report binders.

"*Collateral?*"

"Yeah. Stuart Beattie beat me to that, so his last name is fitting."

"Who is Stuart Beattie?"

"An Australian filmmaker."

Jermaine pulled out another binder and flipped open the cover. "*Dreamgirls?*"

"Now, come on," Corliss said. "I thought about making a movie out of it, too, right after I saw the play. I was nine years old and my aunt June, the only one who believed in my talent, rest her soul, flew me to New York City to see *Dreamgirls* at the Imperial Theatre on Broadway. I'll never forget that experience. It was August eleventh, 1985—the closing day for *Dreamgirls*."

He pulled out yet another binder.

"*Looking for Mr. Goodbar*."

"That's a remake of an old movie that was produced in the late '70s. I was six or seven when I saw it on television late one night, and it stayed with me."

"You're a real movie buff—how come I never knew that?"

She shrugged. "Why do you think I made you take me to the movies every weekend? Or buy all those DVDs?"

"Well, I knew you liked movies. I just didn't know you wanted to write them. Why didn't you ever tell me?"

"I don't know. I guess I didn't feel like being laughed at."

"Who would have laughed at you?"

"Believe me, people have."

"We're not throwing this box out." He looked inside. "There must be fifty manuscripts in here."

"And I have another box filled with over a hundred rejection letters, so let's just get rid of it."

"No. You never know what could become of this. Dust this stuff off, and take it to the Dream Job Seminar."

"The what?"

"Haven't you heard about the Dream Job Seminar being sponsored by 1FM?"

"1FM?"

"You don't listen to the *Sweet Georgia Brown Morning Show?*"

"Nah, please. I'm a Marvelous Marvin fan. You listen to Sweet Georgia Brown?"

"I sure do. I listen to her in the mornings on the way to work and Michael Baisden in my office in the afternoon."

"I definitely would have thought you were a Marvelous Marvin kind of man."

He frowned. "You should know better. He's too negative and too cocky. I listened to him once and couldn't take any more. Now I listen to Georgia Brown. Before her, it was Tom Joyner. And besides, Georgia bakes those cookies. You have to love her for that alone."

"What cookies?"

"There's a downtown bakery that sells the best damn chocolate chip and walnut cookies I have ever tasted. Georgia makes the dough."

"Better than the Doubletree cookies?"

"Yes, better than the Doubletree cookies."

Corliss laughed. "Remember when we used to rent a room at the Doubletree just so we could get their cookies?"

"We didn't know they sold them," Jermaine said, "but we enjoyed much more than the cookies—at least I did."

"I did, too."

"Anyway, she sponsors Cookies for a Cause. Eighty percent of the profit from the cookies goes to assisting homeless families. And besides, she goes to my church."

Corliss waved her hand, "That's why you listen to her."

"No, she's good. Her team is good. Cammy from Marvelous Marvin's show is on there."

"Is Cammy on there? I might have to listen, then, if my girl Cammy is on the show, because I can't get with that new girl Marvin brought on. First, he had some chick named Destiny. Now I don't know who this new one is, but she doesn't have a clue. And he's not the same anyway. He's not even funny anymore." She sighed. "So what's this about a dream job seminar?"

"It's coming to Cobo Hall. There will be editors, agents, talent scouts, and producers. You need to check it out. Georgia talks about it every day on her show. Just tune in tomorrow morning. You'll hear all about it."

"**G**ood morning, y'all. This is Sweet Georgia Brown making sure you keep dreamin'. I'm excited about the upcoming Dream Job Seminar and my Cookies for a Cause. Who would have thought the chocolate chip cookies I've been baking for years would explode into this?"

"It's a phenomenon, girl," Cammy said. "I know I'm hooked . . . to the cause, of course."

"And the calories," Tonya said.

"The seminar is this weekend at Cobo Hall. Are you going to be the next Jennifer Hudson? An overnight success?"

"I'm sure Jennifer doesn't think it was overnight," Cammy said.

"The point is, you have to dare to dream. Whatever you

want to be—a radio host, an actor, a movie producer—whatever. It really could be possible. Look at Shonda Rhimes, the woman who wrote *Grey's Anatomy*. She used to work day jobs in advertising, office administration, and counseling before making it in the business. She worked. Just because you're working during the day doesn't mean you can't dare to dream at night."

"Or during the day," Tonya said. "Shoot, I used to. My job title was receptionist, but I told myself I was getting paid to dream. It's okay to work and dream at the same time."

"Remember, it's this Saturday at Cobo Hall. Come one, come all, and don't forget your dreams. And for those who aren't in the Detroit area, we know you have dreams, too, which is why our Dare to Dream seminar is going on the road in the fall. Dare to dream y'all . . . dare to dream."

While Corliss waited in the lobby for her interview to be the new team leader, she read the book Georgia had recommended on her show, *Dream Careers: How to Quickly Break into a Fab Job!* Sweet Georgia Brown and 1FM were sponsoring a three-day seminar to help people land their dream jobs.

More than anything, Corliss wanted to be a screen-writer.

"Corliss, we're ready for you," an older woman said as she opened the conference room door.

Corliss quickly shoved her book inside her large hand-bag and walked confidently into the room. Even though she couldn't care less if she got the position, she still wanted to look and act her best as practice for the seminar.

She sat in the middle of the long conference room table across from the panel of four conducting the interview.

"Would you like to start by telling us a little bit about yourself?"

"Sure, I've been working here for seven years, and I'm the top collector in the company."

They nodded. "Very impressive," the only woman on the panel said. "Well, I'd like to start our interview. It is situational, and we'll start most questions with, 'Tell us about a time when . . .' so we'd like you to provide examples, and we may ask you to elaborate. If you need us to repeat the question, just ask us. It is very important you answer every question. Also, we will be writing as you speak, so don't be too concerned when you see us looking up and down at our papers. Do you have any questions for us before we start?"

She shook her head. "No."

"Tell us about a time you had a conflict you were able to resolve. What steps did you take? What was the final outcome? Would you have done anything differently?"

Corliss blinked.

Her mind had already drifted. She was thinking about the coming weekend and the seminar.

"Could you repeat the question?"

"Yes. Tell us about a time—"

"Yes, I remember now—about a time I resolved a conflict and the steps I took. Does it have to be something that happened at work?"

"No, it can be from your personal life."

She took a moment to think. The only thing that came

to mind was her current situation with Dante. Meeting him had turned her life upside down.

"It doesn't have to be a recent conflict," one of the men further clarified.

"Well, I did have a recent conflict with my ex-boyfriend. He didn't contribute much to the partnership, and I decided to sever all ties. I asked him to leave, and he wouldn't. I had to get the law involved, and he left, but then he began stalking me. My son's father was very concerned, so he offered us his home. I had to move out of my apartment and rearrange my entire life." She realized after saying it that it wasn't the best example to give.

"What was the final outcome?"

"I now live with my son's father—platonically. My ex-boyfriend was issued a restraining order and can't come anywhere near me. And I am starting to put my personal life back together."

"Would you have done anything differently?"

She thought for a moment.

"Yes, I would have never left my son's father for my ex-boyfriend. I regret that decision to this day, and hopefully one day, he will forgive me."

The panel remained quiet, their faces stiff.

Then the woman who asked the question smiled. "Good answer. Moving on to the next question—"

"Girl," Sharon said when Corliss returned to her cubicle, "why didn't you tell somebody it was your birthday? Looks like someone sent you a dozen roses."

"Someone sent me roses?" Corliss asked excitedly as she snatched the card and read silently. *Happy birthday to the woman who brought my son into this world—may your day be as bright as all the days you have given me since he was born.*

"Who sent them?"

"Jermaine. And this is totally not like him. He has never sent me roses."

"Not even on your birthday?"

"No, not even on my birthday."

Corliss arrived to an empty house. Jermaine had called a few minutes before her shift had ended and told her he was taking Jelani to his mother's house to spend the night. He had a surprise for her. She assumed he would take her to dinner, even though she didn't feel like going out—not when she would have to turn around and go to work the next morning.

She had asked him to give her a hint, but all he said was, "It's something you can use."

A few minutes after Corliss arrived, Jermaine pulled up.

He covered her eyes with his hands and walked her into her bedroom. "Surprise," he said, uncovering her eyes.

Her eyes focused on the computer program propped up on the desk. She rushed over to pick it up. "You got me Final Draft. Version Seven."

"Yes, I did. But I got you a whole lot more than that. What about the Sony laptop and the docking station? Not to mention a twenty-seven-inch monitor? And the desk that took me all day to put together?"

"Thank you. It is such a nice computer. And this monitor?" She ran her hands along the edge of the laptop and widescreen flat panel monitor. "You went all out."

She grabbed his cheeks and gave him a quick smack on his lips.

"Can I get a real one?"

"A real kiss?"

"Yes." He closed his eyes and leaned toward her, and she did the same.

"So are you my birthday cake?"

"If you want me to be."

"I do." Corliss started licking his neck and worked her way down. She removed his shirt and unbuckled his pants. After he stepped out of his pants, she pushed him onto the bed.

"What are we about to do? Make another baby?"

"Not another baby—we're about to make love," she answered.

He watched as she pulled her dress over her head, removed her bra and panties and straddled him. Corliss knew Jermaine enjoyed their lovemaking. When they used to fuss and fight in their relationship, all she had to do to make it up to him was climb on top so he could watch her take what she wanted.

She was the more experienced one. They had first met five years earlier at Yesterday's Club in Southfield. Before Corliss, he had had only two girlfriends—one all through high school and the other all through college. Then Corliss, who he said would be the one to last the rest of his life.

She was happy in the beginning.

He wined and dined her.

Didn't press for sex.

And when the time came and they finally made love, she understood why—Jermaine was insecure about the size of his penis. He mentioned it before she could—not that she would have, because he wasn't that small. His size didn't bother Corliss, even if she was used to being with much larger men. What troubled her was he wasn't into oral sex, and it became a problem. But she was starting to realize she'd much rather have a man who loved her than one who was just willing to lick anywhere on her. Jermaine loved her—that much she knew.

"Do I satisfy you, baby?" he asked as she rode him.

"Yes, baby," she moaned. For some reason the sex was feeling unusually good.

"Does this mean we're back together?"

"Do you want me back?" she asked. "Will you take me back?"

"I never wanted us to be apart."

She reached her climax once he said that. And watching her come made him do the same.

While Jermaine was at work and Jelani at his grand-mother's, Corliss sat motionless in her bedroom, watching *The Shawshank Redemption* yet again. She had seen the movie so many times, she'd lost count. She had the same reaction every time—overcome with emotion. For Corliss, what stuck most was when Morgan Freeman's character, Red, said, "Let me tell you something, my friend. Hope is a dangerous thing. Hope can drive a man insane."

Corliss could certainly relate. She had hoped for many things. She hoped she and Jermaine would marry. It seemed they were becoming closer, and he was learning to trust her again. Then there was her other hope of breaking into Hollywood. *Such a big one*, she thought. It was the only one she had for herself careerwise, and she didn't want to apologize for her own desires—didn't want to think small like her parents had. She wanted to believe anything was possible, even though her parents taught her the only thing she should dream of was security. To them, security meant working the same job for thirty years and retiring at seventy. That wasn't Corliss's dream at all.

She snatched the CD with her latest screenplay from her computer, and placed it inside a clear case. "I'm going." She headed out the door and downtown to Cobo Hall.

Corliss stood in front of the massive Dreamworks kiosk while her eyes bounced between *Dreamgirls, Disturbia, Norbit,* and *Shrek the Third.* They were among the many movies playing on the flat screen monitors attached to the elaborate Dreamworks backdrop.

"Wow." She stood in awe until a young woman armed with brochures approached her.

"Impressive, huh?"

"Very. One day I want to have a movie playing on the big screen."

"Then hurry to the workshop just starting in room 101A-C called Becoming a Screenwriter. I hear there are some high-powered agents and producers inside."

"101A-C. Okay, thanks, I'm there."

"Right outside the doors and to your left," the woman said as Corliss rushed off.

"So you want to write an Oscar-winning screenplay?" the man said as Corliss entered and took her aisle seat in the last row. "You want to become the next Stephen King. You've seen his movies. You can do it, right? He's good, but I'm better. If you are, we need to talk and fast," the man said, and the audience laughed. "Is it possible? Of course. Can I accomplish my goals all the way from Detroit or Cleveland or Chicago, wherever you're from? Or do I need to move to Los Angeles? I'm here to tell you anything is possible. No, you don't have to live in LA if you want to become a screenwriter. Would there be more opportunity if you did? Probably. But this weekend is all about possibilities—your dreams and daring to go for them.

"Let me tell you my story. I grew up in a middle-class family. My parents were both educators in the public school system. My father's biggest dream was to become a school administrator, and hey, there's nothing wrong with that. Only, it never happened for him, so guess who he imposed his dream on? You guessed it—me. I didn't want to work in education. I barely got my own education.

"I wanted to write. I had always known I wanted to write, and when I went to college I majored in English. Did my parents mind? No, because I could be an English professor. They upgraded their dreams with me. They wanted me to go all the way through until I earned a doctorate and could teach at the university level. Only guess what? I never received my bachelor's. And I'm not saying this to encourage people to drop out of school. I'm letting you know I dared to dream.

"A screenwriting magazine held a contest searching for the next big screenwriter. 'Send us your screenplay and a twenty-five-dollar entry fee and you could become the next—' Back then, I was young and believed in all those contests. Thank God I did, because I won. Now, that was just the start, because I got the money and an agent, but the screenplay itself sat on a desk and never got produced until ten years later. I haven't told you my name yet. I'm—"

"Dennis Hoefner," Corliss said along with the man. She had already read his story a few years earlier. He had gone on to write numerous screenplays, and won an Oscar for *All Is Well*, the screenplay that took ten years to produce.

"And you still may not have heard of me because screenwriters are only known, usually, among the industry, but you have heard of my films." He named his top-grossing movies and the audience gasped. "I would much rather you know my movies than know me. My friends and family know me. I need movie buffs to know my films. Dare to dream . . . and dream big, because if it can happen to me, it can happen to anyone."

Corliss was conked out on the sofa when Jermaine arrived home from work a little after eleven. She woke up when she felt his hand stroke the side of her cheek.

"How was work?" she asked.

"Busy. We sold a lot of cars, which is always good."

She smiled. "That's good."

"How was your day? Did you go to the seminar?"

"Yes."

"You did?" He smiled.

She sat up on the sofa. "Thank you for telling me about it."

"Thank Georgia."

"I would thank her if I could. It made me want to go for my dreams. No matter how far-fetched."

"Wait a minute. Your dreams are not far-fetched. I want to own a dealership—and I will. This is despite hearing people say minority dealerships aren't successful. I don't care what they say. I'm going to own one, and it will be successful. And you're going to be a screenwriter."

She smiled. "Thank you for believing in me. And thank you for giving me another chance to show you how much I truly love you."

Georgia grabbed a quick bite in the promenade of the Guardian Building. She loved the quaint space and the Avalon International bakery's inexpensive pastries and baguette sandwiches, as well as Illy's coffee, which was some of the best Georgia had ever tasted.

The meeting lasted an hour. Georgia and her morning team sat around Priscilla and listened to her vent about Thomas's expectations for the station.

"Ladies, personally, I think all of you are doing wonderful. Georgia, you are refreshing and inspiring. I read the e-mails. In fact, I'm personally going to nominate Georgia for the Marconi Award."

Because of Marvin, Georgia was well aware of the prestigious Marconi Award, named after Italian inventor

Guglielmo Marconi, who was credited as being "the father of radio." Marvin was envious of Tom Joyner, who had won the award in 2004 for Network/Syndicated Personality of the Year, making him the first black person to ever win it. It was now Marvin's mission to win one.

"You're nominating me?" Georgia asked after setting down her Illy's coffee cup.

"Absolutely. But, ladies, I called you here to prepare you for the lunch meeting with my dad. He is from the old school, and he wants a man or two to mix in with the team. As much as he doesn't like the idea of a female morning show host, he doubly doesn't like the idea of an all-female morning show team. He wants to bring on some testosterone. Sell my father at all times. Let him know an all-female morning show team has a niche and can be successful."

Georgia wasn't very hungry, so she opted for the Mosaic Greek salad, stabbing her fork through crispy greens every time Thomas said something out of line.

They had all gathered at Mosaic Restaurant in Greektown—Priscilla, Thomas, Cammy, Tonya, and Georgia.

"You ladies are doing well," Thomas said. "I just have one suggestion. I love that Cookies for a Cause thing. It's a cute gimmick."

"It's not a gimmick. I am very passionate about helping the homeless. My brother is homeless."

"That's even better—it's a gimmick that will seem believable once your audience learns you have a homeless brother. Although I'm sure they'll wonder why you allow him to remain homeless."

"That's his choice. I'd take him off the streets anytime if he'd let me. All he has to do is call. And again, Cookies for a Cause is not a gimmick."

"Okay, well, it seems like one. It would be one thing if you worked for Betty Crocker or Duncan Hines, but you don't. You're a morning show host for 1FM, WFOR, The Force. What are you baking cookies for?"

"Because I love to bake. Now there's a demand for my cookies."

"But is there one for your show? You're in fifteen markets right now, which for a few months on the air is great, but let's put it into perspective—Marvin's in one hundred and fifteen."

"And he's been on the air for five-plus years," Georgia said.

Thomas continued, "I have a strong suspicion the majority of your listeners are women, and we need more than just women listening to the show. How are we coming along with finding a man to add to this mix?"

"My neighbor Art could do it," Georgia said. "He's a stay-at-home dad, a great guy."

"We need a man who men can relate to. Who in the hell can relate to a stay-at-home dad?" Thomas asked.

Georgia twisted her face at the same time she jabbed her fork into a Kalamata olive and block of feta cheese. "I don't know about that," Georgia said, "I read an article—"

"Please," Thomas said, throwing both his hands up,

"save those damn articles. That's all you ladies talk about— articles and reality shows. Get some scoop. In the meantime, it's time to start up a big contest."

"We already give away a thousand dollars a week."

"Try a thousand dollars an hour for one thousand hours. We'll have a contest with a *Deal or No Deal* spin to it, and one of those lucky thousand-dollar winners will also become a millionaire. I know 102 Hitz will come out soon with one of their own, so let's beat them to the punch."

"Georgia, you're doing well," Priscilla said, encouragingly.

"Yes, you are. You all are," Thomas said, "but we can always be doing better. So ladies, let's concentrate on becoming number one. The Arbitron ratings will be out before you know it. And that book tells the true story."

Chuck E. Cheese.

It was Jelani's birthday, and all week he could barely contain his excitement about going to Chuck E. Cheese. Corliss wasn't into any kiddy stuff. She hated places with rides, grown people dressed in costumes, even cartoons.

Corliss hadn't been in Chuck E. Cheese a full ten minutes before her head started pounding. Too many screaming kids and arcade games—and Jermaine ran right into the middle of it all.

She grabbed a handful of tokens from the table and played ski ball to clear her mind. After several minutes, Jermaine snuck up behind her.

"Boo!"

She turned around, her hand to her chest while the

other clutched her cell phone. "Don't do that! You know I don't like that."

"I'm sorry. What's gotten into you?"

"Nothing."

"Are you sure? Are you okay?"

She wanted to tell him the truth. That living with him wouldn't cut it. She wanted him to forgive her so they could move on and become a family, but if he could be stubborn, she could be, too. She still had a good living arrangement—no rent, but also no ring.

"How much longer do we have to stay here?"

"It's Jelani's birthday and we haven't been here that long. Try to hold out."

"There's a movie theatre across the street. I think I'm going to go over there and see *Disturbia*. The next show starts in fifteen minutes."

"How do you know?"

"I just called them."

"But it's Jelani's birthday."

"I just feel like seeing a movie. I just want to dream."

He looked deep into her eyes and nodded. "Okay, I'll take you over there. Call me when you're out, and I'll pick you up."

"Are you sure? Am I being selfish?"

"I know you don't like Chuck E. Cheese, and you have been here almost thirty minutes, which is longer than I thought you'd last. If you want to see a movie, that's fine. By the time it's over, we'll be packing up anyway."

"Are you sure?"

"I'm positive, baby. I'm going to ask you again. Are you okay, because you don't seem like it."

"I've been listening to the *Sweet Georgia Brown Show*."

"No more Marvelous Marvin?"

"No more. She just makes me want to go after my dreams. She is so positive and I get so excited. Then I become frustrated. I feel trapped. I hate my job, but I need my job. I have to work. I need the money. But all I can think about is how I have to get up tomorrow and deal with the same mess. I know everyone else deals with it, too, but it's so hard for me. I'm sorry. I'm just venting."

He put his arm around Corliss. "You never know what tomorrow may bring. Always remember that."

Marvelous Marvin arrived at the radio station just before six a.m. As he pulled into his reserved spot, his cell phone started to ring.

He knew before answering who was on the other end.

They wanted their money.

The worst part was he didn't have it. The first and second mortgages had been kicking his butt. He still had a sneaking suspicion the FCC was investigating him. Everything in his life was falling apart fast.

"I'm going to have the money like I always do. I just need a little more time," Marvin said.

"Let me ask you something," the man said. "I never asked you this before, but did you ever watch *The Sopranos*?"

"No."

"No? Are you out of your fuckin' mind? Who didn't watch *The Sopranos*? *Never*?"

"I did a few times, but I wasn't a *Sopranos* fan."

"Well, I *am* a *Sopranos* fan, because that shit right there was as real as it gets. You know what I mean? Do you remember the episode 'Everybody Hurts'?"

"No, Vincent, I don't."

"Okay, I've seen every episode of *The Sopranos* at least two dozen times. I watch the shit in my Maybach sometimes. 'Everybody Hurts' aired in the fourth season—the sixth episode."

"You are a big fan."

"Oh, yeah. I could write a book on *The Sopranos* easily and break down every episode and give my opinion as an organized-crime-family expert. But let me explain to you the relevance of that episode. You say you've watched the show a few times—do you remember Artie Bucco?"

"No."

"No? Artie Bucco, the chef. He was one of Tony's best friends—they went to elementary school together."

"Vincent, I have to get on the radio. What are you getting at?"

"Because in the episode 'Everybody Hurts,' Tony finds out Artie needs money. Tony gives him the money, even though Artie never came to him asking to borrow it. Artie attempts suicide when he can't pay Tony back, but doesn't die. When Tony visits him at the hospital, he tells Artie it's okay, and that he'll assume his debt. I'm telling you this to prove a very small point—you're not my best friend and we didn't go to elementary school together. We have no connection. You are not family. And you owe me a lot of fuckin' money.

"Now, I am a patient man, but I'm not a very nice one. If not for the fact you have always paid me back with hefty interest, your show would already be off the air, because you wouldn't be alive to still host it. I need my money and I need it quickly."

"Two weeks. I'll get you your money in two weeks."

It was Monday, which was prank-call day for Marvin, but he didn't feel like making one. Not after his conversation with Vincent. Some of his listeners called to complain that Marvin didn't seem to care much anymore.

"I mean he calls himself 'the hardest-working man in radio,' but lately he's not doing a thing."

"He doesn't call himself the hardest-working man in radio," the new female team member said.

"Oh, I'm sorry, that's Tom Joyner—the man I guess I should be listening to," the caller said, slamming the phone down.

Nothing seemed to faze Marvin, who filled the entire four hours with music and commercials and absolutely no talk.

"Is Marvin on vacation?" another caller asked.

"He's been in meetings most of the morning," the same female member of his morning team stated, "working on a new contest to roll out to y'all. Just keep it locked right here so you won't miss our announcement." Marvin hadn't been in a meeting, and they certainly weren't working on a new contest, because they had just finalized the one Marvin suggested—four sponsors each donated five hundred thousand dollars to participate in the biggest giveaway in radio history—two million dollars given away in forty days, with one one-thousand-dollar winner going on to become a millionaire.

Marvin sat at the controls, unmotivated to move.

He appeared dazed.

He was thinking about his wife, the debt he owed, and Single Barrel Jack Daniel's whiskey.

That night, he went to Flood's Bar and Grill on Lafayette and sipped on Dewar's White Label Scotch Whiskey instead. Several listeners of his show approached him. Many recognized him from his reality-show days, or even further back to when he performed at Bea's Comedy Kitchen down the street. And a giant billboard of Marvelous Marvin hung in the parking lot adjacent to the bar. Marvin was popular in several cities, but in Detroit, he was a celebrity.

He sat at the bar and contemplated his life—wondered if it was almost over. He thought about Georgia and smiled, about his children and almost cried. He didn't want them to grow up fatherless. He even thought about Chloe, his only daughter—it would be too late for him to try to mend their distant relationship if he didn't pay off his debt.

Marvin had to do it and do it quickly—two weeks was all the time he had. Bill would notice the Visa cards missing immediately. There would be no way he wouldn't, especially when the cards were kept in a safe in Bill's office, and the only other person to know the combination was his assistant. So Marvin had two dilemmas: how to get the combination, and then how to get into Bill's office. It all had to happen soon. Bill had taken off the latter part of the following week, so all Marvin had to deal with was Bill's assistant, who had a big crush on Marvin anyway.

He peered across the room, past the local band performing, over to a group of ladies celebrating a baby shower.

"You have to know Nina to understand why," the woman who had been eyeing Marvin said, after she had finally gathered enough nerve to join him. She sat beside him on a bar stool. "Let's just say, I wouldn't be surprised if her baby needs some rum in his milk, because Nina hasn't let her pregnancy stop her from getting her drink on."

The woman's name was Crystal, and she was a thick woman—not fat, just wide with a flat stomach and an extremely round ass, Marvin noticed. "And what about you?" he asked. "Do you have any kids or want any?" Flirting always helped Marvin's mind forget about his troubles.

"Me?" the woman said. "No, I don't have any, and yes, I wouldn't mind having one or two one day. No rush."

"Can we go somewhere tonight and practice?"

She looked over at the booth where her friends sat—the three of them stared in her direction, smiling. She took a sip of her vodka tonic, removed the lemon from the glass, and began sucking.

Marvin stood, straightened his tie, took his fedora off

the stool beside him and adjusted the fit after placing it on his head. Tonight, he just wanted a little companionship. Sure, he could always call Destiny, because she would always be there willing and waiting. Or he could call the lucky lady he had met at the casino whose Century 21 realtor card he had taken. She had been starstruck, also. But why call either, when the woman sitting beside him, who giggled constantly and laughed at everything he said, was more than willing?

He opened his wallet and tossed two one-hundred-dollar bills on the bar.

"Did you drink that much or are you tipping that big?"

"I'm Marvelous Marvin, baby, and I don't mind paying for good service."

They left the bar, and he escorted her to his car, opening the passenger side as she slid in. He walked around to the driver's side, entered, and stuck his key in the ignition, but didn't move. Where was he going to take her? To which hotel? One of his usuals, maybe? But he didn't even want her. Wasn't even horny. He was just going through the motions, and the motions had gotten him in big trouble lately.

He turned to the young lady and said. "You know what, I'm sorry, but this is a mistake."

"What do you mean a mistake?"

He leaned over her lap and opened his car door. "I'm married."

"I know. To Georgia. You talk about her on the radio all the time. And we're just practicing, remember?"

"No, we're not."

"You just lost a listener."

"I have over eleven million . . . I'll be okay."

As the woman stormed off and Marvin drove off, he planned his next move. He was going to take the debit cards—he had no other choice. He didn't want to die. Especially now that his father was so proud of him. And he definitely had to stick around to show Georgia just who the "Boss of Radio" was.

Marvin knew what needed to happen. He had already pressed the station to pay him more money, but they were unwilling to renegotiate another contract this year. But they did like his contest idea.

"That other radio station is just like the banker from *Deal or No Deal*—they're not offering any big money. We're giving away two million dollars, and all you have to do is be our tenth caller every hour to qualify. Do you honestly think I'd let some new station give away more money to my listeners? I don't think so. It's so simple. All you have to do is be our tenth caller, and you automatically win a Visa debit card for one thousand dollars. Then, you are automatically enrolled in our one-million-dollar Memorial Day giveaway. Instant gratification, because that's how we like it. Our lines are opening right now." He took his headphones off and queued up an old Alicia Keys song.

As he approached Bill's office, he noticed his assistant placing a large box in the floor safe. He assumed it held the debit cards. She had a piece of paper in her hand with the combination. She closed the safe and stood.

"Is Bill here yet?"

"No, sir. Not yet this morning."

"You don't have to call me sir. I feel old when you do that, and I don't want to feel old." She smiled. It was obvious to Marvin she had a crush on him, and even though she was a college intern too young for his taste, she held the key to solving his financial troubles. "So tell me, how does an old man like me get to go out with a pretty woman like you?" He took one step closer.

She shrugged. "I guess ask."

"Will you?"

"Will I what?"

"Go out with me?"

Her smile widened even more. "Of course."

"Well, let me write down your number," he said as he snatched the paper from her hand.

"No! No, sir. Not on that."

"I'll just take a piece of it."

"Hey, Marvin," the female member of his morning team said. "We're back on the air in thirty seconds."

"I'll be right back," Marvin said, folding the combination.

"But sir, I need that paper."

"I'll bring it right back," he said as he disappeared be-hind the door with the on-air sign flashing, leaving her waiting helplessly on the other side. Fifteen minutes later, Marvin surfaced with one of his business cards and handed it to the young lady. "Call me sometime."

"But what about that piece of paper?" she asked as she took the business card from him.

"Oh, was there something important on it? I threw it away."

"Yes, it was very important. I mean, I just need it back."

"Let's go get it out of the garbage then," he said, as he widened the door to the studio and allowed her inside.

She stooped down and found the balled-up piece of pa-per resting on top and sighed a big sigh of relief.

"I'll call you," she said.

"Take your time," he responded.

"What?"

"I'm looking forward to hearing from you soon."

She smiled and left the studio.

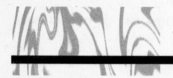

"Don't forget, I have to watch that movie," Chloe reminded Georgia as they rode down Jefferson toward home. She had been telling Georgia for nearly a month that her essay about *An Inconvenient Truth* was due on April thirtieth. Georgia had heard Chloe the first six times, but her mind was so clouded lately, she found it difficult to concentrate on anything other than the Arbitron winter book that would be released in two days. Soon, Georgia would finally have a progress report.

"Didn't I order that off Amazon weeks ago?"

"You were supposed to, but it's too late for all that now. The thirtieth is this Monday."

"Why didn't you remind me, Chloe?"

"I did. Several times." Chloe realized they had just

passed their normal route. "And why are you going this way?"

"What way?"

"Toward the old house."

"What am I doing? Okay, I have to get a grip. You need the DVD. It's too late for Amazon, so we'll go to Blockbuster. But I also need the imported chocolate for my cookies. And only two specialty stores in Michigan sell it. The one in Grosse Pointe is sold out, and the other is way out in White Lake. I have the address programmed in the navigational system. It's next to a Meijer."

"Perfect, Meijer sells videos."

It took them nearly an hour to drive all the way to Highland Road in White Lake, Michigan.

"You want to talk about an *inconvenient* truth?" Georgia said as she pulled into the Meijer parking lot, exhausted from all the driving. "This drive certainly qualifies," she mumbled. "Look at the boys back there, conked out. I'm going to run inside Baker's Rack, and then Meijer for your DVD and some groceries. They're holding the DVD at customer service. I need you to stay here with the boys."

She was reaching for a box of Pearl tampons in Meijer when someone caught her eye—a woman who didn't quite look like a woman. Actually, she wasn't a woman—the person was a man dressed as a woman. He was with a boy who appeared to be around twelve or thirteen, but it was hard to tell, because he kept his head down. They were both dirty, and the man pushed their cart overflowing with groceries.

Georgia stood stiff for a moment and then arched on tiptoe and tried to peer over the shelves, searching for someone who could help. She was in a large store filled with people, but who could she tell? Who would believe that one of the brothers who had been abducted five years ago was in the store right now? She had heard the story on the news, and for some reason, it had never left her.

A young couple passed her in the midst of their own private laughter. She stuck her hand out and made a sound and they looked, but she said nothing. She followed behind the man and the child, but not too closely. She didn't want to draw their attention.

"I thought you said five minutes," Chloe asked. "It's been a good ten."

Georgia dropped her red basket on the floor and grabbed Chloe's arms. "Chloe, did you leave Edrik and Haden in the car?"

"Yes."

"Go back there and wait for me." That's all she could say. Her heart raced. Nothing like this had ever happened to her before. She couldn't think straight.

Georgia's eyes raced in the direction of the man and the child moving toward the exit with the cart full of groceries. "That's okay, we've got to go."

"Okay, what's wrong?"

"Keep your eyes on that boy and that man."

"That woman you mean?"

"No, that's no woman—that's a man."

"Who are they?"

"I'll tell you when we get to the car."

They discreetly rushed toward their car, which was in the same direction the man and child were headed. She finally saw the man and the boy walk by her own car to the one parked directly in front of theirs—a silver Dodge Shadow. That's when she noticed another boy's head pop up from the backseat.

Georgia held her heart. "Oh my God," she whispered, her hand trembling. "Chloe, it is them. Don't look at them. Walk to the car and get in. Act normally."

Georgia's hands shook as she used her remote to open the car door.

Chloe did as instructed.

"Keep your eyes on that car. Do not let them out of our sight," Georgia said as she started her engine. She waited for the car to back out of its spot and then pulled forward, following behind.

"Can you tell me who they are?"

"Get your cell phone out and call the police."

Chloe was afraid. She had never witnessed Georgia act this way.

She pulled out her cell phone and dialed 911.

"Put it on speaker," Georgia said.

"Nine-one-one, what is the emergency?" a young man asked.

"The two brothers who have been missing for five years, who were abducted from the Simmon's department store on Gratiot and Twenty-Six Mile—the Bright brothers—I'm driving behind the man who abducted them. He has two children in the car with him right now. Please send some help."

"Ma'am, are you referring to James and Kyle Bright who were abducted on December twenty-fourth, 2002, at Simmons department store?"

"Yes!"

"Where are you right now? What is your locale?"

"We just left Meijer in White Lake."

"You are on Highland Road?"

"Yes."

"And what direction are you traveling?"

"North. I should be traveling south if I were going home, but I'm traveling north because I want to help those boys. But we need the police to help us."

Chloe sat in the passenger side, extending the phone toward Georgia, but away from the view of the windshield.

Georgia kept a fair distance behind the Dodge Shadow. "I can't believe they are still driving that Shadow."

"Can you provide some landmarks for us please?"

"We are on North Milford Road, and we are in the middle of nowhere."

"I need a landmark."

"I don't have a landmark. Okay, wait, he's stopping. He's stopping at an On-the-Go gas station."

"On North Milford Road?"

"Yes, he is stopping to get gas." Georgia pulled up to the front of the gas station. "What do we do now?"

"We have dispatched some state police officers to the location. What is the perpetrator doing now?"

Georgia looked out her rearview mirror and watched as the man left the gas pump and headed for the station.

"He just walked inside the station."

"We have one trooper and a local police officer less than five minutes away and two more troopers less than ten minutes away. We need to transfer your call to the local FBI office. Will you stay on the line, please?"

"One of the troopers just pulled up. And a police car just pulled up, too," Georgia said. She was so excited she leaped from her SUV and ran toward the officers. "He's inside!" Georgia yelled. "That's his car right there. The boys are in the car. Get the boys out of the car."

The man walked out with a gun in his hand and bullets started flying. The police officer swerved his car, jumped out, and knocked Georgia to the ground. Three more police cars swerved into the gas station, and within minutes, nearly a half dozen local and state authorities were on the scene.

The man walked toward his car on an obvious suicide mission as officers exchanged several rounds and riddled his body with bullets. He lay on his back in a pool of blood.

Georgia noticed the two boys peeking out the back window. "Will you get the boys out of that car?" Georgia asked as she brushed the dirt from her outfit and attempted to stand. "Would someone call their parents and tell them their children are safe?"

"**S**he sponsors Cookies for a Cause, and now a popular radio host can add another good deed to her resume—solving a five-year-old kidnapping case. Sweet Georgia Brown, the nationally syndicated morning radio show host, displayed plenty of courage, and even more guts, this evening. I'm Denise Vance with your local channel four news here to tell you more about this incredible story, and introduce you to the woman who brought an end to five years of torment for one local family. You might recall . . ."

The story was on every station Marvin turned to—and so was Georgia.

"Hello, I'm Diane Saunter with the CBS national news, and we have a truly heartwarming story to open tonight's broadcast. Popular national radio show host Sweet Georgia Brown isn't making news for anything she's said on-air, but for what's she's done as a concerned citizen. Many of you might remember . . ."

Marvin's cell phone buzzed on the coffee table. His entire management team had been calling.

"She's going to be on *Larry King Live*," Bill said. "Do you know what all this publicity will do for her career?"

"Yeah, I know. And she deserves it. Everyone will definitely know her name after today."

"Marvin, are you okay?" Bill asked.

"I'm fine."

Marvin hung up and changed the channel, catching the end of Georgia's interview on *Inside Edition* where she explained how she felt she was destined to reunite the two brothers with their parents. Each event had lined up exactly as it was supposed to—waiting until the last minute to purchase the DVD, which led her to the Meijer that was beside the only Baker's Rack that carried the imported chocolate she included in her gourmet chocolate chip cookies. It all put her in the path of the abductor. "This is life-changing," Georgia said as her eyes began to water. "I'm so happy for that family."

"And we're so proud of you."

The media just couldn't get enough of her.

"Remind our viewers. You're on the radio every morning from six until ten, and I'm sure you have quite a radio show, because you are quite a woman," a reporter from the *Nancy Grace* show said as he spoke to Georgia over the phone. "Have you talked to the parents or the children since they were reunited?"

"It's only been about six hours, so not yet. I'm sure they have a lot of catching up to do first."

"Is there anything you want to tell them?"

"I know what it's like to search for someone and wonder if they're okay. My brother is homeless, but that is by choice, and this incident wasn't. I'm just so happy that I could assist."

After watching the television continuously for hours, flipping from station to station, searching for anyone discussing Georiga, Marvin finally decided to break away and turn it off.

He'd had enough. Not just with the reports, but with his life.

He felt himself spiraling. Something was going to catch up with him, he was sure of it.

He walked to the portable bar and poured a martini. He took one sip and set it down. He had a bad taste in his mouth and it wasn't from the drink, but from all he had done. And now he was embarrassed. A few news stations played bits from his show when he had insulted his wife. One late-night talk show host called him Moron Marvin.

He knew the truth—he hadn't been true to himself. And now, he was getting ready to pay for it all. He couldn't explain what he felt, just that he knew something was about to happen. He had done Georgia wrong and done his daughter wrong.

*   *   *

The next morning, Marvin started his show with an open letter to Georgia.

"Listeners, good morning. I've spent the past five years insulting my wife. For five years, I've lied to each and every one of you. Georgia is nothing like I've described her. The problem was, the more I talked about her, the more I believed what I said. For five years, I've broadcast from this studio as Marvelous Marvin, but what is the definition of marvelous? Webster's defines it as, 'such as to cause wonder, admiration, or astonishment; surprising; extraordinary.' And that, I am not. I used to feel that way when I was married to Georgia. She made me feel like Superman—I felt like I could do anything when I was with her. I love you, Georgia, and I'm so sorry I used my radio show to spread lies about you. You deserve everything wonderful. You don't deserve me—you deserve much better."

He turned off his microphone and stood. Marvin was ready to leave the studio for good, but first, Bill needed to see him in his office.

In Bill's office, they sat in silence waiting for the other to speak. Bill looked stern.

"Did you take over a half million dollars in Visa cards from this station? I'm giving you an opportunity to just admit what you've done."

Marvin was tired of lying. He'd lied to Georgia for years, all the while thinking he had gotten away with something when, in fact, the wool was being pulled over his eyes. "Yes, I took some of the debit cards."

"Some, Marvin?"

"But I had planned on giving them back."

"Now that you're caught anyway, right?"

"Take it out of my check. I make enough." If there was a way Marvin could give all the cards back he would, but it was much too late for that. He had already sold all of the debit cards.

"Evidently, you don't. And besides, you no longer have a check for me to take it out from. I would never have a thief work for me."

It was then the police arrived, and Marvin saw his demise flash quickly before his eyes.

The police read him his rights, and Marvin remained placid as they placed his hands behind his back and handcuffed him.

"You're not so marvelous, Marvin," Bill said as he watched the police escort him out. "You're not marvelous at all."

"You're right. I'm not."

"**O**h, wait a minute, let me get my digital camera," Jermaine's mother said as she rushed into her dining room and snatched it off the buffet table. "Jermaine bought me a digital camera, honey—for no special occasion at all—just because. And you don't need film."

"Mom acts like those just came out," Jermaine whispered to Corliss.

They stood in his mother's small entryway. They had dropped by on their way to dinner at the Whitney Restaurant, former home to lumber baron David Whitney Jr., located on Woodward Avenue near the VH1 Brian McKnight concert at the Fox Theatre in downtown Detroit that they were attending.

His mother rushed back into the entrance. "Jelani, go stand between your parents."

Jelani positioned himself between his parents.

"Look at that—one big happy family. That's what you all are. Keep posing. I have a lot of images left. I can take five hundred pictures if I want to. Say cheese, Jelani."

"Cheese, Granny." He grinned from ear to ear.

"I feel like I'm going to the prom," Corliss said.

"The prom? A wedding, honey."

Jermaine twisted his face and gave his mother a strange look. He was afraid she would let the surprise out of the bag.

"Let me take a few more pictures. Step outside on my front porch beside my hibiscus plants. See, the great thing about digital cameras is, after you take the picture, you just hook it up to your computer and transfer the images. You can e-mail them out to your friends and family. I'm going to get the printer next. I mean *my son* is gonna get one for me." Jermaine's mother winked at Corliss. "Because he loves his mother. Isn't that right, son?"

"Yes, Mom. That's right."

"Daddy loves me, too," Jelani said, looking up at his father.

Jermaine rubbed his son's head. "That's right, little man, I love you."

"And Mommy."

"And your mommy, you're right," Jermaine said as he looked over at Corliss. "Definitely."

"Mmm-hmm—I raised a romantic son. Where y'all going to eat?"

"The Whitney."

"Child, the Whitney? On Woodward?"

"Is it expensive?" Corliss asked.

"Yes, ma'am." Jermaine's mother took Jelani's hand and walked toward the front door. "Well, enjoy your evening. Jelani and I have a date with the Cartoon Network, don't we?"

He nodded and waved good-bye to his parents.

Corliss and Jermaine entered the multilevel mansion.

The great hall was illuminated with crystal chandeliers, and a three-piece string ensemble played Bach. The spectacular grand stairway offered a stunning glimpse of the rich woods and gold and silver-washed plaster featured throughout the restaurant.

They had reservations to dine in a secluded romantic corner in the library among the leather-bound volumes of Whitney's personal collection. Jermaine had carefully planned this moment. At the suggestion of a party planner, he had picked this restaurant and arranged for the appetizers to be on the table when they arrived.

Her eyes popped when she opened the menu.

"Did you see the prices of these meals?" she whispered to Jermaine.

"Yeah, baby. I have it covered."

"But baby, forty-four dollars for a steak—the Detroiter?"

"Is that what you want?"

"And that doesn't even come with a salad. You have to buy that separate."

"Don't worry about the price."

"But I'm used to Ponderosa prices."

He leaned toward Corliss. "I make over a hundred and fifty thousand dollars a year—we can splurge every now and then."

She gasped. "You make how much? I thought the auto industry was hurting badly." The waiter approached. "Well, I'll take the Detroiter, then." She closed the menu. "With the blue cheese soufflé salad and a lobster bisque soup."

"Well, damn."

"You said I could have whatever."

"You can, baby."

Their waiter arrived with a plate of bread covered by a silver cloche. Tucked inside the tuxedo-folded linen napkin was an engagement ring. He then set the bell-shaped metal cover on the table, stifled a smile, and left.

"Corliss, we've had our ups and downs, but I have realized during the time we were apart that I can't live my life without you and my son in it every day, every step of the way." He lifted the cloche and revealed the open Tiffany ring box holding an emerald-cut three-stone diamond ring.

"What's that?"

Jermaine stood and walked around the table to Corliss. He got down on one knee and said, "Will you marry me?"

Corliss began giggling into her napkin as her eyes searched the room and delighted onlookers.

"Will you?"

"Yes, baby. Yes, baby. I'll marry you."

He slipped the ring on her finger and kissed her hand. She stared at it.

"Do you like it?"

"Yes, I love it."

"Only the best for you and Jelani. Oh, and one more thing."

"There's more?"

He removed a set of keys from his suit pocket and slid them in front of her.

"What's this?"

"Remember when we pulled up to the valet and you mentioned how much you liked the black 300C SRT8 parked in front of us?"

"Yeah."

"That's your car."

"You planned all of this, Jermaine?"

"You think?"

"The man who never sent me flowers until my birthday can do all of this?"

"Anybody can send flowers. And if I had made the type of money I make now, I would have done romantic things."

"You know what? It's not about what you did or didn't do, because you have always been consistent in the way you love me." Tears ran down Corliss's cheeks. "And I'm going to spend the rest of my life with you. I love you."

"I love you, too, baby. And there's just one last thing."

"What? There can't be any more."

"I want you to pursue your dream."

"What are you saying?"

"You don't have to go to Hollywood. If you make enough noise, Hollywood will come to you."

"What do you mean?"

"I know you don't like your job, so you don't have to do it anymore. Effective tomorrow, you're starting your new job as a screenwriter, and when you finish your script, I'll find a way to get it produced independently if I have to take out a loan. Whatever it takes, because I believe in you."

"Are you saying I can quit?"

He nodded.

She leaped from their table and shouted, "Yes! Yes! Yes!"

"Damn, I didn't even get that kind of reaction to my proposal."

"This is a reaction to everything. Thank you."

Corliss had planned this moment for years.

She had decided to write her exit like a screenplay. She knew she would offer her first customer an extension, a practice Trish highly frowned upon, even though customers qualified for one per year. And she would also request time off at the very last minute. The company required a month's notice—something Corliss couldn't stand, because things came up, and you didn't always have a month to plan them out.

For the first time, she couldn't wait to get to work. She wondered if she would stick to script, or if she would improvise and leave at lunch to never return. She had alternate endings, not sure which one she would use.

*　　*　　*

INT. OFFICE—DAY

A large call center in a modern well-lit facility. Collectors are on a predictive dialer system collecting customer payments while team leaders walk around cubicles keeping an eye on employee production.

Corliss (on the phone with a customer)
I'm going to see if we can give you a two-month extension on your car payments.

Customer
Do you really think they'd do that for me?

Corliss
I don't see why not. You've only had one extension out of thirty-eight payments, so I'm sure we can do that.

Customer
You are truly an angel. And God will bless you very soon. What did you say your name was?

Corliss (Corliss uses Jermaine's last name.)
Mrs. Townsend.

Customer
When those other people call me—especially that Miss Trish with her old nasty attitude, calling herself the supervisor—I don't even pick up the phone, because they treat me so bad. But you talk to me like I'm a person just going through

some bad times right now. I know I'm behind on my car
payments, but I'll catch 'em up. I need my car to get to
work. With my husband dying and my daughter getting hit
by that car, everything just came down on me all at once.
So if you could get me that two-month extension, I sure
would appreciate it.

Corliss walks over to Trish's desk and folds her arms, listening to Trish's phone conversation.

Corliss (to Trish softly)
Excuse me, I don't mean to interrupt you, but I have a
customer on hold.

Trish gives Corliss an irritated quick up and down glance.

Trish (to friend on phone)
Girl, let me call you back after I handle this. Stay by the phone;
I'm going to call you right back.

Trish slams the receiver down and swivels her chair to face
Corliss. Then she looks her up and down again and shakes
her head.

Trish (cont'd)
Okay, so you have a customer holding, *and*—

Corliss
I told her I might be able to offer a two-month extension. She
is very late.

Trish

Why are you getting soft all of a sudden? I'll tell you what
extension I can give her—a four-digit one. 7561.
Have her call me. She'll pay what she owes after
she talks to me or she can turn in that car.
And after I talk to her, I need to talk to you.

Corliss walks back to her cubicle. Trish walks over to
Corliss's desk.

Trish

What's taking you so long to transfer that call to me?

Corliss

She hung up.

Trish

She hung up?

Corliss

Yes. She hung up. But while you're here, I need to take the
next two weeks off.

Trish

We don't grant two weeks off, and we definitely don't grant
time off at the last minute. Besides, there's a training class next
week I need you to attend.

Corliss

Is it mandatory?

Trish
I need you to attend.

Corliss
That's fine.

Corliss turns away from her, but quickly spins back around.

Corliss (cont'd)
Oh, by the way, today will be my last day.

Trish
Excuse me?

Corliss removes a Post-it note from the tower of Post-its on her desk and writes, "Today IS my last day."

Corliss
So you won't forget. Have a productive day . . . because I sure will.

Corliss stands, straightens out her clothes and sticks the Post-it note on Trish's forehead.

Georgia couldn't believe it—Marvin had been arrested. Now it was his turn to appear on the news. He had confessed to stealing a half-million-dollars' worth of Visa debit cards that he then sold to his cousin Pookey—who the media classified as a street hustler—for fifty cents on the dollar to pay off his gambling debts. Georgia had no idea Marvin even had a gambling problem. Her phone started ringing, but she didn't answer. She didn't feel like talking. She hated to see Marvin's downfall. As mad as he could make her, there was a large part of her that he would always own.

At the pretrial hearing, Bill and Georgia talked briefly.

"It's a shame, you know," Georgia said, "that a man who did so much for 102 **Hitz might** wind up in prison."

"He took money from us, Georgia."

"He shouldn't have done that, I agree. But prison, Bill? Marvin was at his lowest. Everyone deserves a second chance."

"Did you give him one? Are you going to?"

"Marvin and I will always be friends. We have children together. But friends is what we'll remain."

"Well, Marvin and I won't even be that."

"Am I still your friend? Yours and Beverly's?"

"Of course, you are. You didn't steal from my station—other than ratings, but that was business."

"Then, please?"

"Georgia, what do you propose I do? Drop the charges?"

"I like that idea. I really do like that one."

"He took a half million dollars from my station. I can't just drop the charges."

"How much more do you think you will lose if you let him go to prison?"

"Okay, and if he doesn't, do you think people will want to hear what he has to say?"

"Marvin's listeners are so loyal that if he tells them it was one big prank, they'll believe him."

Bill thought about what Georgia said and came up with a solution of his own. "I'll drop the charges on one condition—you and Marvin host a morning show together on 102 Hitz."

"You know I can't do that."

"Why can't you? When does your contract expire?"

Georgia laughed. "As a matter of fact, I'm getting ready to negotiate my contract."

"Having you as the morning show host of 102 Hitz would be worth five hundred thousand dollars. What do you say? Is it going to be Marvin and Georgia in the morning or Marvin behind bars morning and night?"

"Bill, please don't be so cutthroat."

"We're talking five hundred thousand dollars. It's business, Georgia. Business."

"I have to bring my girls with me, Cammy and Tonya."

"I never wanted Cammy to leave in the first place. So you're sweetening the pot. Do we have a deal?"

She thought about it, and shook her head. "No. I want my own radio show. I want to prove that a woman can succeed in radio. If I cohost with Marvin, somehow it will look like I needed him when, in fact, he needed me. I don't want to host with Marvin. But, I don't want him to go to prison. I want him to get help for his gambling problem."

"Well, if you're not going to cohost, we don't have a deal."

"But I also know you would like to get out of the business if the price is right. What if I could find someone to take over 102 Hitz?"

"I'm listening."

"Someone who will pay what you want for it *and* make up for your losses."

"Marvin shouldn't get off that easily. He should pay for what he did, if not by serving time, then at least by paying back the money."

"He will. Leave that part up to me."

"Okay, so what do you want from me?"

"I want for you to drop the charges."

"And what if your buyer doesn't bite?"

"Then it will have to be *Georgia* and Marvin in the morning."

After throwing out the case, the judge pounded his gavel.

Marvin appeared stunned.

"How the hell did that happen?" he asked Bill as he approached him.

"You need to ask Georgia," Bill said.

Marvin and Georgia locked eyes and exchanged smiles.

"I'm going to negotiate coming to 102 Hitz."

"Does that mean you and I are going to try to work things out?" Marvin asked Georgia.

"No, Marvin, it doesn't mean that. It means you and I might host a radio show together, and that's all it may ever mean. I'm enjoying my new life."

He watched as she left the courthouse with a spring in her step and her permed hair boucing. "I still love that woman," he said to Bill.

"Well, *that* woman may very well take your job if you don't step up and pay back all the money you took from the station and your listeners. The only reason you have a job is because of that woman."

"Georgia?"

"Yes. Sweet Georgia Brown."

Georgia walked into the large conference room followed by Cammy, Tonya, and Art.

"You brought someone along?"

"Yes, I did."

"Arthur Lewis," Thomas said, recognizing Art's face from the many articles that had been written about him through the years. "You were an awesome attorney. Then you just dropped out of sight."

"This is Art, my next-door neighbor—the one I told you was a stay-at-home dad. The one you said no man would be able to relate to."

"You didn't tell me he was Arthur Lewis."

"My wife and I started a family," Art said. "One of us needed to stay home, so I took a step back so that she could take a step forward. My kids just started nursery school and I'm starting my own practice—home-based. And Georgia is my first client. So let's get these negotiations under way. We've seen the Arbitron ratings."

"Have you?" Thomas said, sitting up in his executive chair.

"Yes, we have." The Arbitron ratings had just been released. Georgia had claimed the number-one position in urban radio for Detroit, Dallas, Cleveland, and Atlanta. Marvin had placed just below her. "We're very excited. As you are well aware, my client and her team were never under contract with your station."

Priscilla grinned. "Get to your bottom line. How much are you asking for?"

"Well," Arthur said, straightening his necktie. "It's not really about the money per se."

"It's always about the money," Priscilla said.

"Not in this case. The *Sweet Georgia Brown Morning Show* is a trademarked name that Georgia Brown owns."

"When did that happen?" Thomas asked.

"I took care of that for her almost as soon as she didn't sign on any dotted line with your station. Essentially, Georgia is a brand name—a household name—and she can take that brand name anywhere. She has decided to take her show to 102 Hitz."

"Didn't I tell you?" Thomas asked. "I saw this coming. Let me guess, Marvin and Georgia are going to have a show together?"

"But I thought he was going to prison," Priscilla said.

Thomas waved aside his daughter's comment. "Marvin and Georgia together." He turned toward his daughter. "Why didn't you have our attorneys draft up an agreement?"

"You were the one who said you didn't want to enter into negotiations until the first ratings book was released. Don't you remember that?"

"Well, we're leaving the market again, I guess."

"Not necessarily," Arthur said. "You see, I also represent Bill Stanley and Bruce Richards, who are looking to sell their Detroit affiliate station to the right bidder."

Thomas grinned. "You haven't lost your touch. What exactly are we talking about?"

Arthur took some legal paperwork from his briefcase and leaned forward as he went over the terms, including the five hundred thousand dollars Marvin owed 102 Hitz. But Marvin wouldn't get off so easily, because he would have to sign a separate addendum to Sweet Georgia Brown and her Cookies for a Cause, agreeing to donate ten percent of his income to a minimum dollar amount of five hundred thousand dollars.

At that moment, it felt good being Sweet Georgia Brown—almost too good to be true.

"And so," Arthur said, as he took a break reviewing the legal documents, "do the terms sound reasonable? Might we have a deal?"

"I might be able to work something out," Thomas said. "We'll let you know."

"Well, don't wait too long because Sweet Georgia Brown

is a trademark. So is Cookies for a Cause. I'll leave you my card with my contact information."

They hadn't quite made it out the building before Art's cell phone rang.

"Arthur Lewis. Yes, we can certainly meet tomorrow to firm things up. Certainly, I can check with Bill and Bruce and see if they're available. Well, now, I know acquiring a radio station will take time. Yes, I know you have the money. Thirty days is reasonable. Of course, I hope your attorneys will look it over. And your accountants. Of course, that's standard, that's business. Well, let's get down to more business tomorrow. Shall we? All right, then. But, let's have this meeting at my client's convenience in the GM Renaissance Center—fair?" He ended his call and high-fived Georgia, Cammy, and Tonya. "We're doing big things. We're about to do even bigger things." He walked like George Jefferson toward his BMW that had just been pulled up to the front of the building. "I still got it."

"Yes, you do, Mr. Lewis," Georgia said, laughing.

One Year Later

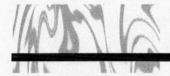

Corliss sat at her desk putting the finishing touches on her manuscript. She quickly glanced at the clock. Her radio, set to WFOR, The Force, would turn on at six to the *Sweet Georgia Brown Morning Show.*

"No other station does it quite like this," the highly excited prerecorded male's voice said over firecrackers in the background. "We're 1FM, home to the top two urban morning show hosts in the world—WFOR, The Force, hosted by Marconi Award winner Sweet Georgia Brown, and 102 Hitz, with the one and only Marvelous Marvin. Keep it locked. Don't touch that dial."

Life was wonderful. Corliss had a supportive, loving family, and she was doing what she loved to do full time—working toward her goal of writing a movie script so powerful that Hollywood would have to come knocking.

She thought about how grateful she was at the exact moment Georgia Brown played "I'm Grateful" by Yolanda Adams.

"I'm grateful. So thankful to be in the land of the living."

Corliss began singing along with the song.

"Are you grateful?" Georgia asked. "This step is so important—saying thank you. Telling God what you appreciate about Him and what He has done to turn your life around, because He has turned my life around and I am so truly grateful to Him and to you—my listeners. Always keep listening because you never know what you might hear."

Georgia played several gospel hits, because it was Monday, and she believed she needed to keep people's minds on God at the start of the week.

Corliss's head bobbed and her heart filled with the spirit as her fingers clicked away at the keys, completing the final word of the last scene. On only two hours of sleep in the past twenty-four hours, she was finally ready to hit print.

Acknowledgments

Through it all, God has been there for me. And this year I am especially thankful for all the blessings that I have received. Truly, one year has made a tremendous difference in my life, and I am so very thankful.

To my family: My parents, Ben and Velma Robinson. I know you would much rather me strive to become an executive for a major corporation rather than a full-time writer, but this is my passion and I have to be true to myself. Thank you for loving me and trying to understand what motivates me. To my sister, Janice—what happened to the novel you were writing? Never abandon your dreams. I love you, sis. To my nephews, Sterling Robinson and Brandon Robinson, I love both of you very much and want each of you to have the best life ever. No dream is too big. To my angels in heaven: My brother. I miss you so much, but I feel your presence every day in my journey through life. Aunt Billy and Uncle Sherman, may you rest in peace. Thank you for your insight on life and your understanding of me. Please continue to whisper in my ear. I'm listening.

To my best friend in this whole wide world: Shawn B. We've known each other for how many years now? And you know me pretty well. You keep my mood in check and remind me of all of the things that I need to be thankful for when I sometimes lose sight. And I remind you to slow down on that Hayabusa! You have had too many close calls on that bike. You're getting older—you may need to park it (LOL).

To Bishop T. D. Jakes, for teaching about the power of faith; your words have helped me make it through so many different trials and tribulations.

To my agent, Marc Gerald, and to Earl Cox of writers andpoets.com for getting my book into Marc's hands. Thank you for taking a chance on a new, unknown, and previously self-published author. You are both proof that everything happens for a reason.

To my editors at Penguin/New American Library, Kara Cesare and her assistant, Lindsay Nouis, I truly can't say thank-you enough. From start to finish, you were both there, and all of your comments and suggestions helped me tremendously.

To the many people and organizations who continue to support me in my journey: To Brian C., a new friend who has made such an impact on my life in such a short time. It is so fun talking and texting with you. I hope you always remain in my life. You are an incredible person, but you already know all that because you have such a big head (LOL). Oh, and by the way, who are Frankie Beverly and Maze? Name one song. I know that was well before your time. To my many MySpace.com friends; to D. Manor aka Dee M. Thai of Lipserviceink.com; to all of the urban radio show hosts across America, who are far too many to name; to Heather Covington of Disilgold.com; Marlive Harris of thegrits.com; Pia Wilson-Body; Symphony Parson; Anthony Body; Kenyea Dudley; Chandra Sparks-Taylor; Stacy Luecker of Essex Graphix; the Sistah Circle Book Club; Rawsistaz.com; Circle of Sisters Book Club; Nubian Sistas Book Club; A Nu-Twistah Flavah; Mahogany Book Club; Book-remarks.com; Tulsa Sistas Sippin' Tea Literary Group; Brothas Well Read; Dial Book Club; OOASA online book club; Dewhana Jones; Agatha Clark; Cynthia Taylor; Regina Smith; Charmette Brown; Tony Wright; Sandra Davenport; Belinda Bynum; Kyra Brown; Gregory Chastang; Shaft and Keesha Washington; Derek Burke; Valissa Armstrong; Chris Elliott; Tamyra Anderson; Gerald Leigh; Laverio Richardson; Nekosher Dillard; San Antonio Black Magazine (sablack.com); A Place of Our Own (apooo.org); Black Issues Book Review; Cushcity. com; Emma Rodgers; Til Pettis of Jokae's African-American Books; James Lisbon of AMAG, Inc.; Desiree Harris; Carbette Miller; Loose Leaves; Janet Brotherton; Jocelyn Lawson; Mosaic Books; and Pamela Walker-Williams of Pageturner. net. Oh, I definitely can't forget to mention Green "Ricky" Moss III, one of the first people who believed in me. And invested in my dreams. The comedy venture didn't work, but it's not over till it's over! Thank you for your faith in me. And to those whose names I may have forgotten to mention, it always happens, so please forgive me.

To my author friends, **Cydney Rax, Electa Rome Parks, Joy King, Meta Smith, and the many** authors who have inspired me through your individual progress and the creative stories you write. Let's continue to support each other and grow our readership.

To everyone who picks up this book and decides to purchase it, for allowing me to walk one step closer to my dream of writing full-time.

Thank you and God bless.
—*Cheryl Robinson*

Sweet Georgia Brown

cheryl robinson

A CONVERSATION WITH CHERYL ROBINSON

Q. What was your motivation behind writing Sweet Georgia Brown?

A. It was my goal to write an uplifting novel. So often, we are confronted with trials and tribulations in life and we all need to expose ourselves as often as we possibly can to things that make us feel good. This novel was my "feel better" contribution.

Q. How did Sweet Georgia Brown *evolve?*

A. Characters pop into my head all throughout the day and some stay around long enough for me to get to know them. Georgia was one character who made her presence well known. Every day I thought about Georgia, but I didn't know exactly who she was. I knew certain things. For instance, I knew that she was married with children and that she was a housewife, but I wasn't sure who she wanted to be deep inside.

Q. What did you discover was Georgia's motivation?

A. Georgia wanted her own success. She was very proud of her husband and the fact that he had finally realized a dream for himself, but she was losing sight of her own dreams. She was lost in the day-to-day routine of being a wife and a stay-at-home mom who put everyone else before herself, and she decided that she wanted to come first. And the closer she came to turning forty the stronger her desire became to pursue her own goals.

Q. What message do you really feel passionate about passing on through Sweet Georgia Brown?

A. First of all, always make room in your life for your dreams and have them no matter your age. That was another important message I wanted to convey: that dreams don't have an age limit or a unique profile, which is why I made Georgia a middle-aged housewife raising three children to prove that anyone can change their lives if they so desire. Follow your dreams and get excited about life and the many possibilities that it holds. And in the process, be kind to others.

Q. You and Georgia are the same age. Was that your experience the closer you came to turning forty?

A. I have been going through a transformation that is

unbelievable even to myself. I evolve almost by the minute now. By nature, I'm quiet, but quiet has its place. And it doesn't have a place at all when you are trying to succeed and let people know about you and the gift that God has given you. I was raised to be humble, but I was confused when it came to being humble and being confident. There is a difference. There's nothing wrong with believing in yourself and your gift. Fear is also a theme in the book, because I believe fear holds people back from achieving their dreams. I have a fear of flying that has really held me hostage and that holds me back as well. I've found that you have to work really hard to make your dreams a reality and sacrifice sometimes. I don't watch television. I used to be a reality show junkie, but I had to give up TV in order to find even more time to write. My evenings and weekends belong to my characters, and in the end I believe it has been well worth it. Georgia worked her way there, and anyone with a dream is working their way there. However, Georgia had somewhat of a Jennifer Hudson experience, which is always nice, and always possible. Georgia did become an overnight success in a way.

Q. What made you decide to make Marvelous Marvin Brown a radio host?

A. Actually, that evolved as I was writing. When I first sat down to write this novel, the only thing that I knew about Marvin was that he was a comedian, and I was very excited that I finally was able to write about a stand-up comedian, because I know a little something about that lifestyle.

I have a genuine love for comedy that has stemmed nearly twenty years. When I was in my early twenties I opened a production company named A Penny Away From Being Poor Productions. Once a week, I rented out Club Penta, which was a small intimate club in the Fisher Building in Detroit. I booked comedians to perform there. Some of the guys I booked then went on to star in movies; Faizon Love is one example. Even though he was from New York, he had a close friend in Detroit and he was living there for several months. I knew he was a star from the first time I saw him perform on stage and I produced a thirty-minute show, *An Evening with Faizon Love*, that was a big success. I was happy. . . . I really saw myself back then becoming a casting agent/manager, but things took a negative turn and one chapter of my life closed and remained that way for several years until I started writing several years later.

Q. How did you draw on your personal experiences of owning a production company for comedians for background in this book and why did you leave the business?

A. Well, first of all I was a female manager in, at the time, a male-dominated field. Stand-up comedians in the nineties were mostly men. It was very hard for me to find female comedians to book, and I would book comedians who came from all over and not just locally. For comedians, everything revolved around stage time. If one comedian was given more stage time than the other, there was a problem; everyone was trying to be my friend and I thought they were genuine, but I found out people aren't always who they seem to be. My passion for comedy was becoming more and more of a business and it wasn't fun any longer. I was approached by an investor to take my act on a larger scale by touring big-name comedians throughout college campuses, and that's when I learned an important lesson, which was never walk before you crawl. And I wasn't just walking— I was skipping, leaping, and running—and the comedy tour didn't turn out at all the way I had imagined it would.

Q. Are there any central themes in Sweet Georgia Brown *that relate to experiences in your own life?*

A. For a long time after that experience, I felt like another person could control my fate, but that's because my faith at the time wasn't as strong as it should have been. Now I know that no man on this earth is more powerful than God, and I don't have fear that a person can destroy what's meant for me to have. My character Georgia is the same way. When entering an arena with a lot of established on-air personalities and some stiff competition, especially from her own husband, she focused on being herself and touching those who were open to experiencing someone new. And as a result she surpassed the achievements of even her own husband in a very short time.

Q. Are you working on a new novel? And any final thoughts for your readers?

A. I'm always working on something new so, yes, I have a few things going. I'm negotiating with a few characters who are trying to have their stories told.

As for my readers, I appreciate you so much. I appreciate the e-mails that are sent to newfictionwriter@ msn.com telling me what you thought of my novels. I appreciate you visiting my Web site at www.cherylrobin son.com and my MySpace page at www.myspace.com/ cherylrobinson. You have so many books to choose from and the fact that you selected mine as one to occupy your time makes me want to guarantee that you will enjoy it. When I write, I think about you, the reader, and I want to entertain and enlighten you. So I hope I have done that.

Keep reading!

QUESTIONS
FOR DISCUSSION

1. The novel *Sweet Georgia Brown* was divided into three parts. In part one, who were Georgia and Marvin? What, if anything, motivated them then and how do you feel about their financial turning point?

2. In part two, Marvin and Georgia have money. What do you think about Marvin after his success? Is he the same man? Does he still love Georgia? Does Georgia still love him?

3. How do you feel about Marvin using his radio format to put down his wife? Was that just a part of his act? And if so, should Georgia have just told her friends and family to mind their own business since her husband was successful?

4. What do you think was the final straw to make Georgia decide she had had enough and that she was going to leave Marvin to start her own life?

5. Who were your favorite and least favorite characters in the novel? Please explain why.

6. What do you think of Chloe? Does she represent in your mind a "typical" teenager?

7. Why do you think Chloe and Georgia bonded so well? Were you surprised by their connection?

8. In part three, Georgia is a host of her very own morning show. Do you feel she earned this show or was given the show because of who her husband was? Did you ever get the sense of whether or not radio was Georgia's true passion?

9. In your opinion, what was the central theme of the novel, *Sweet Georgia Brown*?

10. Take a moment and share your passion/dreams with the others in the group if you dare. How attainable do you feel your own dreams are?